Kissing Babies

at the

Piggly Wiggly

Also by Robert Dalby

Waltzing at the Piggly Wiggly

Kissing Babies

at the

Piggly Wiggly

ROBERT DALBY

★

G. P. PUTNAM'S SONS
NEW YORK

G. P. PUTNAM'S SONS
Publishers Since 1838
Published by the Penguin Group
Penguin Group (USA) Inc., 375 Hudson Street, New York, New York 10014, USA •
Penguin Group (Canada), 90 Eglinton Avenue East, Suite 700, Toronto, Ontario M4P 2Y3,
Canada (a division of Pearson Penguin Canada Inc.) • Penguin Books Ltd,
80 Strand, London WC2R 0RL, England • Penguin Ireland, 25 St Stephen's Green,
Dublin 2, Ireland (a division of Penguin Books Ltd) • Penguin Group (Australia),
250 Camberwell Road, Camberwell, Victoria 3124, Australia (a division of Pearson
Australia Group Pty Ltd) • Penguin Books India Pvt Ltd, 11 Community Centre,
Panchsheel Park, New Delhi–110 017, India • Penguin Group (NZ), 67 Apollo Drive,
Rosedale, North Shore 0745, Auckland, New Zealand (a division of Pearson
New Zealand Ltd) • Penguin Books (South Africa) (Pty) Ltd, 24 Sturdee Avenue,
Rosebank, Johannesburg 2196, South Africa

Penguin Books Ltd, Registered Offices:
80 Strand, London WC2R 0RL, England

Library of Congress Cataloging-in-Publication Data
Dalby, Robert.
Kissing babies at the Piggly Wiggly / Robert Dalby.
p.   cm.
ISBN 978-0-399-15428-7
1. Mississippi — Fiction.   2. Political campaigns — Fiction.   3. Domestic
fiction.   I. Title.
PS3554 . A4148K57   2007   2007000540
813' . 54 — dc22

Printed in the United States of America
1   3   5   7   9   10   8   6   4   2

Book design by Amanda Dewey

This is a work of fiction. Names, characters, places, and incidents either are the product of
the author's imagination or are used fictitiously, and any resemblance to actual persons, living or dead, businesses, companies, events, or locales is entirely coincidental.

While the author has made every effort to provide accurate telephone numbers and Internet
addresses at the time of publication, neither the publisher nor the author assumes any
responsibility for errors, or for changes that occur after publication. Further, the publisher
does not have any control over and does not assume any responsibility for author or third-
party websites or their content.

For the incredible network of Cudd'ns

Kissing Babies

at the

Piggly Wiggly

1.

THE BATTLE BEGINS

By the time mid-September of the year 2001 rolled around in the quirky little town of Second Creek, Mississippi, two things were readily apparent. The first was that the oppressive heat the new millennium had ushered in had more than worn out its welcome. The second was that most Second Creekers were having trouble believing that the seventyish Mr. Choppy Dunbar was actually going to take on the solidly entrenched and self-serving Mr. Floyce Hammontree in the February 2002 mayoral election—the result of Second Creek's special charter that allowed it to march to its customary different drummer and vote around Valentine's Day.

But no matter when the vote was going to take place, what did Mr. Choppy really know about Mr. Floyce's specialty—the down-and-dirty business of local politics? Mr. Choppy's résumé consisted entirely of running the family-owned Piggly Wiggly for many decades, but he had recently shut it down in the face of withering competition from the sprawling MegaMart out on the Bypass. This, despite the game rescue efforts of Laurie Lepanto Hampton and her club of sixtysomething wealthy widows—the Nitwitts.

It had all seemed so promising at first—such a lark, a breezy adventure looming on the horizon. Ever so diplomatic Laurie, then the president of the eclectic group, had sweet-talked silver-haired retired ballroom instructor Powell Hampton into setting up dancing and flirting hours for all the female customers in the aisles of the Piggly Wiggly. The plan had been to drum up more business for the struggling store with the offbeat ploy. After a few weeks of publicity, CNN had come calling to capture the proceedings and broadcast them nationally. But that had not been nearly enough. There had been way too much dancing and harmless flirtation and not enough shopping and bagging of groceries.

On the bright side, Laurie and Powell had fallen in love during all the brouhaha, gotten married in the Piggly Wiggly itself, and then graciously accepted Mr. Choppy's offer to become his campaign managers and help him bring down Mr. Floyce's corrupt municipal machine. And now they had returned from their dreamy and restful honeymoon down in New Orleans and Jamaica and were ready to go at it full bore.

"We're going to win this battle. I'm sure of it!" Laurie proclaimed shortly after she and Powell had marched straight into Mr. Choppy's cluttered office for their first posthoneymoon strategy meeting. It was strange seeing all the Piggly Wiggly shelves completely bereft of food—even stranger missing that comforting ripe-produce smell that had always greeted them.

Nonetheless, Laurie and Powell took it in stride, their smiling faces nicely bronzed by the tropical sun they had recently enjoyed.

"All kinds of campaign ideas occurred to me during our honeymoon," Laurie continued. "But I think Powell and I would like to hear what you've come up with so far before we go any further."

The couple took their seats across from Mr. Choppy, eagerly awaiting his update on the decisions he had made in their absence. He did not disappoint.

"As you know, we have about five months until the election to pull off this feat," Mr. Choppy began, putting his big calloused hands atop his messy desk and leaning forward. "And as I'm sure you saw when you pulled up in the parkin' lot, I've had that temporary banner made and strung it in front of the old Piggly Wiggly logo."

The big white cloth banner announced in red block lettering: Hale Dunbar Jr. — Campaign Headquarters.

"We've got to get this campaign into high gear right away, since Mr. Floyce has the advantage of bein' the long-standin' incumbent. There are a lotta folks out there who are on the take to him, and that won't be easy to overcome. We all know it, even if we can't prove it. But I gotta believe he's got a flaw or two we can exploit."

The couple straightened up a bit in their chairs, and Powell said, "We poke around for his soft underbelly, huh? Well, we're both ready to work hard on your behalf. We're nicely rejuvenated by our honeymoon."

Mr. Choppy quickly looked them up and down. "Yeah, I gotta say you two are the picture of health — not a hint of sunburn or peelin' skin between you. Me, I never could spend any time at all in the sun. I've always fried up like an egg in a skillet from the time I was a pale little boy."

"A little dab of sunblock works wonders these days," Powell replied. "The trick is not to overdo—with either the sunblock or the sun, I mean. We also bought a couple of souvenir straw hats down in Negril and put them to good use." He paused and gave his wife a wicked wink. "We indulged everything in moderation, except romance."

Mr. Choppy winked back, nodding agreeably before continuing. "Well, the first thing I wanted to emphasize to y'all is the use of my Christian name both on the banner outside and on the campaign trail as well. I know you'll both prob'ly call me Mr. Choppy outta habit, and you're welcome to, of course. I figure that most everybody else'll call me that, too, after all these years. But as I said before you left for your honeymoon, I'll be runnin' for office as Hale Dunbar Junior. No more references to my damned missin' finger and nickname—at least not in the official campaign literature we'll hand out."

He held up the nub on his right-hand index finger and shook his balding head soberly. "I spent way too much of my life what-iffing over the woman who caused me to chop this off way back when. But, as you know, my Gaylie Girl came down from Chicago when she saw that CNN story and finally set things right. That's all behind me now—I don't run a grocery store or fillet steaks for folks any-more. Besides, Mr. Choppy just isn't an appropriate name for the mayor of Second Creek, Mississippi. Doesn't have any—oh, what's that word all the talk-show commentators like to use these days, Miz Hampton? Sounds somethin' like gravy or gravity."

Laurie was unable to suppress her amusement and gazed fondly at Mr. Choppy with her bright blue eyes and a tilt of her

sun-streaked coiffure, giving him her customary winning smile.
There was no other way to put it—she positively adored this
pudgy, cherubic-looking man who had been a treasured friend of
the family for decades. "You must mean *gravitas*. Of course, I
know what you're getting at, but there are some that might say
Mr. Choppy is a perfectly appropriate name, considering the history of our crazy little town."

Indeed, Second Creek's reputation as a magnet for eccentric
people and weather patterns alike preceded it. In some mysterious fashion the place seemed to attract both, and no one had ever
come up with a plausible explanation for the unpredictable
storms and tantrums of both the meteorological and human variety that had characterized it over the years and made it such an
irresistible, if off-the-beaten-path, tourist attraction.

"That may well be," Mr. Choppy continued, "but nevertheless,
all our campaign fodder will refer to me as Hale Dunbar Junior."

"No quarrel with that. You're the boss," Powell replied,
stretching his long legs and pursing his lips briefly while he considered further. "Come up with any catchy slogans yet?"

"Matter a' fact, I have. What do you think about Vote for a
New Outlook: Hearty and Hale Dunbar Junior? I know I turned
that phrase around on its ear a bit, but it sticks with you,
don'tcha think?"

Laurie and Powell mulled it over, their eyes cutting from side
to side thoughtfully.

"I like it," Laurie finally offered. "It has humor and energy."

"Agreed," Powell added.

Mr. Choppy took a deep breath and settled back in his chair
a bit. "Great. Because we're gonna need an energetic, dynamic
approach. It's only been a week or two since I declared my

intentions, but it's gotten back to me already what sorta tactics Mr. Floyce'll use against me in the campaign. When he heard that I intended to run against him, he was pretty ticked off, I can tell you. I'm sure he expected to run unopposed for the umpteenth time. Guess he thinks of the position as his birthright by now."

Laurie drew back slightly, an incredulous look overwhelming her pretty face. "How did you find all that out so fast? Were you a fly on the wall of his office?"

"No. But a little birdie told me, and at this point, I'd rather not reveal my sources. Let's just say that I have it on some authority that Mr. Floyce will use my age as an issue against me. Maybe not come right out and put it that way. But he'll hint that I'm too old and not vigorous enough for the job. Not to mention that I have no experience in government and politics. I'm sure he'll keep peckin' away at it—claimin' that I'm inexperienced and over the hill at the same time. Have his political cake and eat it, too, so to speak."

Powell stirred, looking deeply offended. "Well, we won't let him get away with that, will we? We folks in our sixties and up are perfectly capable of running any show in town. Hell, most all our presidents have had that kind of mileage on them. Some before and some after they left office, but none of them were what you'd call spring chickens. A relative youngster like Mr. Floyce—what is he, pushing fifty or something by now?—will just have to be taught a valuable lesson, it seems to me."

Laurie rubbed her hands together with gusto and gave both men a mischievous smirk. "I think I may have one of my perfectly brilliant schemes simmering up here already." She pointed to her temple for emphasis. "I'll run it by the Nitwitts as soon as I can."

A smile exploded across Mr. Choppy's face. "I was hopin' you'd find a way to get those wonderful ladies involved as soon as possible. They sure got the word out about waltzin' at the Piggly Wiggly with Mr. Hampton here. Our little plan didn't fail for any lack of their tryin'."

"I can certainly attest to that," Powell replied. "I had the tired feet to prove it. We had everyone from Lady Roth on down coming out of the woodwork for a while."

Mr. Choppy looked especially thoughtful for a moment or two, his brows arching expectantly. "Do you think we should enlist Lady Roth's help? Or would it turn too many people off to have her on the warpath against Mr. Floyce?"

Laurie set her mouth firmly. "My gut feeling is that we definitely enlist the help of the Nitwitts in the months ahead but that we not openly court Lady Roth. She's just too much of a wild card when it comes to daily life and everyday behavior. Now, if she should come to us at some point and beg to participate, perhaps we can find a role for her in the campaign. But unless that happens, I suggest we steer clear of her histrionics."

"You make some mighty good points there, Miz Hampton," Mr. Choppy replied. "I'm thinkin' back now on all the dancin' Lady Roth did in the aisles with Mr. Hampton over the summer. I have to admit she was a sight to see, all dressed up as different characters like Mary Todd Lincoln and Eliza Doolittle and the like. The other customers either loved her or hated her. There was just no in between." He glanced up at the ceiling and laughed vigorously. "Remember the day she came in with that grocery list where she'd written 'one blueberry' on it? I did a double take when I read that, but I okayed it to keep the peace, and we actually sold her one lonely little blueberry that day. God knows what she did with it. I suspect it was just for show. When you come right down to it, she's all about showmanship, and there's a reason for everything she does."

"She does boggle the mind," Laurie added. "But trust me, I do think I have an interesting idea for the Nitwitts to consider, and I promise I'll bring it up at the next meeting."

"And when would that be, Miz Hampton?"

"It's this coming Friday afternoon, matter of fact. I promised the girls I'd meet with them and give them all the juicy details of the honeymoon." She paused to give her husband a coy glance. "Well, not all the details. Anyway, they're all coming over to my house for liquor, lunch, and lollygaggin', as we Nitwitts like to put it. I'll choose my moment carefully and then spring my suggestion."

Powell reached over and patted his wife's shoulder gently. "I know that tone of voice, honey. It's got the Devil's touch in it. Is your newest brainstorm going to be a tad on the scandalous side?"

"How perceptive you are! Here we've only been married a couple of weeks, and you've got all my vocal nuances down pat."

Powell drew up his long, lithe body with a triumphant expression on his face. "Ah, but we've known each other much longer than that—two or three years, off and on, if I recall correctly. Did you know I had my eye on you when I first moved down from Memphis?"

"You never told me that."

Powell chuckled richly. "I spotted you first from afar while you were shopping at the Piggly Wiggly fondling the tomatoes." He paused to cross his heart. "True story. You looked so appetizing with that cute little figure of yours—a tomato fondling tomatoes. I figured you then for the good dancer you are. Just to get an intro, I even contemplated that corny old ploy—crashing into your grocery cart with mine."

"Did you really?"

He held up his right hand. "It's the God's honest truth. But reason prevailed, and I kept my cart to myself. Fortunately, we were introduced soon after that at Miss Kittykate's funeral."

Mr. Choppy intervened, looking thoroughly captivated. "You two were just meant to be—that's all there is to it."

"No doubt about that now," Laurie replied, gazing affectionately into her husband's eyes. "But enough of that. What I'm going to propose to the Nitwitts may not meet with their unanimous approval the way my dancing in the aisles of the Piggly Wiggly did. Some of the girls may require a bit of convincing along the way."

Mr. Choppy perked up visibly. "When you put it like that, it makes me want to be there to hear your new scheme for myself."

Laurie gently wagged a finger. "No flies on the wall here. I don't even think Powell should be present when I trot out my idea. It could end up being a very delicate situation. Trust me."

Powell made a mock frown and looked at her sideways. "So I'm to take a walk around the block during your little Nitwitt to-do?"

"Something like that. Believe me, it's for the best. I know my Nitwitts."

"I can't argue with that," Powell said. "You kept them under control quite admirably for the better part of seven years and three consecutive presidential terms. That was no small accomplishment. You'd make a splendid UN ambassador."

Laurie grasped his hand warmly and tilted her head in his direction. "I'm not that good. I'd still be president if I hadn't married you, of course. But since it's a widows' club, I felt very strongly that taking on a second husband required me to renounce my throne."

Mr. Choppy folded his arms and sat in silence for a moment, observing the affectionate looks passing between his two campaign managers. He knew that if he succeeded in loosening Mr. Floyce's stranglehold over Second Creek, Laurie and Powell Hampton would be instrumental in helping him do so. He could not have chosen a more intelligent and articulate couple for his long-shot quest.

"Well, I'll certainly look forward to your feedback on your Nitwitt meeting, Miz Hampton," Mr. Choppy said. "Meanwhile, I've drawn up a schedule for printin' up flyers and buyin' some time to make radio speeches and such. I'd like to get together with you, Mr. Hampton, and we can discuss my platform and have you turn all of it into somethin' that'll sound good over the air. You did a great job writin' that radio commercial that invited all the ladies to come in and dance with you at the store. You got a real way with words, and I'll need all the help I can get in that department. I never got real good grades in English, you know."

Powell nodded crisply. "We can go over that next, if you like. It'll take nothing less than our very best to unseat Mr. Floyce after all these years."

"Don't I know it." Mr. Choppy momentarily sucked in his cheeks, then exhaled dramatically. "Incidentally, this'll be the last time you'll see all those empty shelves out there. I've just sold 'em off, and I intend to replace 'em with some tables and chairs I've rented. Then I'll have some phone lines put in for the workers who'll volunteer to do battle for us down the line. Maybe some of your Nitwitt ladies callin' up everybody they know, Miz Hampton?"

"That'll be my top priority," Laurie replied, looking very pleased with herself.

Mr. Choppy's reply had a sense of urgency to it. "I feel like I'm doin' the right thing in takin' on Mr. Floyce and all, but I know we've got some difficult work ahead of us. After all, the heart and soul of our beloved Second Creek are at stake."

2

THE BIG, BAD BAGMAN

M r. Floyce fidgeted behind his imposing mahogany desk in
his municipal chambers, distractedly fingering his pencil
mustache as his Rolex ticked toward ten in the evening. Across
from him sat his longtime attorney and confidant, Eljay
Jeffers, a morbidly obese specimen of middle-aged Southern
manhood who was constantly perspiring and florid of face. A few
minutes earlier they had dismissed Minnie Forbes, Mr. Floyce's
fussy little secretary, finally allowing her to go home to her husband, Charley, after taking notes on yet another tension-filled
session of general grousing regarding Mr. Choppy's election challenge.

"I don't want that nine-fingered sonuvabitch comin' any-
where close to me on Election Day when the vote is tallied,
Eljay," Mr. Floyce said, the irritation clouding his voice.
Heretofore, he had considered Mr. Choppy a harmless oddity,

not even an afterthought in the scheme of things. But no longer. How dare that over-the-hill steak jockey threaten Floyce Yerby Hammontree's preeminent position as mayor emeritus of Second Creek!

"He won't," Eljay offered. "We got all our ducks in a row. Hell, our contributions to Hanging Grapes A.M.E. Church alone should shore up the black vote but good."

"Damn well better," Mr. Floyce replied. "Brother Willyus V. Thompson's had his hand out enough."

Eljay snickered, his tone full of condescension. "Unfortunately, it's just the cost of doin' bid'ness. How did he put it to you last time you saw him?"

"He goes, 'This bid'ness of savin' souls requires the proper settin'.' And then something about running out of room to stage all their potluck suppers in the social hall. Time for an expansion for his hungry and righteous flock or some such. Heh. Minus his commission, of course." Mr. Floyce paused and firmly set his jaw. "All I gotta say is that Brother Thompson better deliver that entire black precinct down in Ward Six, or we cut him off!"

Mr. Floyce's memories of previous campaigns in some of the town's fundamentalist churches flashed before him. He had the routine down pat. He would show up and clap his hands to the raucous, up-tempo hymns and pretend to be mesmerized by the guttural rhythmic chanting that the various pastors practiced with sweaty showmanship. Then he would cap that off with a "Praise the Lord!" every now and then to convince the flock that he was a genuine believer—filled to the brim with zeal—and he was usually home free. Of course, a little green behind the scene to win over the brown of the town, as his bagman, Eljay, liked to put it, never hurt either.

"Brother Thompson knows what side his bread is buttered on but good," Eljay answered. "He'll come through for us as usual — his faithful flock will be signed, sealed, and delivered come Election Day in February."

Mr. Floyce nodded, but there were several wild cards out there amongst the black believers. The Reverend Quintus Payne of the Marblestone Alley Church of Holiness, for instance, had refused to succumb to Mr. Floyce's fevered performances in the pews of his church, remaining stubbornly above the political fray. What Mr. Floyce could not control made him nervous, particularly come election time.

"I was just thinkin' about some of these churches and bid'-nesses that won't play our game, Eljay. We got a healthy percentage of the good ole boy and the black vote locked up, but I still worry about all those goody-goodies out there. And then some of the older generation of women out there have the warm fuzzies for that old grocery store coot, particularly those foolish Nitwitts. Still, I don't think it's anywhere near enough to get him into office. Not by a long shot."

Eljay sopped up some of the sweat on his forehead with a handkerchief and then shrugged his big, hulking shoulders. "Nah, I can't see Mr. Choppy pullin' this off, no matter what. You got too many favors to call in from blacks and whites alike."

"Yep. And we just got through pavin' Lower Winchester Road down in Ward Six, too. All those folks out that way have been after me for the better part of six years to asphalt their cabooses straight into The Square. No more gravel washboard for 'em now, though. That's our insurance."

Mr. Floyce finally allowed himself to relax a bit, hitching up his seersucker pants and stretching his legs out underneath the desk. Plotting with Eljay always took a lot out of him, dredging up memories of payoffs and bribes and other acts of questionable legality they had pulled off on a regular basis over the many years of his reign. And, yes, every one of those stunts had come off without a hitch, but there had been some close calls, and it was a nerve-racking business to boot. Sometimes he had lost some sleep, but none of it had ever seemed to faze Eljay one iota. The man was as unflappable and stealthy as he was bombastic and overfed. He seemed to have swallowed his conscience whole, turning it into more belly fat. Even better—he never left a hint of a paper trail, nor any suggestion that Mr. Floyce had been behind any particular transaction. That was his gift and the main reason the two men were literally thick as thieves.

Eljay finished scribbling a brief note to himself in his little black book, stuffed it into the pocket of his moist white shirt, and settled his girth back in his chair, sighing vigorously. "Hoo, boy, I think we covered all the bases tonight!" Then he wiped off more sweat, eyeing his friend shrewdly. "I'm just curious, though. What ever happened to all those big-time Vegas act dreams you had? I remember the time you and Jo Nelle came back from one of your trips out there, and you and I managed to get away from the wives for some bourbon and branch together one night. You were mighty high on stand-up comedy back then, as I recall, and you even ran a coupla routines past me. Frankly, I thought you might be onto somethin'. You given up on those headliner notions for good?"

At first Mr. Floyce seemed a bit taken aback by the comments but he recovered quickly, leaning forward and lowering his voice as if someone might be eavesdropping on them. "It's like this, Eljay. I recently signed that contract with all the Mississippi MegaMarts to sell my Miss Delta Floozie CDs, and they've told me that if my little ditty does well statewide, they might consider regional, even national, distribution."

"Yeah, I saw that in *The Citizen* a coupla weeks ago — 'She's a Doozie, She's a Floozie.' I've heard you sing it two or three times in The Square. Pretty neat little tune."

Mr. Floyce indulged a self-satisfied chuckle and nodded. "I enjoy trottin' it out every June, when all the ladies get themselves up like streetwalkers and compete for the trophy. Only this year we had a friggin' drag queen win it, and I couldn't do a damned thing about it."

"What's the world comin' to, huh?"

"Well, all that aside, I have to confess that singin' that little song of mine once a year for the benefit of all those tourists in The Square and havin' it so they can buy copies in all the MegaMarts out there doesn't really satisfy my showbiz desires. It's like I'm just bidin' my time until I get the big break and get to do what I really want to do, you know?"

Eljay nodded but looked slightly skeptical. "You'd never know it from the way you've been reactin' to Mr. Choppy's announcement. I think you like your job more'n you let on."

"That's different," Mr. Floyce replied. The tone of his voice had gone from candid to indignant in a flash. "I'll leave office when I'm damned good and ready to leave and not a moment before. I've been runnin' this crazy town for the better part of two decades now, and I think I've done a bang-up job. The very idea of that glorified ex–grocery store clerk challengin' me just makes my blood boil. Who the hell does he think he is? Besides, with Floyce Junior in college now, I've got extra expenses to keep an eye on."

"Folks've always liked the Dunbar family, you gotta admit," Eljay returned, deciding to play devil's advocate. "Mr. Choppy's father was very much admired because of all those charitable things he did over the years, especially those food donations after our more spectacular storms. My own mother, may she rest in peace, swore by the man. Said he had a heart of gold."

Mr. Floyce screwed up his face. "That was Hale Dunbar Senior, and he lived a long time ago in the days of dinosaurs and dragons. This is Hale Dunbar Junior, and he's peein' on my territory right now, in the present, as we speak, and yada, yada, yada. It goes without sayin' that this dog don't like it one damned bit!"

Eljay's great belly shook with laughter, and he rolled his eyes, clearing his throat noisily at the finish. "That's the spirit, Floyce. I've never known you to back down from a fight. Matter of fact, in all the years we've been friends, I've never seen you lose a scrap."

"Don't expect me to start now. Mr. Choppy'll be dead meat— no pun intended. First of all, we'll stonewall him when it comes to his stupid notion of debates. I hate all that politically correct crap. Did I tell you he sent me a letter last week askin' if I'd cotton to that idea? Discuss the issues, I mean. In some kinda open forum, he said. No doubt run by those preposterous Nitwitts like some gigantic tea party!"

Eljay grew unusually quiet, taking his time to reply. When he finally did, there was no hint of humor in his voice or face. "Yeah, you mentioned all that the other day. I understand what you're sayin' about those ladies, but I'm sure you know better than to get on their bad side. They all got plenty of money their husbands left 'em, and they got social position to boot. Considerin' how they all came to Mr. Choppy's rescue with that goofy dancin'-in-the-grocery-store scheme, they're bound to get behind him in this race. If I were you, I'd tread lightly with that bunch — give 'em the other side of the street."

Mr. Floyce turned up his nose as if he had just caught a whiff of something putrid wafting by. "Easier said than done. That Laurie Lepanto — uh, Hampton she is now — rounded 'em all up this past summer to swoop down on me like harpies the day the old Grande Theater was scheduled to be demolished. Hell, man, the damned roof had caved in from a thousand pounds of pigeon poop. But, no, they even wanted me to halt the demolition and practically go out to Hollywood to get all the actors and writers from Mississippi to agree to restore it. Can you imagine? Women like that just have too much time and money on their hands, and you and I both know what they really need to get rid of that sour taste in their lives."

Eljay cackled, then pursed his ample lips and whistled. "I'm surprised you'd ever let 'em get under your skin that way. They're basically harmless when you get down to cases."

"Yeah, I know. But it was just the way Laurie Hampton put things to me that particular day. She implied her first husband knew all kinda things about the way I've been runnin' this town."

"Roy Lepanto? I never knew him to raise his voice to a soul. He didn't know squat about anything except insurance and life-expectancy charts. She was just bluffin' — tryin' to throw her weight around like all those silly women do."

Mr. Floyce shook his head, looking genuinely irritated. "All I'm sayin' is that meddlin' biddies can be very hard to ignore sometimes, particularly when they get their minds made up with their noses in the air."

Eljay lifted his great bulk out of his chair with a grunt and caught his breath. "Well, we both agreed earlier that those

Nitwitts wouldn't be near enough to get Mr. Choppy across the finish line. Let's don't lose any sleep over that. And I think you may be right about stonewallin' on the debate idea. Unless—" He broke off suddenly and did not seem inclined to resume his train of thought.

Finally, Mr. Floyce could bear the silence no longer. "Unless what? Quit keepin' me in suspense!"

"Hold on now. I was just thinkin' it all the way through. Suppose we use a reverse psychology on him?"

Mr. Floyce slowly rose from his desk and looked Eljay straight in the eye. "Okay, spill it."

"What if we don't stonewall? What if you answer his letter and tell him you'll agree to his idea of a debate with him? The ball would be in his court then. Sure, he'd get some extra exposure, but that could end up bein' his kiss of death. No matter who the man thinks he is or wants to be, he is what he is—an ex-butcher and grocery store owner. He's got no special speakin' skills that I know of. No real knowledge of what it takes to run municipal government. Maybe we should give him enough rope and let him hang himself in front of God and all of Second Creek. Hell, I've got confidence you can wipe the floor with him one on one. You've been sweet-talkin' the voters for almost two decades now."

"You bet I have."

"So whaddaya think?"

Mr. Floyce's brain went into overdrive. Eljay might just have something. After all, why should he be afraid to take advantage of his strengths? Over the years, he had been able to talk his way out of just about anything. And who knew? When he'd finally had his fill of local politics and feathered his nest sufficiently, he just might be able to talk his way into that brilliant showbiz career he'd always said he wanted.

"Okay, let's go for it. I'll have Minnie send him a letter tomorrow and tell him the debate is on at a date to be determined. Bet that'll make his day!"

"Ha!" Eljay proclaimed. "When the time comes, he won't know what hit him!" Then he noisily smacked his lips, peeling them back into a malicious grin that was too white and perfect, hinting of dentures. "You still keepin' a touch of booze around these days? Break out the bourbon, and let's have a little nightcap before we go home to the wives."

Mr. Floyce smiled broadly, moved to his desk, and opened the right-hand bottom drawer, where he customarily stowed a fifth of Wild Turkey, along with several mother-of-pearl shot glasses Jo Nelle had bought him on that trip they'd taken to Cancún. Each man in turn slammed back a bit of stinging liquid courage and produced a satisfying "Ahhh!"—confident that the upcoming campaign would be nothing short of a snap.

★

Charley Forbes stood in the kitchen doorway of his modest little tract house on the south side of Second Creek, watching his hardworking wife, Minnie, pull up into the carport. Neither of them had ever really liked the development they lived in— New Vista Acres, it was called. But there was nothing new about it, nor did it have any vistas to recommend it. The closely spaced tin-type houses throughout the subdivision— ranchburgers, the builders liked to call them—each baked in the broiling sun on dusty soybean fields that a bankrupt farmer had been forced to sell off to an opportunistic developer some thirty years earlier. Not everyone in Second Creek lived the charmed life.

"God, I hate it when he keeps you this late," Charley said to his wife of thirty-three years as she trudged through the door. He could clearly read the exhaustion in her drooping shoulders and grim demeanor. "That man has absolutely no sense of time. He's a damned slave driver." Charley watched her drop her purse and notepad on the kitchen counter, then retrieve a can of caffeine-free soda from the refrigerator. "What was it this time?" he continued as he watched her pour the soda into an ice-filled glass and then take a healthy sip.

"What else? That infernal reelection campaign," she replied, suppressing a small belch with her mouth closed while shaking her mousy little head. "Mr. Jeffers was there again, mostly trying to calm Mr. Floyce down and reassure him about various things. Sometimes I get the feeling that they're speaking in code, though. There's a lot that passes between 'em I just don't understand. But I write it all down anyway, just in case I have to use it later on to type a letter or something."

Charley followed his wife into the nearby low-ceilinged living room, sitting beside her on a small sofa sorely in need of reupholstering. "Well, I can't believe that whatever it was couldn'a waited until tomorrow morning at a decent hour. He sure gets his money's worth for what he pays you, honey."

She rattled her ice cubes, twitched in place in birdlike fashion, and took another generous swig of her soda. "He's promised me that raise this year for sure."

Charley clenched his fists, and his craggy face darkened further, giving a dead-on imitation of a featherweight boxer just itching to get at his next opponent. He'd been known to let his temper get the best of him and had been given a ticket more than once for his road rage antics. "He's been feedin' you that line for three years now. I wish to God there was some way I could bring in more money so you could up and quit. I've said it before, and I'll say it again—Floyce Hammontree has never given a damn about anybody but himself."

Minnie nodded reluctantly. "He still has a lot on his plate. Anyway, we need the job and the money. We do what we have to do. That seems to be our lot in life."

Charley sat quietly for a while, wincing as he quickly reviewed their financial situation. He'd been promised that morning shift supervisory job at the catfish plant six years ago, and the extra pay would have enabled his little Minnie to finally quit her position as Floyce Hammontree's number-one lackey. But at the last minute he had been unceremoniously passed over for the owner's son, an inveterate womanizer who was supposedly going through a messy divorce and needed the money to keep his head above water.

Well, so what? Charley Franklin Forbes needed the money, too. He'd given Second Creek's largest employer—Pond-Raised Catfish, Incorporated—almost twenty years of loyal, backbreaking service, and what had he gained in return? The same old deadening, messy shift-worker job decapitating catfish that meant living paycheck to paycheck. It just wasn't right that two people who had worked as hard as Charley and Minnie Forbes had over the years still had so little to show for it. True, their kids had offered to help them through the various rough spots, but the couple had always refused such handouts. Their children had young families of their own to support, and these days that wasn't easy.

"Let's get some rest, honey. It's been a long day," Minnie said after she had finished her soda.

Charley took the cue and refused to stir the pot any further, leaning over to kiss her gently on the forehead. But he patiently waited for his beloved wife to fall asleep before stealthily lifting back the covers and easing out of bed later that night. He quietly made his way back into the kitchen. Minnie's trademark notepad was right where she had left it on the counter. Charley picked it up and clicked on the little light above the stove next to the exhaust fan. He spent the next ten minutes or so thoroughly perusing Minnie's most recent entries and committing the gist to memory.

Her predictable modus operandi was to write down everything under the sun—the fallout from a limited and compulsively ordered mind. Sometimes she even took note of sound effects such as a lengthy coughing spell that someone had endured, followed by a detailed description of that person heading down the hall for a drink of water. Most of what she transcribed was tedious, meandering, and of little consequence. But once in a while she picked up on something significant, and Charley definitely felt that to be the case again tonight.

3.

TESTING THE
NITWITT WATERS

Laurie was trying her dead-level best to read the body language and facial tics of the recently elected president of the Nitwitts—her successor, Myrtis Troy. The two of them were sitting across from each other, having a confidential discussion and late-morning libation out on the glassed-in back porch of the Troy mansion, Evening Shadows. It was here, with fresh gardenias and other blooms picked from the gardens surrounding her boxwood maze, that the always sociable and stylish Myrtis had customarily held forth as hostess over the years. At first it appeared that she was going to stonewall indefinitely with an ongoing series of noncommittal phrases such as "Well, I just don't know," "You've caught me off guard here, Laurie," and "Are you serious?"

But eventually Myrtis shifted her weight in her chair, took a generous swig of her Bloody Mary for courage, and got off dead center. "I don't suppose I'd mind too much, although you have to admit this goes against all our training as shining examples of Southern womanhood. You're not supposed to ask, and you're only supposed to tell if there's some sort of medical emergency that might justify it."

Laurie stirred her toothpick-stabbed olive around in her drink and smiled. "I understand. We Southern belles are supposed to be so calculating in that regard."

Myrtis put her drink down on the nearby end table and took a deep breath. "It's never been a particular affectation of mine, of course. I have other tendencies, and I'll be the first to admit it. Becoming president of the Nitwitts has caused me to take a long, hard look at myself, as you've probably observed."

"You've been doing a magnificent job since I stepped down," Laurie replied, knowing quite well what Myrtis meant. Only recently had Raymond Troy's widow stopped regaling her friends with glib, pretentious accounts of how much money she'd been left and how much she spent on everything—from shoes to antiques, soup to nuts. Without question, the dollar signs in her eyes seemed to have faded somewhat, much to the relief of all her friends.

"I appreciate that. Coming from you, that certainly means a lot."

Myrtis offered nothing further, however, and Laurie continued to force the issue. "When you said that you wouldn't mind, was that your way of suggesting to me that the others would? I thought there might be a mixed reaction when I first came up with the idea. How do you see it?"

"Some of them would mind, I think. Oh, maybe our Wittsie might not. She's never been particularly vain about anything, as far as I know. You know how scatty she is."

Indeed, the spindly and somewhat absentminded club secretary, Wittsie Chadwick, who had voluntarily stepped down years ago as president because the responsibilities were starting to overwhelm her, was as straightforward as they came. Myrtis was probably right about her. But the rest? They were a different-feathered flock entirely, and Laurie quickly reviewed them in her head.

First up was Novie Mims, their world traveler, who had never been particularly forthcoming about anything except her interminable slide shows. Her relationship with her now-departed husband, Geoffrey, had always been somewhat shrouded in mystery, nor had she ever offered as much as a crumb about the whereabouts and activities of her only son, Marc.

Next, Denver Lee McQueen—she of the god-awful but finally abandoned oil painting pastime—had recently revealed to the group her prediabetic diagnosis and had become inordinately preoccupied with trying to melt away some of her generous poundage. She had taken to hounding them all relentlessly on the subjects of healthful recipes and sticking her fingers for blood, to the point of distraction. Would she be amenable to revealing yet more private information about her life?

And finally there was Renza Belford, who wrapped her privacy around herself like the fox furs she usually wrapped around her shoulders in public. Not to mention that Renza had always had a perceptible nose-in-the-air attitude about life in general. It was no exaggeration to say that this sleek and fashionable woman likely thought of herself as just a little bit better than everybody else. As a result, it also seemed likely that Renza's fastidiousness just might require her to take a dim view of Laurie's new scheme.

That was the lot, and Laurie suddenly realized that the task ahead of her might be a bit more formidable than she had anticipated. Myrtis had always been a fairly accurate bellwether of the group's reactions.

"I assume you're going to bring this up when we all get together Friday at your place," Myrtis resumed. Then she offered a lingering wink. "Of course, everyone is just dying to hear all your honeymoon details."

"Yes, I did promise, didn't I?"

"That you did. And we're not going to let you off the hook."

Laurie drained the last of her Bloody Mary, devoured her olive, and gave her friend an amused glance. "Well, never fear. I do intend to deliver—within reason, of course. Powell would want me to keep a few things out of the public domain. But I'm also perfectly serious about this latest ploy of mine. It could end up being just what Mr. Choppy needs to put him over the top when the election campaign starts up in earnest."

Myrtis's expression was the picture of skepticism. "You really think so? You know that I've always admired your many schemes over the years. You generally came up with just what the doctor ordered for the club. But this one? I just don't know, Laurie. I just don't know."

★

Come Friday noon, Renza Belford was the first to grace Laurie's little tea party with her presence, sweeping into the foyer of the tidy Victorian raised cottage that Laurie had shared first with Roy and now called home with Powell. Fashionably attired, immaculately coiffed, and swathed in her customary fox fur even in the heat of late summer, she lost no time in revealing that she was in the midst of a crisis.

"I'm absolutely wrung out, Laurie," she began, making straight for one of the parlor sofas. She plopped herself down with a resolute sigh.

"You could take off that fur for starters," Laurie replied, following close behind and taking a seat beside her. "And what ever happened to hello?"

Renza drew back slightly but quickly recovered her wits. "Oh, I didn't mean wrung out from the heat." Despite the clarification, she immediately removed her fur and set it aside. "And here's a belated hello for you. By the way, you look exquisite as usual. I love that shade of blue you have on. It definitely suits you and your cute figure. Brings out your eyes, especially." Then she paused briefly to sniff the air and flash a smile. "And that must be tomato sauce I smell on your stove. Wait—a touch of garlic, right?"

"First-rate sniffer you got there."

"Well, I'm sure whatever it is you're serving will be delicious. Now, down to my complaint. You just wouldn't believe what horse apples I've been through this week. My LaGrande just up and quit on me after what seems like eons. You know, she's been coming to me since just after Lewis and I were married and our children were mere babies. I thought LaGrande and I would fly over the Second Creek Cemetery and look down from above on all our mourners together one glorious day."

Laurie was unable to restrain herself, blurting out the conspiratorial comment that burst into her brain. "How very Egyptian! Planning to take her along to starch your shroud in the afterlife, were you?"

"I fail to appreciate your morbid humor today, Laurie. You could be a bit more sympathetic. Reliable people are just impossible to come by these days. I don't know how you've managed all these years without. I know you could have afforded help. Your Roy did well enough in the life insurance game, and my Lewis, being the successful realtor that he was, always insisted that I pamper myself. Of course, I did my best to accommodate him, and I really think he doted on my extravagance."

"Extravagance was never my thing, Renza. I've always preferred to do the cooking and cleaning myself. My mother was the same way. She always said that if you wanted things done right, you should do them yourself. Roy and my two girls never complained, and neither has Powell so far."

Renza looked unimpressed, her nose tilting upward in customary fashion. "Well, for my part, I'd rather pay someone to scrub the toilets and chase down the furballs under the beds and furniture. Anyway, LaGrande shows up Monday morning and tells me that she's moving away to Memphis to keep company with her sister, whose husband just happened to keel over and drop dead from a heart attack after stuffing himself with barbecued ribs and potato salad."

"Oh, how awful!"

"Yes. It seems they waited around too long thinking he just had a bad case of indigestion. So I've been scurrying around trying to find a replacement on such short notice."

"And have you found one?"

"Yes, but that's not the half of it. She's this sweet young thing named Vidalia Williams from somewhere out in the county. Anyhow, she showed up promptly this morning and did a very competent job dusting and vacuuming and scrubbing everything I asked her to, but I'm frazzled to within an inch of my life."

Laurie frowned, then leaned in skeptically. "If she was so competent, why are you so frazzled?"

"Because," Renza began with an exasperated edge to her voice, "I had to straighten everything up before she came."

"Run that by me again?"

Renza gathered herself, rearranging her fur on the sofa and then shaking her head impatiently. "Since you've always done for yourself, you wouldn't understand. But you simply cannot have servants seeing how messy things get in between visits. You have to preclean before they walk through the door. That's always been my policy."

Laurie burst into a wide grin, raising an eyebrow. "No wonder this Vidalia person did such a good job. You did most of the work for her."

"Yes, well, I'll probably relax about it as time goes on, but you have to make that first impression count with servants. You have to make it clear that you have high standards from the start, and the only way to do that is to let them see how clean you expect things to be. Otherwise, they take advantage of you and try to get by with as little as possible. Despite our many years together, LaGrande had gotten positively surly about doing extra things like minding the grime around the baseboards. Perhaps it's best she moved on, now that I think about it."

"Now, that's the Renza Belford I know and understand," Laurie replied after mulling things over briefly. "Very Nitwittian in outlook, through and through."

"So glad you approve, dear. And now that I've explained everything to your satisfaction, I believe I'd like a taste of whatever spirits you had in mind for us today," Renza added. "I'm parched after explaining the entire house to Vidalia."

"I've mixed us all some delicious milk punch today, and it's coming right up."

Five minutes later, Laurie and Renza were sipping milk punch in the parlor alongside Denver Lee McQueen, who was the next to arrive, full of the latest details on her battle with the bulge and related health problems.

"I really shouldn't be having this milk punch, girls," she was saying, trying to get comfortable beneath the pedestrian tent dress that concealed her still ample figure. "Not just from the calorie angle, of course, but the alcohol isn't conducive to my proper blood sugar levels. But perhaps one won't hurt. I've been a very good girl this past week. I've eaten plate after eternal plate of al dente vegetables and boneless, skinless chicken breasts sautéed in extra-virgin olive oil. You'd think something that's essentially naked like that would be more exciting to taste, but my God, how I've begun to miss the good old days when I could crunch something deep-fried without a hint of guilt!"

"Then you think you've gotten this prediabetic thing under control?" Laurie said.

"Well, I have lost four pounds over the past two weeks. I'm sure you can't tell, though. Sometimes I think it's a lost cause. My bone structure doesn't help one iota. It's not just these big shoulders of mine either. I wake up to my full moon of a face every morning in the mirror, and I curse whatever gods may be that I must have been playing hooky the day they handed out cheekbones."

That produced a healthy outburst of laughter just as the doorbell rang. Laurie rose to admit the remaining Nitwitts—Myrtis, Wittsie, and Novie.

"So you've started without us?" Novie quipped after the usual greetings were exchanged and the newcomers had settled in all around the room. "Back up and repeat whatever naughty little honeymoon incident you were describing, Laurie. We heard all the whooping and hollering at the door."

"No, it isn't what you think, Novie. I hadn't even started in on the honeymoon," Laurie explained as she headed for the kitchen. "Denver Lee was just bringing us up to speed on her current bouts with the sugar bug. Meanwhile, you girls just relax while I fetch you some milk punch."

Soon, everyone was sipping blissfully, allowing Laurie's doctored-up whiskey to work its magic while bits and pieces of the honeymoon trip emerged. "We decided to ride the streetcar on the way to dinner at Commander's Palace," Laurie was saying. "Just a simple, inexpensive thing to do out of all the elaborate choices you can make in New Orleans, but we enjoyed it. All the different architectural periods of the city pass you by along St. Charles Avenue. We got a great look at the Garden District, letting the breeze blow against our faces through the open window. You do that sort of thing when you're in love as a sort of reflex action."

Novie grew restless, wriggling her pigeon-breasted little form in her seat. "Enough about breezes and the scenery. How was the romance? Where did y'all stay?"

"The Royal Sonesta in the Quarter, and the romance was just fine and dandy, Novie. Powell was always very attentive during our courtship period, and he was not found lacking in that department in New Orleans or later on in Negril. I'd say our ratio of indoor to outdoor activity was roughly two to one. Lots and lots of room service."

"Did you take pictures?" Novie continued, suppressing a chuckle. "You know, I've been to Jamaica, but I wanted to see the grittier side of things, so I spent most of my time in Kingston while I was down there. You know me. I prefer adventure to predictability. I don't like doing the really touristy things."

"Yes, I remember your Kingston slide show quite well. Very *National Geographic* in content. And to answer your question, we did take snapshots, but we haven't developed them yet. I'll have you all over again when we do."

Laurie ignored the disappointed expressions and slumped postures and continued to paint elaborate verbal pictures of the historic houses, antique shops, beaches, and palm-dotted landscapes she and Powell had enjoyed throughout the respective stops of the honeymoon. Eventually she ran out of material, and the Nitwitts ran out of questions. Time to get down to the business of broaching her ploy for Mr. Choppy's election campaign.

"Ladies," Myrtis began, clearing the way after Laurie had signaled with a decided tilt of her head. "As club president I'd like to turn the floor over to Laurie, who has something for us to consider regarding helping Mr. Choppy out during his upcoming election bid. Laurie?"

"Should I take notes?" Wittsie said, looking suddenly bewildered as Laurie rose and moved to a spot in the middle of her Persian rug. "I mean, I didn't come prepared for that. . . . No one mentioned any club business. . . . You know how I am. . . . Oh, dear . . . did I just forget?"

Laurie gave her a thoughtful glance and smiled. "No, you didn't forget your secretarial duties, Wittsie. I did discuss this briefly with Myrtis beforehand, but this isn't really an official club matter yet, since I'm technically not even a member anymore. I just thought I'd run my idea past all of you, and if you decide to run with it, then you can take it from there."

She now had their undivided attention, and she could tell by the benign and respectful expressions on their faces that they had no idea what was coming. Though she was no longer president, it was clear that they still looked to her for leadership. So she just took a deep breath and plowed ahead, blurting it out all at once—deliberately not leaving any room for commentary or questions. She was afraid that if she got interrupted, she might lose heart. When she had finished, the silence was deafening.

Myrtis finally broke the stalemate. "Well, what do you think, girls?"

Renza cleared her throat pointedly. "You first, Myrtis. It seems you've heard all of this before."

"For the record, I don't think I'd mind doing it," Myrtis replied. "After all, it's to help Mr. Choppy out, and we all did our best for him at the Piggly Wiggly, whether we were dancing or shopping."

"Dancing or shopping was one thing. This is something entirely different," Renza added, aiming for indignation. "I think it's in poor taste, myself."

Myrtis pointedly locked eyes with Laurie and then continued. "Well, you're entitled to your opinion, of course. How about the rest of you?"

Wittsie stirred uncomfortably, speaking softly and in her usual discombobulated fashion. "I don't think it's that big a deal. . . . I mean, yes, if Mr. Floyce is going to make such an issue of this, it might become a big deal. . . . That just doesn't seem right to me . . . but we could throw it right back in his face. . . . Couldn't we just—"

"Horse apples! I don't care what anyone says," Renza interrupted. "I'm not going to reveal my age like that. Of course, I think I look damned good for my age. I'm certainly not ashamed of it. But that's not the point. This just seems, well, too off the wall, Laurie. Frankly, it's the first idea you've ever come up with that I just don't think has staying power."

Laurie chose not to be argumentative, knowing better than to antagonize certain members of the group. "Well, perhaps you're right, Renza. But could we hear from Novie and Denver Lee first?"

There was an awkward silence, but finally Denver Lee spoke up. "I do think it's a bit tacky, Laurie. A radio campaign where we all talk about how proud we are to be—let's face it—over the hill? Okay, okay. I know that's not the way you put it just now. There's nothing wrong with aging gracefully, and God knows, I was as big a fan of *The Golden Girls* as the next mature woman. But here you're asking us to reveal our approximate ages as a testimonial to the viability of Mr. Choppy. Don't you think that's a bit apples and oranges?"

Laurie smiled graciously. "Thanks for the input." Then she turned to Novie. "And what about you?"

Novie finished the last of her milk punch and surveyed her peers with an imperious air. "This may surprise you all, but I see nothing wrong with Laurie's idea. The bottom line here is to help Mr. Choppy oust Mr. Floyce, and if Mr. Floyce is going to make Mr. Choppy's age an issue and somehow sneakily claim that he's too old to be mayor, I think we ought to rally around him, ladies. Attacking someone just because they have a few rings around the trunk is downright mean-spirited. I thought Reagan handled all of that in devastating fashion in that debate he had with

Mondale back in the eighties. I have no problem revealing to Second Creek that I am sixty-six years old and can still hold my shrimp fork without a session of physical therapy, thank you very much. I'm for it all the way."

Renza made a brief hissing sound. "You'd go anywhere and do or say anything as long as you had a camera in your hand, but I'm not going to tell every Tom, Dick, and Harry out there in Radioland how long it's been since I arrived in my birthday suit."

Then Laurie adopted her traditional peacemaker mode. "I can respect that, Renza. No one's saying that you have to participate—that is, if you all decide to do this. My suggestion would be that those who choose to reveal their exact ages in the radio spots can do so, and maybe the rest can just pitch in and man the phones at the Piggly Wiggly. Mr. Choppy says that's going to be very important, too. He knows how well connected we all are and hopes we can help him get out the vote among our friends."

"And you say Powell will help us write these spots so that they sound professional? I know I wouldn't begin to know where to start putting a radio commercial together," Myrtis added.

"Of course he will," Laurie replied. "He's officially in charge of all that. I'm sure you all remember that come-hither spot he created to get all the ladies dancing in the aisles this summer. He and Mr. Choppy are in the midst of planning the rhetoric of the whole campaign, and I know he'd be delighted to work with each of you again. Believe me, he'll present you in a totally flattering way."

"I absolutely adored our rehearsals at the Piggly Wiggly," Novie said. "What fun gliding down the aisles the way we did.

Your Powell is one smooth operator, and I felt as if I were danc-ing in the clouds."

Laurie smirked, wagging her brows shamefully for effect. "In more ways than one." She was very much aware that she was the envy of the group, and she had tried hard not to gloat once she and Powell were out of the bag and in the sack, but there were times when she just couldn't seem to help herself. Every woman should have it as good as she did right now.

Then Myrtis made an executive decision, calling for an impromptu vote on Laurie's suggestions. "And Laurie," she con-tinued, "would you be kind enough to get Wittsie a notepad and pen so she can record all of this?"

The directive sent Laurie scurrying into the kitchen to rum-mage through a couple of junk drawers, but she eventually emerged with the necessary secretarial items. The group was quickly canvassed—minus Laurie, who could no longer vote. The result was three yeas from Myrtis, Novie, and Wittsie, and two nays from Renza and Denver Lee.

"How about we leave it like this for now?" Myrtis began after reviewing the scribbles on the piece of paper Wittsie handed over to her. "We'll all help with the phone banks as we can work it into our schedules, and those who wish to pursue a radio spot can get together with Powell and work out the copy to their liking."

Everyone seemed agreeable to that arrangement, and then Laurie announced that it was time to settle in around the dining-room table for baked chicken spaghetti, buttered green beans with sliced almonds, homemade cornbread muffins, and the mandatory sweet tea to wash things down. Although Laurie insisted she could manage things all by herself, her words fell on deaf ears, and all six women quickly crowded into the kitchen, getting in one another's way. It was almost as confounding as the deferential debates the Nitwitts always had over whose turn it was to pick up the tab when they all dined out.

"It's my turn to pay!" was the opening battle cry on such occasions. Followed by "Nonsense, this is my treat this time!" And then, "I won't hear of it!" Or, "I absolutely insist!"

More often than not, of course, they had all settled for going Dutch, but not before going through the requisite paces worthy of a bad theatrical audition.

Finally, Laurie brought order to confusion by giving each woman her own assignment—something to carry out into the dining room or something to shut off in the kitchen or haul out of the fridge—and soon they were complimenting their hostess in between bites.

"I keep forgetting to get your recipe for this marvelous chicken spaghetti," Novie said after taking a sip of her tea.

"Oh, it's just your basic spaghetti recipe," Laurie explained. "The secret is to saufe the chicken with the onions before you put the whole thing in to bake."

"I'll have to mind the size of my portion, Laurie," Denver Lee offered. "Pasta turns to sugar, you know. But I'm fine with the green beans—even a second helping—and you notice I'm not having any sweet tea—just ice water. I hope you don't mind that I poured a tumbler out of that big pitcher you had in the fridge."

"Oh, of course I don't mind. And I must do better in the future about remembering you have special needs now. I'm so accustomed to fixing everything under the sun. Roy, Lizzie, and Hannah always ate whatever I put on their plates, and Powell has maybe the world's best appetite."

"And not just for food, we understand," Novie quipped. There was a ripple of laughter around the table, and the luncheon conversation continued to drift further into the pleasantly mundane. It was a familiar scene—the six of them discussing the state of Second Creek and its environs while enjoying good food and one another's company. For her part, Laurie considered her mission mostly accomplished. At least a couple of the Nitwitts, along with herself, were going to go to bat in a very personal way for Mr. Choppy during the campaign. Furthermore, she knew Powell was her ace in the hole. When word got back to the holdouts about what fun it was to work with him on the radio spots, she figured peer pressure might just do the trick and bring the rest of them on board.

4.

THE MOLE AND
OTHER MATTERS

Mr. Choppy was sitting behind his Piggly Wiggly—aka campaign headquarters—office desk, checking his watch for the umpteenth time over the last fifteen minutes. It was now quarter past six on a late September Saturday evening in Second Creek. The record heat wave the town had been experiencing was finally beginning to dissipate, and there was a refreshing nip in the air at long last. Could the unpredictable storms of a Second Creek winter be far behind?

Mr. Choppy's mole was supposed to have shown up right around six for the latest inside report on Mr. Floyce's plans. Powell Hampton was keeping Mr. Choppy company for a brainstorming session, scribbling on a legal pad and trying out different combinations of words for campaign slogans. After much deliberation, Powell had told Mr. Choppy that he felt the Vote for a New Outlook: Hearty and Hale Dunbar Jr. idea was just a little too cutesy for their objectives.

"I like the new outlook part, but let's stay away from puns, why don't we?" Powell had suggested. "We want the public to take you seriously, and we already know that Mr. Floyce is going to do his damnedest to make sure that doesn't happen. Let's don't give him any additional ammunition. I can picture him saying something like, 'See? Even Mr. Choppy thinks his candidacy is a big joke.'"

Mr. Choppy had deferred to Powell's judgment and quickly charged him with the task of coming up with something appropriate. "I guess we're back to that word *gravitas*, huh?"

And Powell had smiled, put pen to hand, and immediately gone to work.

At exactly 6:21, Charley Franklin Forbes sauntered into the office with a scowl on his weary face and his hands tucked into the pockets of his jeans, looking very much as if he wanted to deck someone. Mr. Choppy and Powell stood up, the perfunctory introductions were made, and the three men quickly got down to business.

"Sorry I'm runnin' a little late," Charley began, settling into his chair. "Minnie and I had another big blowup about her job. Seems we're always fightin' about it these days. That's why I'm willin' to do whatever I can to help you get that stingy, manipulatin' sonuvabitch outta office, Mr. Choppy." He dug down into his pocket and handed over a folded piece of paper. "Those are my latest notes straight from Minnie's pad. Hope you find 'em useful like the last two times. I'll keep on doin' this as long as you think it'll help out."

Mr. Choppy opened it up, scanned the writing, and then gave it to Powell for a look-see. "So he'll resort to somethin' as trite as kissing babies this time out, huh?" Mr. Choppy remarked, shaking his head. "That'll be a first. Don't recall he ever did that before."

Powell finished with the paper and rested it in his lap. "He didn't need to. After all, he's been unopposed for so long. But in a way it makes sense. We already know that he's planning to make your inexperience and even your age an issue, though I think he'll have to be careful about his approach there. I also think what he may be striving for here is to associate himself with youth and vitality for contrast. What better way to do that than to schedule a bunch of photo ops with young couples and their adorable babies and youngsters. It may be corny, it may be old school, but it's worked for a lot of politicians who haven't had a lot else to offer over the years."

Mr. Choppy nodded with an air of resignation. "I see what you mean. No better place to find 'em than out in the aisles of the MegaMart, too. Frankly, I think some of 'em live out there."

Charley straightened up his scrawny body a bit and warily cocked his head to one side. "So did I do good?"

"Yeah, you did," Mr. Choppy replied. "We need to know as much about his campaign as we can ahead of time. You don't know how much I appreciate you takin' the time to come to me in the first place. You're a godsend." Then Mr. Choppy turned to his campaign manager for feedback. "Do we need to counter this?"

Powell sat in silence for a few moments, running his hand through his silver hair while concentrating hard. Finally, he said, "If Mr. Floyce is going to be scheduling glad-handing and baby-kissing sessions out at the MegaMart, I say we do the same thing. Laurie can get the Nitwitts to round up all the young couples they know to trot out their reproductive handiwork. Hey, if Mr. Floyce can kiss babies out at the MegaMart, you can kiss babies at the Piggly Wiggly."

Mr. Choppy was unable to suppress his laughter. "So this'll be a kiss-off, more or less?"

The other two men joined the laughter, and Powell said, "That's one way to look at it, I suppose. It's all about image, though. You'll want to appear in touch with Second Creekers and concerned about their well-being. You and I know that you really are concerned in a way that Mr. Floyce never could be. You know this town like the back of your hand, and you really do care what happens to all the people in it. You won't be faking any of your kisses, in any case."

"But Mr. Floyce sure will be!" Charley put in suddenly. "He's the biggest fake east of the Mississippi River, far as I'm concerned. He'll be out there schmoozin' the hell outta everyone and tryin' to sell 'em a ton of his Miss Delta Floozie CDs while he's at it. He's all about the money and the power, and he'll fight like a dog to make sure he keeps 'em both."

"Yep. He's likely to get nasty without appearin' to," Mr. Choppy replied while retrieving a file folder from his upper right-hand desk drawer. Then he thumbed through it and pulled out a newspaper clipping, momentarily holding it up in front of his face and giving it a thump with his finger. "You gotta hand it to him, though. He's slick as they come. Talkin' Littleman Mullins and the MegaMart into that Miss Delta Floozie CD contract for the entire state of Mississippi was quite an accomplishment. That song stinks up the place in my book 'cause it really doesn't make much sense unless it's June and you're in The Square watchin' the Miss Delta Floozie Contest. It's gotten downright sickenin' to watch him emcee that thing every year. Betcha Bert Parks is turnin' over in his grave."

Charley's head bobbed up and down vigorously. "But you better believe Littleman Mullins'll get a nice kickback on every sale."

"Pretty good bet," said Mr. Choppy. Then he settled back in his chair, folded his hands, and rested them in his lap. "I guess Littleman Mullins has come a long way, truth to tell. I can remember years ago when he first came here to manage the new tire store over on Cypress Street. Now he's worked his way up to manager of the local MegaMart and all that comes with it. He's a go-getter in his own right—I'll give him that—and I'm sure he saw this CD thing as an opportunity to make more money for the store and get more publicity. Maybe he thinks he can get a little higher up in the MegaMart chain if this works out for him."

Charley briefly rested his chin in the palm of his hand while drumming his fingers on his cheekbone. "We all wanna get ahead. It's just I'd like to do it the right way."

Mr. Choppy sat up and leaned in. "Don't you worry, Charley. I'll be as good as my word. If I get elected, I'm sure I can find a spot for you somewhere in my administration for helpin' us out the way you have. I know this is all about givin' your Minnie some well-deserved time off."

"No special favors, though, Mr. Choppy. Just somethin' you think I might be qualified for. I don't want you to do it the way Mr. Floyce does. I'll do any sorta hard work you think I can do if you get in. Hell, if I can cut the heads off catfish for twenty years and still keep my head together, I can do near about any-thing!"

"I'm sure you can," Mr. Choppy replied.

Charley rose from his chair, offering his hand to both men in turn. "Well, I better be headin' on home. Minnie and I didn't have so bad a set-to that she won't have supper waitin' for me, and she'll be ticked off if she has to hold it too long. Saturday's always fried chicken and corn on the cob with baked custard for dessert. Minnie takes good care of me, despite workin' all hours of the day and night for Mr. Floyce. Maybe she might not like me sneakin' around readin' her notes the way I have, but I don't care. She deserves a break, and if this is the way I can maybe get it for her, so be it."

"I can fully appreciate that," Mr. Choppy said. "Now, you take care of yourself, and let us know if anything else comes up."

★

After Charley had left, Mr. Choppy grabbed an envelope from the file folder he had just retrieved and handed it over to Powell. "I'd like you to take a look at this letter. Got it in my mailbox this mornin'."

Powell scanned it quickly, then looked up from his lap with a shrewd expression. "So Mr. Floyce has agreed to your idea of a debate after all. Interesting."

"You think this is good news, don'tcha?"

Powell took his time while his instincts kicked in. They told him in no uncertain terms that this missive from Mr. Floyce might well be a Trojan horse. It would be prudent to think everything through carefully. "I'm slightly surprised he agreed to it. I think the conventional wisdom about the incumbent giving too much exposure to the challenger is that it's not a good idea. Mr. Floyce is evidently very confident that he'll win any head-to-head with you."

"I guess I'm not the world's greatest speaker. How are you at coachin'?"

Powell flashed his usual confident smile. "Just so happens I was top dog on my high school debate team. When I was growing up, I liked to argue almost as much as I liked to dance. I argued with my teachers, parents—even my minister. My wife Ann always said I was going to be the first dancing president of the United States someday, and I'd shuffle my way through all those inside-the-Beltway press conferences."

"Sounds good to me," Mr. Choppy said with an appreciative chuckle. "I never had a problem visitin' with all my Piggly Wiggly customers, helpin' 'em find things in the store or listenin' to 'em go on and on about their families. You just gotta help me find a way to translate that into solid campaign talk. Otherwise, I just might be sunk."

"Don't worry. I believe I can do that," Powell replied, handing back Mr. Floyce's letter. Then he turned his attention once again to his legal pad. "I wanted you to review these latest campaign slogan ideas with me, since we've nixed the Hearty and Hale idea for good." Powell tore off the top yellow sheet and handed it over, then sat back in his chair and waited for the verdict.

Finally, the studied tension in Mr. Choppy's face broke, and he looked up. "I think I like this last one the best—Hale Dunbar Jr.—A New Beginning with a Trusted Friend. That's pretty much how I feel about my ambitions."

Powell beamed, then clasped his hands together above his head in a gesture of victory. "You and I are definitely on the same page. That's the strongest one in my opinion, too. And you'll notice that I carefully resisted the phrase 'old friend.' We don't want to play into Mr. Floyce's plans to suggest that you are in any way over the hill and incapable of governing."

"Gotcha. So what's next? How's the radio campaign comin'?"

Powell took back the yellow sheet and made a check mark beside their slogan of choice. "Well, as I told you, Laurie has talked a few of the Nitwitt ladies into making some spots about the advantages of maturity, so to speak. Sometime in December, I'll be getting together with them and working out the copy for the January radio flight. It should be an interesting challenge, since it will basically involve dancing around the subject of a woman's age. Tying it up with pretty ribbons, if you will. I think Laurie did an incredible job getting any of them to agree to it. My Ann was always a tad vain on the subject herself."

Mr. Choppy was amused. He remembered that his own mother, Gladys, had been a devoted practitioner of the age-fudging art, routinely reducing her own age by a couple of years. Once she had passed fifty, however, the subject was completely verboten in the Dunbar household on Pond Street. Substantial presents were still given, and multilayered cakes were still baked. But candles were strictly banned.

"Give me your honest opinion of Miz Hampton's latest idea," Mr. Choppy said finally.

Powell had given the matter a great deal of thought and was thoroughly prepared to defend his wife's latest brainstorm. Having dealt with women far more often than men during his distinguished dancing career, he had developed considerable insight into the female psyche. "I think it just might be surprisingly effective. While it's true that women don't generally like to discuss their age, I plan to package these radio testimonials so that people will sit up and take notice. We should get points for originality and honesty. I'll also work in a bit of humor. I've emphasized to Laurie that we need to keep this particular ploy of ours under wraps until the spots get broadcast. That way we'll get the full benefit of the element of surprise."

"I have to say," Mr. Choppy added, "that I did a really smart thing when I asked you two to manage my campaign. Look at what all you've both come up with already."

"It's our pleasure to try and help you cross the finish line first. Oh, and by the way, I'll do a couple of more generic radio spots for the campaign. We'll talk about your experience as a businessman for nearly five decades, as well as your family's good works in the community over the years. Second Creekers mostly know who you are, but we have to refresh their memories and encourage them to picture you in a different role now."

"You really do have a way with words," Mr. Choppy replied, his face brightening considerably. "You just said it a hundred times better'n I could have."

"We have to run a very smart and down-to-earth campaign, and we should refrain from the negative stuff. Let's just concentrate on your positives, and let Mr. Floyce make all the snide insinuations, if that's the way he chooses to go. It could backfire big-time."

"Amen to that," Mr. Choppy replied. "Maybe some people would call me naïve, but I don't have the stomach for a knock-down-and-drag-out debate with Mr. Floyce anyway. It's just not in my nature. Win or lose, I'll fight the good fight."

Powell glanced down at his watch and gave a little gasp. "Oh, it's almost seven. Laurie will have dinner waiting for me, and she'll want to know all about how it went tonight."

The two men rose from their chairs and headed into the freshly appointed war room of Mr. Choppy's campaign headquarters.

Where shelves and aisles once stood, parallel rows of long tables with phones perched atop them every few feet now awaited his campaign workers to come.

Mr. Choppy came to a halt about halfway to the front door and quickly surveyed the entire setup before turning back to Powell. "I think we're about ready to do battle, don't you?"

"I do. Time to enlist the troops and practice talking you up. Any early takers besides Laurie's Nitwitts?"

Mr. Choppy quickly reviewed the short list in his head and said: "Let's see . . . Hunter and Mary Fred Goodlett called up just the other day to volunteer. I'm sure you know all about their famous bulletin-board courtship in my store. Up until you and Miz Hampton were married in the Piggly Wiggly this past summer, that was the best-known example of a couple gettin' hitched with the blessings of the Piggly Wiggly. The Goodletts also said their daughter, son-in-law, and little granddaughter would also make themselves available to the cause."

"I know all about the Goodletts and your store. Brings a smile to my face every time."

"Yep. It's feel-good stuff," Mr. Choppy replied just as they had reached the front door. "And we do have another volunteer, but I totally forgot to run it past you during our meeting. Lady Roth dropped me a little note offerin' her services the other day. I haven't had a chance to get back to her yet. I'm a little worried about her participation."

Powell grinned. "I think we'll have to handle her with kid gloves. There may be some downside to having her call people up campaigning for you. After all, she has that proverbial short fuse."

"I was thinkin' the same thing."

"Maybe we can come up with something for her to do that doesn't involve her being on the front line, so to speak. I'll discuss it with Laurie and see what she thinks."

"Good deal. When we get together tomorrow, I'll dig up Lady Roth's letter and let you take it home. You and Miz Hampton can make the final decision on how we should handle it."

Then the two men said good night and parted company.

Mr. Choppy was pleased, sighing softly as he watched Powell driving out of the parking lot. It had been a very productive brainstorming session with half of his management team, and he already knew Powell's better half was working wonders with her Nitwitts. As he turned off lights and locked up for the evening, he thought to himself that he just might have a real shot at upsetting Mr. Floyce in the upcoming election.

5.

KISSING BABIES—THE
FIRST VOLLEY

There was nothing particularly spectacular about autumn in Second Creek. Located at the north end of the Mississippi Delta—which had once been defined in literary terms as beginning in the lobby of the Peabody Hotel in Memphis and ending on Catfish Row in Vicksburg—Second Creek and its environs were largely devoid of the vibrant leaf color associated with other regions of the country. The flat fields of soybeans and cotton were flanked here and there by thickets of willow and cypress, along with the occasional stand of hardwoods, but the overall effect was one of wide-open spaces punctuated by bare branches stabbing at the sky.

For some unknown reason, the current blandness of the landscape seemed to be duplicated by Second Creek's weather patterns as well. In a town fabled for its violent and unpredictable weather phenomena, nothing unusual had ever developed during the fall months — at least not that anyone could remember. It was as if Mother Nature herself always sucked in her cheeks and held her breath during this period, saving up her fury for the winter and spring cycles during which Second Creekers frequently had to run for cover.

Against such a backdrop, October gave way to November, heralding the informal beginnings of the mayoral election campaign between Mr. Floyce and Mr. Choppy. The first volley was officially fired by Mr. Floyce out at the MegaMart in a series of elaborate photo ops that showcased his new hands-on persona. On a sunny day that was slightly chilly around the edges, Mr. Floyce and Littleman Mullins held forth just outside the MegaMart's massive automatic front doors.

"Ah, Miz Copeland, so good to see you this morning!" Mr. Floyce began right after taking up his station, dressed in his customary seersucker suit. Even in the colder months, he always fancied that particular fashion statement. He grasped the pudgy matron's hand and pressed into her palm a card with his picture and campaign slogan printed upon it: Keep a Good Thing Going — Reelect Floyce Hammontree. "Is that a new dress you have on?" he continued. "I've always said you wear clothes so well! I hope you'll think of me in the voting booth come February."

Standing beside him and outfitted in his starched, bilious green MegaMart vest and pants, Littleman Mullins was grinning from ear to ear and offered the woman a discount coupon with one hand while gesturing broadly toward the entrance to his cornucopia of merchandise with the other. "Here's a little somethin' that'll getcha twenty percent off anything in the store today, Miz Copeland."

An astute observer would have classified the routine as a barely disguised ploy to buy votes, and the glad-handing continued full force.

"Well, lookee here!" Mr. Floyce exclaimed as a young mother with unflattering horn-rimmed glasses and a dirty-looking pony-tail approached the entrance holding her waddling, bundled-up toddler by the hand. "And how old is this handsome lad, ma'am?"

The woman beamed and picked up the child. "He just made three. Just left the terrible twos behind."

"Ah, yes! Nothin' lasts forever, you know," Mr. Floyce added with a wink. "Now, I don't believe I've had the pleasure of meeting you, young lady. So tell me your name and your boy's name, too."

"I'm Josie Marten, and this is my son, Jacob Ray."

The onslaught continued as Littleman Mullins presented her with a coupon. "Here ya go, ma'am. Use it with our compliments!"

Mr. Floyce retrieved one of his cards and then reached into his pocket to pull out a small red lollipop. "Can little Jacob Ray have one, Miz Marten? Don't want to give it to him unless you say so. I know how you young mothers are always watchin' after cavities and spoiled appetites and things like that."

Mr. Floyce clearly had Josie Marten eating out of his hand. "Oh, no, he can have that," she replied, taking the candy from him and putting it in her coat pocket. "But I'll give it to him later on, after lunch."

Then came the exclamation point. Mr. Floyce leaned in and gave the boy a peck on the cheek while the earnest young photographer from *The Citizen* who had "just happened" to show up flashed his camera on cue. "I hope you'll remember me in the voting booth come February, Miz Marten," Mr. Floyce concluded.

"I certainly will," she replied, heading in with her Jacob Ray in tow.

The pièce de résistance—a carefully plotted photo op that would end up plastered all over the front page of *The Citizen* the next morning—came next. The corpulent Eljay Jeffers and his wife, KayDon, herself a bovine specimen if ever there was one, lumbered into the picture with their overfed daughter, Fayette, and her twin three-year-old girls, Montez and Dorcas.

"Well, here's the entire clan as promised, my friend—dressed up in our Sunday go-to-meetin' clothes!" Eljay proclaimed, stuffed into a three-piece suit whose buttons seemed about to launch into outer space. The truth was, the entourage was woefully overdressed for the occasion—especially the twins, who sported the kind of precocious clothing, makeup, and stiff bouffant hairdos typical of little girls' beauty pageants. Everything was just too contrived and cutesy for words.

"Yes, indeed!" Mr. Floyce replied. "The all-American family!"

Mr. Floyce took an obsessive-compulsive amount of time designing his shot of choice, consulting again and again with the photographer, constantly rearranging people—no small matter considering their combined bulk—and inserting himself in all sorts of distracting positions. Finally, he settled upon himself as the centerpiece of the configuration, squatting down between the two little girls, his arms resting on the shoulder pads of their age-inappropriate outfits. The rest of the Jeffers tribe stood behind them with plastic smiles affixed to their fleshy faces.

"Take one with me smilin' straight ahead," Mr. Floyce said to the photographer, whose facial expressions were beginning to betray his growing exasperation. "Then take two more with me kissin' each of these precious little girls. You know—one kiss to the right, one to the left. We'll keep at it until we find a keeper that shows my best angle."

Fifteen long minutes later, Mr. Floyce was finally satisfied, and the session with the Jeffers clan mercifully came to an end. But the glad-handing, coupon dispensing, and general schmoozing continued throughout the morning as Mr. Floyce made contact with several hundred voters who might end up making the difference between victory and defeat.

★

"Take a look at this," Powell said to Laurie over coffee, orange juice, and Cheerios at their breakfast table the next morning. He handed over the front page of the paper and awaited her reaction.

What confronted Laurie was a picture of Mr. Floyce fervently pressing his lips against the cheek of what appeared to be a miniature streetwalker. "Good heavens!" she proclaimed, thoroughly taken aback.

"The caption says that's one of Eljay Jeffers's granddaughters all dolled up like that," Powell added. "I guess this is Mr. Floyce's idea of kissing babies. Seems more like kiddie porn to me, though. Makes me feel downright queasy."

Laurie put the paper down and took a sip of her coffee. "I suppose this means the campaign has officially begun. I wonder if Mr. Floyce has any idea how predatory that photo actually makes him look."

"Probably not. He's overconfident—even arrogant—about his chances. At least that's the impression I'm getting from the bits and pieces we've received from Charley Forbes."

Laurie looked worried, nonetheless. "Should we maybe rethink the kissing babies thing at our end? I mean, we don't want Mr. Choppy to come off looking like some sort of pervert."

Powell laughed heartily with a toss of his silver head and said: "As his professional handlers, I think we can safely avoid that prospect. Which reminds me—I want to review that list of potential next-generation Piggly Wiggly participants you said you worked up from all your Nitwitt pals at your last meeting. Got it handy?"

"Oh, yes, we were going to do that today, weren't we?" Laurie replied, rising from her chair and heading over to one of the kitchen drawers where she had tucked away a manila folder the night before. "Here it is. A typical Nitwitt list—all over the map!" She returned to the table, opened the folder, and started reading her notes aloud:

"Denver Lee. Says her daughter, Nita, and her husband, Carter Hewes, and their three-year-old son, Christopher, will be visiting her just before Christmas and will be happy to make an appearance at headquarters to help out Mr. Choppy's campaign. That's simple enough." Laurie paused for a breath.

"Now, let's see . . . Wittsie. Says her granddaughter, Meagan, will be staying with her again while her parents do a Charles Dickens Literary Christmas with a tour group in London." Laurie looked up with a decided frown on her face. "I think that's awful, don't you? A teenage girl needs her parents around during the holidays. You remember that Meagan was in our wedding and stayed with Wittsie most of the summer while her parents were gallivanting all over Europe. Roy and I would never have even considered going away on vacation during the holidays without the girls while they were growing up. That's just downright irresponsible parenting, if you ask me."

Laurie resumed her review. "Renza. Her two children, Meta and Cole, and their families are scattered all over Creation, as she so dramatically put it to the group, and none of them can make it to Second Creek during the campaign, it seems." Laurie paused, frowning again and cocking her head. "Don't you think that's odd?"

Powell shrugged. "If they can't make it, they can't make it."

"No, that's not what I meant. It just now struck me that none of our children—the Nitwitts, I mean—not a one of our offspring have chosen to remain in Second Creek to work and raise their families. They've all moved away—every one of them. My Lizzie is in Chicago with her Barry, and Hannah is up in New England with her husband, Kent. As far as I know, none of the others are present and accounted for here in Second Creek either."

"It's probably just a coincidence," Powell replied.

"Or . . . maybe they all needed a break from the craziness of this town. Growing up here is a very intense and unusual experience. I can certainly vouch for that. I had a long conversation with Lizzie on the subject while she was here for our wedding, and she did mention getting another perspective on life living up in Chicago with Barry. But she also assured me that she would very much like to retire here. So maybe the generation below us will eventually return to sop up that special Second Creek gravy in their golden years."

Powell was giving his wife a thoughtful stare, even as a smile crept into the corners of his mouth. "That was very eloquent. I wonder if you should be the one creating the campaign copy."

"Nonsense. That was just one-shot speechifying. You're the one with the verbal staying power," she replied, waving him off playfully. Then she took up her list once again.

"Novie. Nothing from her. She just said none of her family would be able to participate, although she would gladly man the phones and fully intended to follow through on the radio spot. You know, she's just never talked much to any of us about her marriage to Geoffrey Mims, and her son, Marc, seems to have disappeared off the face of the planet. None of us have ever pressed the matter, of course. We've always respected her privacy."

"As it should be."

Laurie sighed stoically. "It's funny in a way. Novie's a slide-showing, wide-open book about her travels all over the world but such a closed case about her family. Some of us have gotten the impression that underneath it all, she's hiding some deep, dark secret."

Powell made a face worthy of a Halloween mask. "Ooh! The mystery of the Mims family deepens."

Laurie gave him a look of mock disdain and continued. "Which brings us to Myrtis. And here the news is positive. She said that her son, Raymond Junior, and her daughter, Roane, would be able to help out in the coming weeks. They both have small children who haven't seen their grandmother in quite a while, so they're definitely going to plan a visit with her out at Evening Shadows."

"And that's the crop?"

"Among the Nitwitts, yes. But there's the Hunter Goodlett family, of course. They'll do anything they can to help Mr. Choppy."

Powell finished the last of his cereal, lifting the bowl to his mouth to siphon off the sugar-flavored milk with the mischievous aplomb of a little boy. Then he grew thoughtful. "I was thinking that with Mr. Floyce's ludicrous photo op example to guide us in the area of what not to do, we should definitely be a bit more subtle in our approach to this kissing thing. You were right to bring it up a few minutes ago."

"I thought so, too," Laurie replied. "Any suggestions as to how we handle it?"

Powell deliberated further. "I don't think we abandon it, of course. But I do think we need to put it in a more natural context. None of this obvious preening and posing, and we definitely do not want to veer into the creepy. We'll just ask our supporters to appear with us at certain venues during the campaign to create that family atmosphere. When *The Citizen* comes calling with their photographer here and there, we will show the Mr. Choppy contingent having a good time together, and the issue of holding and kissing a baby will be an afterthought now and then, not the primary attraction."

Laurie managed a muted chuckle. "I seriously doubt the subject is covered in college political science classes anyhow. Kissing Babies 101? I don't think so."

"On the other hand," Powell added, "image is everything in today's culture. I've never agreed with the policy of style over substance, but it seems to be a fact of life these days. We have to create a pleasant enough style for Mr. Choppy and get Second Creekers to concentrate on why they should vote him into office and Mr. Floyce out, baby kisses or no baby kisses."

Laurie thumbed through her file folder again and located another page of notes, which she briefly held up for emphasis. "I think it's all going to come down to the Town Hall debate with Mr. Floyce on January fifteenth. Do you think you can coach

Mr. Choppy? Those TV interviews with Ronnie Leyton in the Piggly Wiggly this summer for that CNN piece had him sweating bullets. I had to coach him up a bit myself then."

"I think I can calm him down and clean him up, so to speak. You forget that I trained some of the clumsiest men and women on the face of the Earth during my ballroom dancing years. I'll get right to work with him on body language, pacing, and projecting his voice. The rest will simply be a matter of memorizing the brilliant lines I write for him."

"Sounds like a plan to me," Laurie replied with a confident smile. But creases of worry soon appeared in her face as she retrieved a perfumed letter, complete with flowery handwriting on lavender stationery from her file. "We haven't discussed what we're going to do about Lady Roth yet. She didn't really leave Mr. Choppy much wiggle room in this quasi-ultimatum of hers he turned over to us."

Powell sighed, his face a study in resignation. "Well, we just can't ignore her request to help out. If we could just find a way to harness all that pent-up energy of hers in a positive manner . . . "

Laurie silently scanned the letter yet another time, hoping to come up with a solution in the process.

My dear Mr. Choppy Dunbar:

Words cannot express how encouraged I am that you have decided to take on the formidable task of running for the privilege of governing Our Little Kingdom of Second Creek. Would that I were younger and more given to business matters rather than such a consummate slave to the Muses, or I might undertake such a noble mission myself.

In any case, I have decided to lend my full support to your campaign, bringing all of my creative energy to the task, and I trust you will not fail to take me up on my offer. I cast a wide net, indeed, among my acquaintances and shall willingly speak on your behalf wherever I go and whatever I do, urgently pressing them to cast their votes on your behalf.

I shall never forget the stage you afforded me this past summer in the aisles of the Piggly Wiggly, allowing me to impersonate my favorite female figures to my heart's content. Judging from the audience I drew on a regular basis for my performances, I gather that I lent a certain je ne sais quoi to the mundane business of grocery shopping.

It would now be highly imprudent of you not to take advantage of my social position and clout in the upcoming campaign, and I do expect to hear from you on this matter as you prepare your working strategy in the upcoming weeks. It is my belief that we have had more than enough of His Machiavellian Majesty, Floyce Hammontree, and that walking manatee of a sidekick, Eljay Jeffers, over the past fifteen years or so. I would be profoundly disappointed if you did not allow me to put forth my best efforts in helping remove him from office and usher in a bright new era for our beloved Second Creek.

Yours most expectantly for victory,

Lady Roth

Laurie had no sooner put the letter down on the table than her propensity for off-the-wall inspiration suddenly kicked in. "I've got it. Let's allow her to do what she does best—dress in costume and lose herself in a character."

"Do you have something or someone specific in mind? I'd give a mint-condition Buffalo nickel for what's cooking in that brain of yours."

"Nickel . . . nickel . . ." Laurie began, repeating the word several more times. Then she broke off, sucking in air dramatically. "No, not a nickel—a dollar coin. It just came to me this instant. Why not ask her to portray Susan B. Anthony, the great suffragette? We could make her a symbol during all Mr. Choppy's campaign appearances of the importance of women casting an intelligent, informed vote. That way, anything she says would be related to the character she's portraying or that particular feminist slant, and we would avoid the obvious pitfalls of her strong personality in all its condescending glory. I'll suggest to her that she research the part the way she did this summer for all her Piggly Wiggly performances, and everybody should end up happy—or at least harmlessly amused."

"Pluperfectly ingenious as usual!" Powell exclaimed. "I bet you anything she'd go for it, too!"

"She's a frustrated actress at heart. Mr. Choppy told me that her parents absolutely forbade her to pursue a career on the stage when she was a young girl. Seems she's been wandering about looking for curtain calls ever since—that is, until she found the perfect home for them here in Second Creek."

Powell offered a reflective grin. "For that matter, many of us odd fellows have found the perfect home here in Second Creek, and I know that's what Mr. Choppy wants to make this election all about. So let's bear down and get to work. I'll give Mr. Choppy the speech lessons, and you pin down Lady Roth on the character portrayal business."

"Absolutely," Laurie replied, her delicate features brightening. "And I'll bet you a big, fat uncirculated roll of Susan B. Anthony dollars that we pull it all off without a hitch!"

6.

KISSING BABIES —
THE RETORT

It did not take long for Mr. Choppy and Company to respond in exemplary fashion to Mr. Floyce's initial coupon-dispensing foray into campaigning. The occasion was the formal dedication of the Piggly Wiggly as Hale Dunbar Jr. campaign headquarters the following Friday morning. The regional media were well represented, thanks to the whip-smart press release Powell had prepared and sent out. The *Jackson Clarion-Ledger*, *Memphis Commercial Appeal*, WHBQ-TV, and a couple of other mid-South outlets had responded positively, having enthusiastically covered all the dancing-while-shopping activities at the Piggly Wiggly over the past summer.

"Now, this is what I call media coverage!" Mr. Choppy proclaimed. He stood in his gray three-piece suit near the front door, watching the camera crews and reporters pulling up into the parking lot for the ten o'clock ceremony. "I have to hand it to you, Powell. You're a damned fine dance instructor, but maybe you missed your callin'. This turnout looks even better than what we got this summer, and that was way more than I hoped for."

"We thank you for your kind words," he replied, patting his candidate on the shoulder. "But my best is yet to come."

The two men momentarily turned away from the media assembling outside to survey the decked-out war room behind them. An enormous black-and-white blowup of a much younger Mr. Choppy standing in front of the Piggly Wiggly beside his father, the long-departed Hale Dunbar Sr., adorned the back wall. That particular nostalgic touch had been Laurie's idea. She had suggested that it would remind people of the outstanding Dunbar family legacy in Second Creek, one that had encompassed a great deal of generosity following the town's various meteorological catastrophes. Laurie had also insisted that the photo would reinforce the official campaign slogan Powell had created for them: Hale Dunbar Jr.—A New Beginning with a Trusted Friend. That inviting sentiment was suspended from the ceiling in the form of a huge cloth banner.

Although they were still in training, some of the campaign workers had volunteered to sit at several of the phone stations to impress all the media types. Among those who had shown up were Hunter and Mary Fred Goodlett, their daughter, son-in-law, and grandchild, and a selection of Nitwitts—Novie, Myrtis, and Wittsie. Renza and Denver Lee, both of whom were still holding out on participation in the forthcoming controversial radio spots, were conspicuously absent.

And sitting in a distant corner of the room at a small table all to herself was the redoubtable Lady Roth in period costume. A large sign on the wall behind her proclaimed in red block lettering:

Susan B. Anthony Says: Women of Second Creek—Consider Your Vote Carefully!

Laurie finished up visiting with her Nitwitts and the Goodletts at the phone stations and headed toward Powell and Mr. Choppy, gesturing in the general direction of the Susan B. Anthony tableau just as she arrived. "Well, I finally have a chance to ask you how you like my historical project, Mr. Choppy. You have no idea what I went through to convince Lady Roth to go along with it."

"Your husband here gave me a little hint just after Lady Roth arrived a few minutes ago while you were tied up with your Nitwitt ladies," Mr. Choppy replied with a chuckle and a quick arching of his brows. The sight of Lady Roth with a great gray wig perched precariously atop her head and what appeared to be significant padding around the bodice of her dowdy black dress continued to amuse him no end.

Laurie rolled her eyes discreetly and lowered her voice. "Well, let me fill you in on the details. I didn't think I'd ever get her off her preoccupation with Elizabeth Cady Stanton. She kept insisting that it was time to give Susan B. Anthony's nearest and dearest accomplice her own day in the sun. Practically out of nowhere, she kept saying things like, 'Why can't I be Elizabeth Cady Stanton? No one ever pays any attention to her. She never even came close to getting her own unpopular coin.' Finally, I just told her she could be Elizabeth Cady Stanton if that's what she really wanted. At least I had her agreeing to portray a character and not insisting on manning one of our phones. That's the one thing we agreed we must try to avoid at all costs."

"Well, what finally changed her mind?" Mr. Choppy asked, flashing his biggest smile.

"There's never any accounting for Lady Roth's thought processes," Laurie answered. "But I did emphasize that she could use the opportunity any way she wanted. She could talk about the role of women in politics or even her own life experiences. That seemed to click with her, and then she just blurted out something about people maybe not knowing who Elizabeth Cady Stanton actually was versus who Susan B. Anthony was. At that point, it seemed to be a done deal. At any rate, I think we ought to consider informing any interested media that Lady Roth is available for interviews on the importance of the female vote in the upcoming election. Women do make up about fifty-five percent of the town's population, you know. Of course, I can't guarantee that she'll stay on point, but all things considered, I think it's the best we can do and still keep her on our side. We don't want to chance her going over to the enemy in one of her patented snits."

"No harm in slippin' a little Second Creek eccentricity into our first campaign appearance," said Mr. Choppy. "I think we'll still come off a helluva lot better than Mr. Floyce did."

At that point, Powell gave him a gentle pat on the back. "You ready to take them all on?"

"I think so."

"You've been a very apt pupil in our sessions so far. Now, just remember to take a deep breath and go slowly and deliberately. Don't be afraid to glance down at your notes. And here's something to look forward to—I've got a nice surprise coming to tie everything up with a nice big bow after all of this is over."

★

Some twenty minutes or so later, Mr. Choppy walked up to his war room podium and surveyed the media members assembled before him—pens poised over notepads and cameras and recorders rolling. Then he took that deep breath Powell had recommended.

"Ladies and gentlemen," he finally began, his voice surprisingly steady and rehearsed to a pitch a tad deeper than usual, "I want to welcome each of you to the official opening of the Hale Dunbar Junior campaign headquarters here in Second Creek. It is our goal to run a high-profile campaign about the need for change here in our beloved town. All of us who've lived here any length of time recognize that this is a special place." He paused briefly for emphasis as Powell had coached him to do, before returning to the copy that had been so carefully prepared for him.

"As such, it cannot be governed in a careless, business-as-usual manner. To preserve its special charms requires unusual vigilance, as well as understanding and empathy. It is our belief that the present administration, which has had its way for the better part of two decades, has been negligent in these duties, and the town has suffered the consequences. Zoning laws have been grievously relaxed or disregarded outright over and over again for the sake of money and convenience, and there has been an obvious lack of concern for the economic health of all the businesses on and around our tourist-oriented Square, particularly after the development on the Bypass." Once again, Mr. Choppy took a breather and briefly locked eyes with Powell, who responded with an encouraging wink.

"Don't misunderstand our position, however," he continued on cue. "We do not oppose progress in the form of new Second Creek businesses. Every town has to grow or it dies on the vine, and we don't want to discourage legitimate and sound investment in our community. At the same time, we want to preserve the uniqueness of the past, as well as our small-town character. We want the right kind of growth and judicious use of tax money. If elected mayor of Second Creek, Mississippi, in February 2002, I pledge to strike the proper balance between the old and the new so that Second Creekers can continue to take pride in what we have going for us. Here, we're not like everybody else, and that's just fine with us. This town deserves a mayor who really gets and appreciates what we're all about, and I, Hale Dunbar Junior, believe that I am the man who best fits that description. Thank you and God bless. And now I'll be happy to answer any questions you may have."

Several hands shot up simultaneously, and Mr. Choppy began acknowledging them one by one. First off, the freshly hired reporter from *The Citizen*, a rangy bespectacled specimen who identified himself as Rankin Lynch, wanted to know what special qualifications for office the candidate possessed.

Mr. Choppy tugged at his vest smartly and drew himself up with an air of confidence. In their coaching sessions, Powell had assured him he would have to field that question, and it did not faze him in the least. "My main qualification is that I ran a small business here in Second Creek for the better part of forty years, taking over the Dunbar family's Piggly Wiggly from my father when he finally decided to retire. I had been groomed for this all my life, and I understand what it takes to succeed as a businessman in this town. I also came to know and understand the hopes and dreams of all the Second Creekers who patronized my store over the years. With my business and people skills, I expect to become an exceptional mayor, and that's precisely what we need at this time in our town's history."

That seemed to satisfy young Rankin Lynch, and the rest of the media began lobbing a succession of relative softballs throughout the remainder of the press conference. Although Powell had spent some time preparing Mr. Choppy for adversarial questions, none ever appeared. It all went astoundingly well. Even the closing photo op was a seamless logistical exercise—with Laurie, Powell, all of the Goodletts, and the Nitwitts crowded around Mr. Choppy for the quintessential smiling snapshot.

After that, there was an impromptu concession to the kissing babies theme. Mary Fred Goodlett turned and offered up her toddler granddaughter, Casey, to Mr. Choppy for a quick peck on the cheek, but the sequence had none of the suggestiveness of Mr. Floyce's outing with the Jeffers twins. Instead, it came off like the natural, genuine gesture that it was.

"She's been a perfect angel all morning," Mary Fred explained, her voice full of grandmotherly pride. "Not a whimper out of her."

"Little Miss Casey is just adorable," Mr. Choppy said, smiling down upon the beaming golden-haired child.

But there was still one last task to tackle before dismissing the throng.

"Ladies and gentlemen," Mr. Choppy announced, "I'd now like to direct your attention to a special feature of our campaign— Second Creek's own Lady Roth portraying Susan B. Anthony over there in the corner of the room. She sits ready to answer your questions on that important historical figure and her relevance to this campaign. I hope some of you will take the time to mosey on over there and speak with her before you leave, and if you'll allow me, I'll lead the way."

Most of the gathering willingly complied, following Mr. Choppy, Powell, and Laurie to confront this unexpected oracle. No ordinary milquetoast campaign was going to work against the machinations of a pro like Mr. Floyce anyway.

"It has been years since I've been afforded a pulpit," Lady Roth began, once the group had settled around her with mildly curious looks affixed to their faces. "And though I may be long dead, my spirit—the spirit of Susan B. Anthony—lives on in the progress today's women are making day by day."

Here, Lady Roth paused quite dramatically and noticeably altered her facial expressions. Leaning into her audience, she also altered the tone of her voice. "Allow me a brief aside, if you will. I shall speak to you for a few moments now as myself, Lady Roth, not Susan B. Anthony. When I was a young girl, I desperately desired a career in the theater. But I had the misfortune of coming along at a time when girls, as we were then universally designated, were expected to want nothing more than marriage and children. Not that there is a thing wrong with that, you understand.

"But I wanted something more, and I believed that I had the talent to succeed in the theater. My parents intervened, however, and I was forced into a loveless, well-heeled marriage."

Lady Roth then broke off and sat back in her chair, resuming the more rigid posture and intonation of her Susan B. Anthony character. "Today, such parental attitudes would largely be frowned upon. Women are now encouraged to be whatever they want to be. I like to think that I and my dear friend Elizabeth Cady Stanton got the ball rolling in this arena way back in the nineteenth century. And how does all of this relate to Mr. Choppy's campaign, you may well be asking yourself?"

She gently cleared her throat for the payoff as her hushed audience stood mesmerized. "Today, more than ever, it is incumbent upon women not to take for granted all the opportunities now afforded them. They must continue to do everything they can to promote an image of themselves as just as intelligent and thoughtful as men claim to be. Casting an intelligent vote in any election should be part of that. Becoming as informed as possible on the issues is another part of it. I say to you that women always benefit more when the economy, cultural life, and integrity of a community work together as one. Underhanded, under-the-table deals by local good ole boys benefit only the good ole boys and their stout sidekicks."

That particular sentiment produced an audible buzz amongst the media types, and even Mr. Choppy, Powell, and Laurie appeared to be somewhat taken aback by its audacity. At the moment, Susan B. Anthony was being channeled to feisty perfection by Lady Roth, who waited for the whispers to die down before her final statement.

"In conclusion, I would like to say that Mr. Choppy sees clearly that it's time for a change. As aware, intelligent women, we should support him in this just cause. Thank you all very much for listening, and by all means, should you have the inclination, go to your banks and ask for a roll of my dollars to give as stocking stuffers this Christmas. They've all been pitifully undercirculated, and I think it's likely because all the good ole boys resent the hell out of them, if you will pardon my English. That is all."

There was a ripple of awkward laughter, but on the whole the gathering appeared fascinated, if caught off guard. They all lingered for more with Lady Roth, giving Mr. Choppy, Powell, and Laurie the opportunity to move away from the action for a quick powwow.

"Well, what's the verdict?" Mr. Choppy said in a hushed tone.

"Strong stuff," Powell replied. "But I liked it. She was authoritative and cogent and even downright funny there at the end.

It was almost like she'd been a fly on the wall of Mr. Floyce's office. It'll certainly get everyone's attention. I give her a thumbs-up."

Laurie deliberated a bit and then said, "I told her she could research the character to her heart's content, and that's obviously what she did. I also think we did the right thing in going ahead and giving her the floor. She proved just a few minutes ago that she's a team player."

Mr. Choppy shook his head thoughtfully and then gave a little whistle. "It does make me wonder what Mr. Floyce is gonna do once this gets back to him, though."

"We'll take his best shot, regardless," Powell added.

It took a little while longer for the media to tie up a few loose ends with Mr. Choppy, Lady Roth, and the campaign workers. But once they had all cleared out, Powell sprung his big surprise. He and Laurie had just taken their seats across from Mr. Choppy in his office for a final review of the morning's activities.

"I wanted to let you know that I sent out our press release about christening our campaign headquarters to our friend Ronnie Leyton at CNN in Atlanta," he revealed. "I thought he might be interested enough to pick up the story the way he did all the Piggly Wiggly activities this past summer."

Mr. Choppy perked up visibly, leaning forward in his chair, and said, "Have you heard back yet?"

"As a matter of fact, I have."

"You didn't say anything to me about it," Laurie added, giving her husband a petulant nudge with her elbow. "You said you'd keep me posted."

"I just got the phone call from Ronnie this morning while you were in the shower," Powell explained further. "I figured I'd wait until after the press conference was over to let you both know how promising it looks. Ronnie says he can't get over here to cover the early stages of the campaign with his hectic schedule, but he thinks he may be able to interest CNN in covering the Town Hall debate in January. If that happens, he says he will personally put together a piece on the race to the finish line and get them to air it nationally the way they did the Piggly Wiggly story. He says they got tons of positive feedback on all the Second Creek stuff they ran, and that might be enough to swing a sequel with his higher-ups."

Mr. Choppy looked both lost in thought and contrite, shaking his head slowly. "Now, why didn't I think of getting in touch with Ronnie Leyton? He was mighty good to me this summer, even if the publicity wasn't enough to keep my store open. But if my long-lost Gaylie Girl hadn't seen his broadcast, I wouldn't even begin to have the money to consider runnin' for office now."

"Think of it this way," Powell offered. "You got in touch with Ronnie Leyton indirectly by designating me as one of your campaign managers. Smart delegation is essential to good governance, so you're getting in some good practice for all that time you're going to be in office."

"I like the way you think," Mr. Choppy said. "You refuse to let me even project the possibility of losin'."

Powell's reply was immediate and decisive. "Is there any other way to look at it?"

7

THE BOOK SHERIFF AND
THE MIMS FAMILY

The first December meeting of the Nitwitts, plus Laurie, had come to order on the glassed-in back porch of Evening Shadows. Being the Christmas early bird that she was, President Myrtis had already decked the entire Troy mansion with boughs of holly, while potted poinsettias of both the red and white varieties were tucked into every nook and cranny. A towering pine trimmed with silver and gold Victorian bows, ornaments, and angels greeted visitors in the spacious foyer, and what seemed like miles of tiny white lights outlined the elaborate boxwood maze visible from the porch.

All the club's mundane opening matters had been efficiently dispatched and duly recorded by secretary Wittsie. Then it was time to introduce the guest of honor, Lovita Grubbs, the county's crusty and ever-vigilant librarian. So mindful was she of her role as guardian of the taxpayers' money that she had even gone so far as personally knocking on doors to reclaim overdue fines. She had long ago been christened the Book Sheriff. It was a nickname the tall, big-boned woman had come to relish because it suited her natural authoritarian bent. Had she been born after the modern feminist movement had taken hold, she likely would have pursued a career in law enforcement and hunted down criminals with the best of them.

Although Myrtis knew what Lovita's mission involved, the others had no earthly clue. They were prepared for just about anything under the sun, however. Her previous request had consisted of a plea to fund the relocation of the entire South Cypress Branch collection due to a serious infestation of water moccasins. The Nitwitts had agreed to the proposition. What did the Book Sheriff have on her mind this time around? they all wondered.

"Good afternoon, ladies," Lovita began, making eye contact with each of them as they sat around the room contentedly sipping their mimosas and Bloody Marys. "First of all, I wanted to thank each of you once again for being so generous with your club's money this past summer. You came through in splendid civic-minded fashion for your library in allowing us to shut down the South Cypress branch and give all those volumes a safe haven from those horrid slithering snakes."

Lovita paused, waiting for both the giggles and shudders to peter out. "But today I come to you not to solicit but to offer assistance. As I've already explained to your esteemed president, Myrtis, I want to offer my services alongside each of you on Mr. Choppy Dunbar's behalf in the upcoming election. I will do anything asked of me—whether it be to solicit votes over the phone or drive people to the polls on Election Day. Whatever you're going to do, I want to do, too. Of course, I must do so quietly behind the scenes. I can't come out publicly. If Mr. Floyce should win again, my library would really suffer. Nonetheless, I wanted you to know I'm on your team."

There was a smattering of light applause mixed in with polite whispers, and then Lovita continued. "I would like each of you to understand precisely why I am taking sides here. I believe that Floyce Hammontree has been very bad for Second Creek, and today I would like to document that for you from a librarian's point of view."

The group sat up a bit in their chairs, and one or two even put down their cocktails for the inside scoop. "You see, every year I've had to go before His Majesty to present the library's budget, always hoping to get an increase on the patrons' behalf. All those newspapers, periodicals, encyclopedias, best sellers, research titles, and computer terminals that the public has come to rely upon don't come free. But every year I get the same answer from Mr. Floyce. 'We just can't swing it this year, Miz Grubbs. Got us some washboard gravel to pave down in Ward Six this time. Gotta think of the public good as a whole.'"

The color began to rise in Lovita's face as she paused to gather herself. "I suppose I could live with that sort of reasoning as an excuse to ignore the library. But Mr. Floyce would never leave it at that. He'd say, 'There are enough books in there already, Miz Grubbs. All these housewives that want us to keep up with what these romance writers keep churning out need to go to a bookstore and plunk down their own money—that is, if they can tear themselves away from their soap operas.'"

Each of the Nitwitts immediately recoiled and Laurie quickly verbalized what they were all thinking. "How insulting!"

"Oh, it gets worse!" Lovita replied, her voice tinged with passion. "The library budget is the first municipal item he's cut over the years when they have a shortfall of any kind. When I'd show up to protest, he'd feed me some line about my needs being low man on the totem pole and that I need to get a life. Well, the library is my life, thank you very much! He doesn't seem to understand that it's an important educational resource used by most all our high school students and many job-seekers, too. We need someone in there with a more enlightened and balanced view of spending taxpayers' money, and I feel sure that Mr. Choppy will listen to reason in that regard. His family has always had the interests of Second Creekers at heart, and his mother, Gladys, was a big library supporter. True, she was primarily in it for access to the best sellers, but she always managed to donate a little something every year."

Laurie briefly raised her hand and then took the floor. "I can assure you that Mr. Choppy will be fair with you, Lovita, and I know he'll be thrilled that you've chosen to join our team. I'll let him know as soon as possible, and Powell and I can work out something to suit your library schedule. We're looking at starting up the phone solicitation in earnest after Christmas."

"Excellent," Lovita replied. "I can't wait to contribute. Perhaps I can even sneak in on a lunch hour or two and do what I can at headquarters."

There was a polite round of applause, and then Myrtis stepped up, thanked her for the testimonial, and adjourned the meeting. "And now, ladies, let's eat. Oh, and Denver Lee, I've had my Sarah prepare a menu that should be diabetic friendly. There's plenty of fresh fruit, a nice, warm spinach salad with a few feta cheese sprinkles, and some chicken breasts grilled with lemon pepper seasoning—you can have that, can't you?"

"Oh, yes. That sounds perfectly delicious," Denver Lee replied. "And of course I appreciate the extra trouble you went to. My problem is that I'm afraid I'll be mightily tempted by all the other things you'll be serving, especially if you've got any sweets I shouldn't have. I may just end up sneaking something."

Myrtis looked a bit guilty but managed a smile anyway. "I'm afraid I do have miniature turtle cheesecake bites and chocolate-dipped strawberries. Sorry about that."

"Oh, I've been good all week anyway—even lost another pound, if my scales are still working right. Of course, I've practically worn them out lately. Curiosity weigh-ins, I call them. I've become addicted to looking for the slightest hint of progress—practically hour by hour, mind you. In any case, I doubt one strawberry or one cheesecake bite will undo me."

And on that note, the red cider-scented Christmas candles on the back porch table were lit, the generous spread was laid, and everyone proceeded to dig in with gusto.

★

"There's a special reason I asked you to pick me up for the meeting today," Novie was saying to Laurie as they drove away from the massive white columns of Evening Shadows. "I wanted a little time alone with you to talk about something, and I've just now mustered the courage to bring it up."

Laurie came to the end of Evening Shadows's long gravel road, stopped at the wrought-iron front gates, looked both ways, and pulled out onto the asphalt highway. "Well, I'm all ears. What's on your mind?"

"It's about my family. I had a few things I wanted to explain. There's been a new development recently, and I wanted to run it past someone I trusted—that's you."

Laurie took her eyes off the road just long enough to flash a smile at her passenger. "I'm flattered, and I'm sure you know that anything you say to me will be held in strictest confidence. I won't say anything to anyone."

"Oh, I wouldn't mind you mentioning it to Powell. I trust both of you." There was a long, awkward pause while they sped past the surrounding soybean fields. Eventually Novie stopped wriggling her plump little form beneath her seat belt and spoke up. "I know that all of you have been curious over the years about my marriage to Geoffrey. We didn't socialize much with the rest of you while he was still alive, and I've almost never spoken about him since his death. I joined the Nitwitts because I thought it would bring me out of my shell, and it's done just that."

"Oh, you've been a wonderful addition to the group," Laurie replied. "I personally have always admired your willingness to travel alone all over the world the way you do. Some women just wouldn't do it. They'd have to have a companion of some sort. But you—you're so adventurous, always the most fearless among us."

Novie hesitated once again, obviously searching for the right words. "In a certain superficial sense, yes. But in another very important sense, no. You see, Geoffrey and I were pretty happy in the early years of our marriage for the most part. But it was severely strained and took a turn for the worse because of something that happened concerning our son, Marc." She broke off again, sighing and swallowing hard.

"Take all the time you need, dear," Laurie said.

"It's just this . . . Marc came to us while he was still in high school and informed us that he was gay. Neither of us knew how to take it. Geoffrey thought it was his fault, and I thought it was my fault—everything you read from the experts said it had to be. But from that point on, our marriage was never the same. All we did was talk about blame and what we did wrong. But Marc is a very headstrong boy and kept insisting that it didn't have anything to do with either of us. He said he knew he liked other boys way before puberty, and that was that. It was just there, big as life, he said. Nothing went wrong, he kept saying. It just was. But it was still something that was very hard for Geoffrey and me to hear and accept."

"I understand," Laurie replied, trying to sound as calm as possible.

"Anyway, Marc has spent the last ten years or so out in California, where he says people are generally more accepting than here in the small-town South. He's written brief letters to me from time to time, and I've kept him informed here and there of my Nitwitt activities and just recently even a bit about Mr. Choppy's election bid. But I've felt like he's been lost to me most of the time, especially after Geoffrey died and I was left all alone with my unresolved conflicts. I think that's why I've been so willing to travel so much. It takes my mind off all that mess."

Laurie said nothing at first, fully realizing the importance of her reaction to such a difficult revelation. In the end she chose a more oblique response. "What made you tell me all this now?"

"Well, that's the recent development I wanted to discuss with you. Marc phoned the other day and informed me that he's found someone to settle down with, a young man named Michael, and he wants to bring him home to meet me around Christmastime and stay for a while. The two of them even wanted to help the campaign along if they could, but Marc wasn't sure the offer would be appreciated or how Second Creekers might react."

At precisely that moment they passed the Second Creek corporate limits marker, and Laurie turned to offer her friend a reassuring smile. "You're really worried, Novie?"

"You don't think I should be?"

"I most certainly do not. We've had our share of gay people here in Second Creek over the years, and no one's batted an eyelash as far as I know. All sorts of unconventional people have found their way here. I think Marc has underestimated Second Creek all along. Remember Paulina Peyton and her friend and all that interesting pottery they sold in that artsy little shop just off The Square a few years back? What was it called—Paulina's Platters, I believe? And Vester Morrow and his friend Mal Davis have run the Victorian Tea Room to perfection for years. Everyone practically worships the kitchen they cook in. You know, Novie, I think you may have to face the fact that this isn't about the reaction of Second Creekers to Marc and his friend. It's about your reaction to them and all those conflicted feelings you and Geoffrey never resolved."

"It's just different when it's your family, Laurie. It's not abstract anymore. It's not one of those *USA Today* poll questions or the subject of somebody's Sunday sermon. It's your son. The fruit of your loins, the person that's supposed to carry on the family line. It's just . . . hard, that's all."

"I'm sure it's not the easiest thing in the world to hear, but you want my advice? I assume you do or you wouldn't have gone to all this trouble to discuss it with me."

"Yes. I value your opinion very much. Always have."

Laurie drew herself up, firmly gripping the steering wheel. "I think you should welcome Marc and his friend with open arms, and don't worry about what other people think. You should tell Marc the same thing when he gets here. If they'd like to take a turn at the phone banks or help in other ways, Powell and I will be happy to arrange it."

Novie exhaled dramatically while staring at the windshield. "You're a tremendously reassuring person, Laurie. You always have been. I'm quite sure that the Nitwitts would never have made a go of it without your leadership. You've just told me exactly what I needed to hear. I feel much better about the whole thing now."

"Good," Laurie replied, reaching over to give her friend a quick pat on the shoulder. "The first thing you should do when you get home is to phone up Marc and tell him to bring his friend for a nice long visit. We need all the help we can get to oust Mr. Floyce." Then she chuckled under her breath and arched her brows slyly. "Personally, I think it's in the bag now that the Book Sheriff has agreed to ride in on her white horse."

★

Powell and Laurie were sitting beside each other on the living-room sofa, having Irish coffees after her delicious dinner of peppered salmon with rosemary, steamed zucchini squash, and creamed corn miniquiches.

"I was just thinking about what Novie told you this afternoon on the way home from your Nitwitt gathering," Powell began in between sips of his drink. "And it triggers my memories of the ballroom tours of Europe that Ann and I took. Of course, the circuit had its share of gay people—of both genders, you understand. Nobody thought anything of it, and the gay contingent included some of the most delightful people I've ever had the pleasure of meeting. One in particular. He billed himself as the Great Buddha Magruder, and he absolutely lived up to it, too."

Laurie inched closer to her husband and smiled expectantly. "Oh, I love that name. Sounds like some W. C. Fields character. Tell me everything."

Powell indulged a brief, introspective laugh and continued. "His specialty was the tango, although he loved all Latin dances. He was an enormous man—of Orson Wellesian proportions, actually—but you forgot all about that when he took to the dance floor. I've never seen anyone so large look so graceful on his feet. He favored the most flamboyant costumes I've ever seen a man wear—a bit of toreador here, a touch of Carmen Miranda there—but he was no drag queen. He also had the sort of deep voice that would have lost James Earl Jones his voice-over job at CNN. At every banquet, you always hoped he'd be seated at your table."

"I love it," Laurie replied, enjoying the glow from the whiskey and her husband's little tale. "And perhaps I'm perpetuating a stereotype here, but I just realized that I've never known a single gay person who wasn't interesting and creative in some way."

Powell snickered. "Oh, I think it's possible to be gay and dull at the same time, but I agree that you ordinarily don't associate those two terms. At any rate, you said the right thing to Novie about Second Creek's attitude on the subject. Most people just shrug their shoulders and mind their own business. Except maybe Mr. Floyce and his ilk. I thought he was going to have a cow this summer when Mr. Gary Greene won the Miss Delta Floozie Contest in that clever disguise of his. Even had me fooled, and I danced with the guy up close and personal in the aisles of the Piggly Wiggly, remember?"

"How could I forget? And to 'You Don't Know Me,' as a matter of fact."

"A bit of delicious irony, courtesy of Ray Charles, I must admit," Powell added.

Laurie continued to enjoy the buzz from her Irish coffee for a bit longer and then switched subjects. "You haven't told me how your session went this afternoon with Mr. Choppy and Charley Forbes. Any new input from our mole on Mr. Floyce's plans and activities?"

"I'm afraid not. Charley didn't actually show up today. He phoned at the last minute to say that Minnie wasn't in on the last couple of meetings. Seems Mr. Floyce has taken to conferring in Eljay Jeffers's law offices these days, and Minnie's been left out of the loop completely."

Laurie had a wicked smirk on her face. "I'd give anything to know how those two reacted to Lady Roth's comments at the headquarters dedication. I have this mental picture of Mr. Floyce going as red as he did when Gary Greene ripped off his emerald wig at the Piggly Wiggly."

"With the television cameras rolling yet."

They both indulged a retrospective laugh, boosting the effects of the whiskey circulating throughout their veins, and they topped that off with a pleasant Irish coffee–flavored kiss.

Then Powell said, "I suppose we'll find out soon enough what Mr. Floyce's next move will be. He's a quick study, and if we know nothing else about him, we know for certain that he'll go down fighting."

"I think we're holding our own so far, though."

"Yes, we are." Then Powell bit his lip and grew pensive. "But we can't take anything for granted."

They finished their drinks and snuggled on the sofa together, listening to Christmas music—a prelude to the lovemaking that would soon follow in bed.

8.

WINGING IT IN
WARD SIX

M r. Floyce was having trouble with his wife, Jo Nelle, who was being as obstinate as possible on a blustery Sunday morning two and a half weeks out from Christmas. "I don't feel like goin' with you all the way to the end of Lower Winchester Road to that church full of all those hysterical colored people," she was saying while buttering her toast at the breakfast table. Her voice and demeanor were practically dripping with disdain. "They scream and holler like they have epilepsy or something."

"You have to go," he replied, pushing his scrambled eggs around his plate as if they were the culprit in the matter. He absolutely hated it when Jo Nelle got into one of her snits. Then he thrust the front page of *The Citizen* under her nose and called her attention to the paper's first preelection poll. "Forty-nine percent for me, thirty-seven percent for Mr. Piggly Wiggly, and fourteen percent undecided. It's a comfortable lead, but it's certainly not the slam dunk I once thought it would be."

She brushed the paper aside and shrugged. "Polls, schmolls."

"Eljay's bringing KayDon," he replied, not about to let up on her, "and we need to present a united front. We've got it all worked out with Brother Thompson—we've sweetened his pot again, and my mayoral record will be the subject of his sermon today. I want you there. It'll look good to the congregation."

Jo Nelle bristled, determined not to budge an inch. "You know very well I despise this aspect of politics. You do the campaignin', and I'll spend the money."

That much, she definitely knew how to do. She'd been fresh-scrubbed Leland farm girl Jo Nelle Sorrells when they'd first married, but her vanity about her knockout figure and pretty face had emerged soon enough. Mr. Floyce could never make enough money to please her, to keep her in the clothes, makeup, and jewelry she required to sashay about in her daily life. Once she had become First Lady of Second Creek, her self-absorbed attitudes had soared to even greater heights.

"If you want the money to continue to flow, you'll get out of that housecoat, put on your face, do your hair, and make an appearance with me," he replied, raising his voice to her. "You don't have to do a damned thing but sit there in the pew and smile. Eljay and I will do the rest."

"Why are you so all-fired worried about that ridiculous Mr. Choppy?" she said, trying a different approach. "You can't seriously believe he'll beat you. He's just an ex-butcher bumpkin with a missin' finger."

Mr. Floyce made a snorting noise and turned up his nose. "I'm not takin' any chances, that's all. He came off a helluva lot better than I thought he would during that press conference a few weeks back, and all sorts of people have come out of the wood-work on his behalf lately. Some Second Creekers are beginnin' to question my authority, the way I see it, and Eljay senses the same trend."

"You and Eljay think you invented the wheel."

Mr. Floyce narrowed his eyes intently and leaned in on his elbows. "I don't see you turnin' down the considerable fruits of our labor, my dear. You've got everything you've ever wanted because of my long reign—this beautiful house that's way too big for us, all those designer clothes you show off in, all those trips to Vegas and other spots we take every year, and God knows what else. Seems to me you wouldn't want to bite the hand that feeds you so well."

Jo Nelle's features softened a bit. "Maybe I'm just downright bored with it all. You say KayDon is definitely goin' to be there?"

"Yep."

"Then at least I'll have somebody to whisper to out of the side of my mouth."

Mr. Floyce relaxed and sat back in his chair. "I've only asked you to put in an appearance by my side over the years when I've thought it was absolutely necessary, and this is one of those times."

Jo Nelle bit into her toast aggressively, expressing the remnants of her displeasure at being coerced into something she felt was beneath her. "I suppose I'll muddle through somehow."

"Just smile. All you have to do is smile."

"I'll think of somethin' to amuse myself," she added. "Like what KayDon is wearing. When you're as big as she is, you can't find a thing in the stores you can try on that doesn't look like it should be pitched at a Boy Scout Jamboree."

★

Hanging Grapes A.M.E. Church stood at the dead end of newly paved Lower Winchester Road in Ward Six—a rambling white clapboard building with opaque glass windows and a modest black steeple that was home to a congregation of well over three hundred fifty dedicated believers. To Mr. Floyce's way of thinking, of course, it was also home to nearly that many votes, and he could ill afford to take them for granted. Thus, his insistence on dragging Jo Nelle to Brother Willyus V. Thompson's Sunday sermon.

"Brothers and sisters in the Lord," Brother Thompson began in that commanding voice of his, surveying his vast flock from the pulpit. He noted that a few of the faithful were fanning themselves with their fingers every now and then—a tribute to the new heating system bought and paid for by Mr. Floyce's generous contribution from the year before. And on a raw December morning like this, it was certainly coming in handy.

"We got us some very special guests of honor today," Brother Thompson continued. He paused rather dramatically to make eye contact with the two couples perched on the short front pew just below him. Taking up most of the room on the inside were Eljay and KayDon Jeffers, while Mr. Floyce and Jo Nelle occupied what little space was available on the outside edge. All four were dressed in their finest—the men in their most conservative three-piece suits, the women in festive holiday ensembles. Of course, Eljay and KayDon struck a slightly jarring note because of their extreme measurements. Other than that, however, the foursome exuded respectability and attentiveness.

"Let's all please put our hands together, my beloved," Brother Thompson continued, "and welcome His Honor, Mayor Floyce Hammontree, his wife, our First Lady, Jo Nelle, his friend Mr. Eljay Jeffers and his wife, KayDon, to the bosom of our little church and wish these folks good tidings of the season!"

Healthy applause immediately rang out—together with a few Hallelujahs! and cries of Praise the Lord!—and Brother Thompson flashed his trademark generous smile, while vigorously nodding his shiny bald head until all the commotion had died down.

"Brothers and sisters, as we all know, this is the time of year to give thanks to the Lord for his grace and mercy through the birth of Our Savior. But it's also the time to thank those who give of themselves to improve the quality of our lives, praise the good Lord!"

The last phrase echoed throughout the building as a forest of hands shot up and began swaying back and forth. Mr. Floyce and Eljay joined in, but their wives chose the low-key approach and settled for gazing up at Brother Thompson with their smiles frozen in place.

"Today, I will remind y'all what a friend we have in Mr. Floyce Hammontree—yes, indeed we do. Did y'all enjoy drivin' y'all cars to the church today without all the potholes and washboard around that rattle everyone's teeth and shock absorbers alike? Well, Mr. Floyce made that possible. His administration got the job done and paved the way for y'all to get here to praise the Lord a little easier. He's been on the job for y'all down here in Ward Six, and he's put himself out in many other ways here at Hanging Grapes. A modest man like Mr. Floyce won't boast to God 'bout his good works. But I don't have to tell y'all, my brothers and sisters, that one good deed always deserves another. We must reward Mr. Floyce and his good works, both in our hearts and with our votes come February."

More cries of, Praise the Lord!, That's right!, and Hallejulah! rang out, and even more hands began to sway back and forth above heads.

Brother Thompson seized the momentum further. "Ah, yes, my beloved, I see y'all in fine form today. Give it up for the Lord! Let us raise our hands and voices! Thank him for his humble servants like Mr. Floyce, who has done his bidding! Give it up, give it up, give it up!"

And the faithful, every last one of them, gave it up, working themselves into a frenzy. As the emotional explosion reached its zenith, Mr. Floyce began subtly elbowing Jo Nelle until she, too, had joined in, though she found time to elbow him back rather emphatically.

"Oh, yes, my brothers and sisters, the Lord will take notice today of our testimony. He'll see that y'all do not take the good deeds that come through him for granted." Finally, Brother Thompson gestured broadly toward Mr. Floyce. "I will now invite Mr. Floyce to come on up here and speak a few words to you, my brothers and sisters."

On cue, Mr. Floyce smiled, nodded enthusiastically, and reached the pulpit just as Brother Thompson stepped aside. Then he cleared his throat, scanned the throng, and began speaking in a very deliberate manner. That television coverage of Mr. Choppy's unexpectedly erudite performance during the headquarters dedication ceremony had not been lost on him, and he meant to surpass it every time out on the campaign trail. Perfect enunciation was now an essential part of his ticket to victory.

"Ladies and gentlemen of Hanging Grapes A.M.E. Church,"
he began. "What a pleasure to be with you today as we near our
celebration of the blessed event. What I would like to emphasize
to all of you today is that we are all here to serve each other.
That should be our mission in life. And my mission as your
mayor has been to serve you in the most efficient manner possible and with a smile to boot." He paused briefly to catch Jo
Nelle's eye and noticed that she appeared rather bored, causing
him to repeat his last few words with special emphasis. "And . . .
with . . . a . . . smile . . . to . . . boot."

Jo Nelle's glazed stare vanished as she quickly recovered her
smile.

"And let me be the first to admit that my administration has
not always acted as quickly as we would have liked on certain
matters," Mr. Floyce continued. "I therefore beg your forgiveness in being a tad slow in getting the results we all wanted to
see. But forgiveness, too, is a part of this blessed season, isn't it?
That, and your willingness to let me continue to serve your needs
because the truth is, ladies and gentlemen, it takes a great deal
of stamina and vitality to run a town like Second Creek. Not to
mention experience. You just don't wake up one day and decide
you want to be mayor, particularly if you've never so much as
dipped your big toe in the political waters throughout your
younger, most productive years. This business of politics is not
for the retiring soul." Mr. Floyce placed a special upward inflec-
tion on those last two words, wagging his brows and cocking his
head as if sharing some dirty little secret with the congregation.
They responded just as he and Eljay had hoped they would—
reading between the lines, nodding their heads, and whispering
amongst themselves. It was the first time he had trotted out such

rhetoric on the campaign trail, but it would not be the last. He continued to hammer home his themes while refusing to mention his opponent by name.

"It's kinda like people who say they want to be a writer. Everybody says how nice it would be to write, but few actually sit down and do it. But the point is, even if you do try to write and fail at it, you're the only one who's affected. If you get in over your head in political office, you can drag down the lives of thousands of your constituents. Do we really want to take that chance here in Second Creek? In conclusion, let me say that I know we won't let each other down as election time approaches in February. God bless, and Merry Christmas to you all."

Mr. Floyce stepped down as the congregation offered up healthy applause, and he acknowledged them with a solitary wave of his hand before sliding in once again next to his wife.

After Brother Thompson's final words and a stirring closing rendition of "His Eye Is on the Sparrow," sung by a choir resplendent in their red and white holiday robes, everyone adjourned to the nearby social hall for a potluck Sunday dinner. Here, Eljay and KayDon stepped to the forefront and were in their everyday element, moving quickly down the line to heap their plates with steaming chicken and dumplings, pecan cornbread dressing, black-eyed peas with smoked ham, sweet potato casserole, string beans, collards, and yeast rolls. Mr. Floyce took smaller portions of everything but kept right on smiling after he sat down to eat, while Jo Nelle mostly picked at her food, constantly moving it around her plate so expertly that no one noticed she actually wasn't eating anything.

"We'll be startin' up the expansion soon right through that door over there," Brother Thompson was explaining to Mr. Floyce.

They were seated next to each other at one of the many long tables crowded into a room chock-full of people and their meal-time chatter. "As you can see, we really do need the space."

"You know it does my heart good to see Hanging Grapes grow like this," Mr. Floyce replied. "You truly are doin' the work of the Lord way down here in Ward Six, sir."

"I 'speck so. They say this town is special in so many ways that folks can't describe," Brother Thompson added in between bites of his chicken and dumplings. "But sometimes I think it's just a matter of helpin' the other fellow out, no matter what they look like or what they say or how crazy they act."

"Amen," said Mr. Floyce, continuing the mutual admiration society banter with a knowing wink.

By the time everyone had helped themselves to the extravagant dessert table, Jo Nelle had grown weary of her husband's schmoozing and was grasping at straws to amuse herself. Out of desperation, she turned to KayDon at her right and said, "Did I tell you how precious and darlin' I think your outfit is? Wherever did you find it? I just love those little red and green doodads all over it. So Yuletide-ish."

KayDon swallowed a generous mouthful of banana pudding and said, "Oh, thank you. I found it at Lane Bryant at the mall up in Memphis. You know me. I'm hard to fit, but I try hard."

"Yes," Jo Nelle replied, flashing a grin that was far too wide to be sincere. "You definitely have the touch."

★

In the car on the way back to town, Jo Nelle reverted to type and vented about the outing at Hanging Grapes. "I trust you won't require my presence at any more of those. All that greasy, fatty cooking and screamin' and hollerin' and wavin' at the rafters, and did you see what KayDon had on? I could hardly contain myself. She looked like a Christmas tree in drag!"

Mr. Floyce drove on in silence for a while, choosing his words carefully. What he actually wanted to discuss was how smooth the ride was now that Lower Winchester Road had been paved, but his wife simply wasn't going to let him go there. "Thank you for at least keepin' your mouth shut and not sayin' any of that where anybody could hear you. I don't think anyone except me really noticed you weren't havin' a particularly good time. And, no, you won't be required to do anything more than smile and wave here and there for the rest of the campaign. Otherwise, people might get the impression that you're sick and tired of being First Lady of Second Creek."

Jo Nelle looked thoroughly exasperated and folded her arms. "That's basically the truth of the matter when you come right down to it. I was hopin' you'd have made those showbiz dreams of yours you always talked about come true by now. I thought I'd married Mister Big Time, not Mister Small Town, you know."

Mr. Floyce flashed a contemptuous glance but said nothing, and she resumed her rant. "When we first came here, it was only supposed to be a stop on the way to fame and fortune. Okay, so you've made the fortune part with all your big deals. You know as well as I do that we have the money to move away tomorrow if we wanted to. But it looks like you've let us be permanently detoured by this place. Whether you realize it or not, I think you've gotten hooked on all these crazy people and the strange things they do and say. You like to think you have control over them, but you really don't. They're a law unto themselves. Would it really be so bad if you ended up losing this election and were forced to go back to your original dreams? What ever happened to the man I fell in love with—the guy with the endless supply of one-liners that made me laugh so hard?"

Mr. Floyce felt the anger rising in his blood. She had a way of getting to him like no one else ever could, due principally to the fact that she was always throwing tact out the window and reminding him of the truth. "It almost sounds like you want me to lose, the way you're talkin'. Do you really hear yourself?"

"I only know we're not cut out for this place, even if we have lived here for a long time. Even if Floyce Junior grew up here and was happy as a clam. Little boys think weird places are cool. But you and me—we're just not like Mr. Choppy or those inter-ferin' Nitwitts or that bossy Lady Roth. I've never felt like we really belonged here. We're both too practical, and we refuse to stick our heads in the clouds like so many of these people do all the time." She broke off, looking suddenly amused. "Maybe that's what's really responsible for all the peculiar weather around here. That many people with their heads in the clouds are bound to have an effect of some kind."

After another mile or so of silence, Mr. Floyce finally spoke up. "Are you finished?"

She barely nodded, refusing to face him.

"I told Eljay at the start of this campaign, and I'll tell you," he continued. "I intend to leave this town when I'm good and ready and not a minute before—and on my own terms, not some-body else's."

She made a soft guttural noise and said, "Second Creek has a way of making people come to its own peculiar terms."

"I beg to disagree," he replied, determined to get in the last word. "I don't give a damn what Mr. Choppy or Lady Roth or anybody says, I've been good for this town. Nothing would ever get done here if you left it up to all these typical old-time Second Creekers. Like you said, they all have their heads in the clouds and up their you-know-whats, I might add. I know how to get people to do things, to get roads paved, new businesses built, and old buildings torn down if they need to be. The deals I cut benefit me, sure. But they also benefit Second Creek, no matter what Mr. Choppy thinks. I've always been the new blood this place has needed, and that's the record I'm gonna run on, come hell or high water."

And Jo Nelle was finally silenced for the remainder of the drive home.

9.

AGELESS APPEALS

The time had come for Powell to walk the tightrope without
a safety net. Namely, to force a handful of well-to-do, very
opinionated Southern matrons to talk about their age to the general public. It was now of paramount importance that he accomplish this feat. Mr. Floyce's own radio spots had recently
debuted, pounding away at the themes that he and Eljay Jeffers
had so skillfully conjured up.

Throughout the day and into the evening hours, variations on
those themes rode the airwaves as Second Creekers went about
their business in their cars or listening in their homes. "Hello,
I'm Mayor Floyce Hammontree, and I'd like to visit with you for
a few moments. We have a very important election coming up
in a couple of months. You'll decide for yourselves whether my
record of bringing over twenty-five new businesses to Second
Creek in the past two years is worth your vote. You'll decide

whether the time and energy I've devoted to this community for over fifteen years is enough to return me to office. Consider your vote carefully. Public service, particularly in the form of the mayoral office, requires patience and experience, as well as many tough decisions that affect taxpayers' pocketbooks. Don't give this public trust to just anyone—friendly and well intentioned as they may be. Consider whether or not they have the energy and know-how and then vote accordingly on February fifth. Second Creek cannot afford on-the-job training of a retiree. Paid for by the Floyce Y. Hammontree Reelection Campaign."

In addition to this broadcasting bombardment, the latest poll *The Citizen* had taken just one week out from Christmas had shown Mr. Floyce's percentage of those interviewed rising from forty-nine to fifty-one percent, Mr. Choppy's dropping from thirty-seven to thirty-five percent, and the undecideds remaining at fourteen percent. Clearly, Mr. Floyce's message of staying the course was getting through loud and clear. It was past time for the Hale Dunbar Jr. campaign to go on the offensive.

"Right now, just about everything Mr. Floyce is doing is working," Powell was saying to Mr. Choppy as they huddled in front of the big blowup in his campaign office late one evening. "His radio ads, his photo ops, his speeches around town, no doubt whatever he's slipping people under the table—right now, all of it's golden. He even seems to have learned to do the kissing babies thing right. No more fondling little girls made up like tarts—just the time-honored, straightforward shopping center cliché."

Mr. Choppy slumped his shoulders as he searched for something positive to tout. "Well, at least we've gotten that down pat, too." He glanced down at the front page of *The Citizen* on his desk, smiling at the picture of himself holding Denver Lee McQueen's three-year-old grandson, Christopher Hewes, in his arms with a throng of happy-looking campaign workers gathered around him. "If we're doin' nothin' else right, we're kissin' babies and gettin' downright warm and fuzzy here at the Piggly Wiggly—all in good taste, too."

Powell's tone was far from congratulatory, however. "I'm afraid warm and fuzzy's not going to cut it, though. We've allowed Mr. Floyce to define us too much so far. We've been too reactive by playing his game. I've got my work cut out for me with these Nitwitt spots, but it may be our only chance to turn the momentum in our favor before it's too late."

Mr. Choppy shoved the paper aside and took a cleansing breath. It was taking every bit of his will to stay focused on this new and difficult business of politics, and the subtle attacks from Mr. Floyce were beginning to eat away ever so slightly at his confidence. Nonetheless, he held his head up and managed a smile. "So, who do you have to deal with first on these spots?"

"Myrtis Troy," Powell replied. "Tomorrow morning, in fact. Then I see Wittsie Chadwick in the afternoon, and finally Novie Mims the next day. If all goes well, we should have our spots on the air right between Christmas and New Year's."

"And you think you can get those ladies to cooperate fully?"

Powell closed his eyes, rubbing them gently with the tips of his fingers, and said, "Well, at the dance studio, I was able to get some of the clumsiest women in the world to do my bidding. That's what I must tap into again with these radio sessions, God willing. And let me add that I'm going to enlist my wife's assistance for the task. She knows better than anyone else how to soften up her Nitwitts."

"I have faith in you—and Miz Hampton, too." Then Mr. Choppy grew unusually quiet, locking eyes with Powell in a thoughtful pose. "There's somethin' I've been bustin' to talk about with somebody—maybe you, maybe Miz Hampton—but I'm really gettin' nervous about it because it's almost here."

Powell looked slightly quizzical at first but leaned in with a reassuring grin. "I'm here to listen. What's on your mind?"

"It's my widow friend up in Chicago—Gaylie Girl Lyons."

"Aha! The mysterious woman who done you wrong when you were in the throes of puberty way back when!"

Mr. Choppy managed an awkward chuckle and swallowed hard. "But she also made amends this summer when she came down to explain our ancient little fling from her point of view. There are always two sides to every story."

"So what's happening now to make you so nervous?"

Mr. Choppy took a few moments to gather himself before continuing. "Before she went back to Chicago, she asked me to keep in touch with her if I wanted. Maybe let her know my plans since she figured I intended to go through with shuttin' down the store. I guess she wanted to know what I was gonna do with the money she gave me—money she insisted was mine, by the way. I won't go into all that now, though."

Powell shook his head emphatically while wagging his finger. "No need to explain. What's private is private."

"I appreciate that. Anyway, I finally decided to write her a letter to let her know that I was runnin' for office and usin' the money to finance the campaign, and she thought it was a fantastic idea. One thing led to another, and we started talkin' over the phone—not just about the campaign, but about how our lives were goin', and that sorta thing. After bein' outta touch all that time, suddenly we just couldn't seem to stop talkin' to each other. It was like a dam had burst, and the mistakes of the past were washed away."

A sly grin broke across Powell's face. "Are you saying that you and she might be getting involved with each other again?"

"Well, that's the part that's makin' me nervous. You see, she's pretty much throwin' caution to the wind even though I think she's more worried than she lets on about how her family is gonna react. She's actually gonna come down here and spend a coupla days with me around Christmas. In fact, she's flyin' down day after tomorrow to meet me in Memphis, and I don't really know what to expect. I've been outta circulation for so long, if you catch my drift."

"I do," Powell replied with a playful wink. Then his eyes widened in revelation. "Ah, so that's what's behind your new look! I was telling Laurie just the other day that I could have sworn you'd lost some weight lately. At first I thought it might be the stress from the campaign, but now I've seen the light. Am I right? Was your lady friend the inspiration for the sleeker you?"

Mr. Choppy blushed and momentarily hung his head. "Yeah, you figured it out. I've been watchin' my diet and cuttin' out the things I shouldn't eat—not to mention the late-night snacks— and I've dropped about fifteen pounds since the campaign started. I'd gotten a tad sloppy and pudgy there all that time I ran the Piggly Wiggly. Why should I pay attention, though? I had no one to look good for. But that's all changed now."

Powell sat back in his chair and let everything sink in fully. "Looks good on you. So have you made any special plans?"

"Gaylie Girl and I are gonna spend a little bit of time together up in Memphis at the Peabody Hotel, where she first stayed during the war. Turns out there's one of those old-fashioned swing bands playin' in the Continental Ballroom up there all this week—just our kinda music—the type we danced to when we first met. I'm plannin' to drive up and meet her there—she says she's booked a fancy suite for us—so we'll see how it goes. I figure I can take time off from the campaign for the holidays."

"Sure you can. And confidentially," Powell added, "I don't think you should worry too much. Santa Claus can visit you just as well up there as down here."

"You don't think I'm a foolish old coot?"

"I do not. And I can speak with some authority on this subject, having just taken a second swipe at romance myself. When you get to be our age, you take happiness where you can find it without asking questions. I've been very fortunate to have had two wonderful women in my life. I think you should definitely go for it!"

Mr. Choppy expelled what sounded like the weight of the world from his lungs and then plastered a smile on his face. "I'm gonna do my best. Truth is, I feel like a sixteen-year-old kid again!"

★

Powell and Laurie sat next to each other at their kitchen table the next morning, smiling across at their guest, Myrtis Troy. It was nearly ten o'clock, and the room still offered up aromatic traces of the delicious breakfast they had just enjoyed—Laurie's blueberry pancakes with maple syrup, link sausages, and coffee. Along with a ceramic centerpiece of Santa wedged into his sleigh, a pot of mulled cider simmering on the nearby stove added to the cheerful holiday ambience; and to make things even more comfortable for Myrtis, Laurie and Powell had each affixed a pair of those comical reindeer antlers to their heads. They were now ready to begin creating the copy for the first of the Nitwitt radio spots, but it was clear that Myrtis was still a bit unnerved.

"I'm just not sure what you want to know," she began in response to Powell's request that she open the proceedings by talking a bit about herself. "How detailed do you want me to be—and how private, for that matter?"

Powell drained the last of his coffee and took up his notepad and pen with a pleasant smile. "I don't want you to go into anything you'd consider a private family matter, of course. Just the ordinary things about your husband and children will do."

Myrtis seemed to relax a bit, the frown lines softening across her forehead. "Well, I married Raymond Troy, of course. That was light-years ago, in 1958. We had two children, Raymond Junior and Roane, and they're both married and have given me four grandchildren, all of whom I adore. And as you both also know, the whole crew was just here to visit me and helped out the other day at campaign headquarters for a snapshot with Mr. Choppy and a phone call or two on his behalf. Is that what you were after?"

Powell scribbled on his pad while nodding, but it was Laurie who suddenly took up the exchange. "That's just fine, Myrtis, but I happen to know that your Raymond was a man of unusual interests behind the scenes. I know he was a successful lawyer, but there was that little shop of his he bought just for fun. Could you go into detail and maybe tell us a little bit more about Raymond himself?"

Myrtis hesitated, looking skeptical. "Oh, the shop? Are you sure that would really be of any interest?"

"Trust me. I think that's what we might be looking for. Just tell us about it. Have I ever steered you or the club wrong before?"

"Point well taken," Myrtis replied, and then the floodgates opened. "Well, to start with, Raymond was a bundle of contradictions, and he never did anything by the book. He was a good fifteen years older than I was and already a well-established lawyer when we fell in love and got married. My family never had any money to speak of, so I was pretty blown away by his wealth. I guess that's how I got into the habit of bragging for a long time there. I was pretty bad about it, I'll admit."

"Nonsense," Laurie replied. "I'd just classify it as a delightful quirk. We all have them."

"I expect you're right. Anyway, my marriage to Raymond was rolling around splendidly—no problems of any kind with his practice either. And then one day, he comes home brazen as you please with this album from Second Creek Records by the Four Seasons. It seems he'd heard this song on the radio by that same group—I'll never forget it—it was 'Big Girls Don't Cry.' That guy Frankie Valli had a falsetto voice that could have shattered my best wedding crystal."

"Oh, I remember that quite well," Laurie said with a hint of a giggle. "I was a freshman at Ole Miss when that came out. It was all the rage at the sorority house. We fancied ourselves the big girls of the lyrics, and we took a pledge that none of those sexy fraternity boys were going to make us cry that fall. Of course, wouldn't you know it? I remember bawling my eyes out over this tall, dark Kappa Alpha with bedroom eyes by the name of Pawlus Herring the Fourth. He thought he was God's gift to Southern belles everywhere."

Everyone had a good laugh, and then Myrtis said, "Yes, I know the type. But at least you were listening to the Four Seasons as a college student. Put yourself in my shoes. Here's my dignified middle-aged lawyer husband going positively bananas over all this teenybopper music. He'd play it night and day and even come home for lunch from the office just to hear 'Big Girls Don't Cry' and that 'Sherry' song over and over again. At one point he totally bewildered our friends by playing the entire album all through the first dinner party we gave after moving into Evening Shadows. There I was serving filets, Caesar salad, and cheese grits while Frankie Valli wailed like a banshee in the background. People were plugging their ears and later asking for Alka-Seltzer. I thought I would go crazy until I found a solution to Raymond's obsession."

Powell was writing a mile a minute, not bothering to suppress the wide grin on his face. "I can't wait to hear what you came up with."

"Yes, well, I'm not sure how I did it, but somehow I had a brainstorm—the kind Laurie has had so often over the years. I suggested to Raymond that he buy the record shop, let the same people run it for him, and he could go down there anytime he wanted and listen to his heart's content. Anything to get him out of the house with all that noise. Well, to cut to the chase here, he made a fabulous success of the record shop—far better than the previous management—and he changed the name to Ray's Rock and Roll and More. Practically until the day he died, he spent every Saturday down there, helping his clerks sell records to people. He especially liked talking to the teenagers about their music and finding out what they liked to listen to. Some of them even called him Uncle Ray as time went on. Of course, I have no earthly idea where his sudden interest came from. Up until the Four Seasons exploded onto the scene, he listened to nothing but Gershwin and classical music. He did a complete about-face. He would even sing along, trying to imitate that falsetto sound. Even had me doing it at one point. It definitely drove me nuts, but once I got him out the door with it, it wasn't so bad."

"It's funny. I walked past Ray's Rock and Roll just the other day when I was downtown," Powell said, finishing up with his notes. "I knew nothing about the history of the store. Anything else I need to know?"

"There's not too much more. Raymond kept up with the times—graduated from Frankie Valli to Simon and Garfunkel, and then when they broke up, to Paul Simon as his absolute favorite. I sold the store after Raymond died, but the new owners chose to keep the name, since it had become so successful that way," Myrtis replied, sounding thoroughly pleased with herself.

"This is perfect. I know just the tack I'd like to pursue with your spot," Powell said. "I see this as an affirmation of taking on new tasks and interests no matter where you are in life. Your Raymond stepped out of his lawyer's suit and found an interesting and lucrative hobby in the bargain. It's a different version of what Mr. Choppy wants to accomplish with his campaign. Give me a minute, and I'll run my idea past both of you."

The two women waited patiently, studying the way Powell's facial muscles twitched and creased as he steeped himself in his composition. The process seemed to take forever, but eventually Powell looked up, striking a triumphant pose. "Aha! I think I have it. Try this on for size, ladies: 'Hello. I'm Mrs. Myrtis Troy, and I'd like to speak to you Second Creek voters for a minute about Hale Dunbar Junior and his candidacy for mayor.

A longtime successful businessman known to all of us, Mr. Dunbar wants to continue to serve his beloved community in a new role, bringing fresh energy and insights into office with him. Some of you may know that my late husband, Raymond Troy, branched out later in life into the record business—balancing his career as a prominent attorney with running the popular Ray's Rock and Roll and More. Ray succeeded because he loved music and sharing it with his customers, whom he truly cared about. Mr. Dunbar wants to branch out now in the same way—bringing his knowledge of Second Creekers, their lives and businesses, to the forefront and doing what's best for all concerned. His maturity and ambition can be trusted—they are assets, not liabilities. As a woman in her sixties, I'm proud to support Hale Dunbar Junior for mayor of Second Creek, and I invite you to join me in voting for him on February fifth, 2002. Hale Dunbar Junior— a new beginning with a trusted friend.'"

There was a significant pause, during which Powell first locked eyes with Laurie, then with Myrtis. "What do you think?" he said finally. "Could you run with it?"

"I like it for the most part, Powell," she replied after some deliberation. "I'm just wondering how crucial it is that I talk about my age that way. I know I volunteered for the concept, but now that we've gotten down to the lick log, my training as a Southern lady seems to be rearing its genteel head. Can we keep it as it is, except for my saying that I'm in my sixties? Not that that would be a surprise to anyone."

Powell quickly crossed through the word and wrote in something else. "Okay, how's this? 'As a mature and intelligent woman, I'm proud to support Hale Dunbar Junior et cetera.' I think it dovetails nicely with Lady Roth's Susan B. Anthony theme."

Myrtis beamed. "I like that much better. I'd rather err on the part of discretion here. Do you think I'm being vain? I really want to help, but I can almost feel my grandmother waving a perfumed handkerchief in my face and saying, 'No, no, no!'"

"I think it works just fine without the actual number," Laurie put in. "And, no, I don't think you're being vain in the least. Renza and Denver Lee still insist they want nothing to do with this, so maybe they have a point, after all."

"We'll just offer Wittsie and Novie the same option on the actual age thing," Powell added. "Meanwhile, I really think we've got a strong spot here. Your husband's record store is a feel-good story, and so is Mr. Choppy and the Piggly Wiggly."

Myrtis took a deep breath and gave Powell an expectant glance. "So, now that that's settled, what's the next step? When do we go down to WSCM and record this?"

Powell glanced at his notes and made a clucking noise. "We have Wittsie coming over this afternoon and then Novie tomorrow morning. Once we've written all three spots, I'll round you all up for a session right after Christmas. Don't worry about a thing. We'll take our time and do it up right. You'll come off sounding like a million dollars."

Myrtis had a sassy smirk on her face as she said, "Even if I don't, I'm a big girl now. And as we all know, big girls don't cry, and I know my Raymond would want me to take that bridge over troubled water."

★

The midafternoon session with Wittsie turned out to be the proverbial piece of cake—holiday fruitcake, in this instance. Laurie brought out generous slices of her own family recipe, which was more partial to pecans, walnuts, and shredded coconut than candied fruit, and there was a choice of freshly made coffee or mulled cider to wash it all down. Being the guileless person she was, Wittsie cooperated fully with Powell's inquiries about her family and her age, and the appropriate copy for her spot materialized quickly.

"How does this sound, Wittsie?" Powell began from his perch beside her on the living-room sofa. "'Hello. I'm Mrs. Wittsie Chadwick, and I'd like to speak to you today for a moment about Hale Dunbar Junior and his campaign for Second Creek mayor. Some of you may remember that my late husband, Carleton Chadwick, prepared the tax returns for many of you Second Creekers over the years. It was after his death almost ten years ago that I broke through my grief and founded a new social and civic group, which I initially called the Second Creek Widows' Club. We now informally call ourselves the Nitwitts, and many of you are familiar with our good works. I wanted to emphasize to you voters today that it is never too late to start a new phase of your life. Hale Dunbar Junior wants to embark upon just such a phase of his life, after a long and productive business career here in Second Creek. He is seventy-one years strong and seventy-one years committed to this community, and I extend to him all the support of my sixty-five years as a Second Creeker who believes in staying involved at every juncture. His maturity and ambition are assets, not liabilities. Won't you join me in voting for change on February fifth, 2002? Hale Dunbar Junior — a new beginning with a trusted friend.'" Powell paused, giving Wittsie a chance to digest it all. "What do you think? Are you comfortable with the mention of your exact age? We don't have to go there if you prefer not to."

Her response was immediate, though couched in her meandering style. "I have no problem with that. . . . I really liked how you worked Carleton into it. . . . I mean, I'm sure he'd approve. . . . I think I'm doing the right thing. . . . I've just never been one to care about my age or growing old. . . . Of course, I've never felt I was the sharpest tack in the box . . . but I guess you know all about my turning the Nitwitts over to Laurie years ago and dropping back to secretary. . . . Sometimes I get confused. . . . "

"You underestimate yourself, Wittsie. You've done a fine job as recording secretary all these years," Laurie interjected from her favorite armchair.

"I suppose so," she replied, sounding far from convinced and looking quite solemn. "But at any rate, I think the radio spot sounds just fine, Powell . . . unless there's something you think it still needs."

Powell softly demurred. "I can't think of a thing—it's ready to go. I especially like the way I've taken the bull by the horns and not tried to hide the fact that our Mr. Choppy is in his seventies. Let's throw the age thing right back in Mr. Floyce's face. It's nothing to be ashamed of—it certainly worked for Ronald Reagan when he took office. In my opinion, he turned out to be one of our best presidents, gourmet jelly beans and all."

Wittsie flashed a weak little smile and daintily cleared her throat. "Oh, I love jelly beans, especially the weird flavors like buttered popcorn. . . . So did President Reagan . . . not sure which flavors, but he definitely liked jelly beans. . . . You make a good point there. . . . Then, it's settled. . . . But I was wondering . . . I mean, do you both have a few minutes? There's something I wanted to discuss with you."

"My goodness, Wittsie," Laurie replied. "You sound so serious. What's the matter?"

Wittsie took some time to gather her thoughts—seemingly mesmerized by Laurie's superbly decorated Christmas tree gracing a corner of the room with its old-fashioned bubble lights and glittering tinsel. Once she came out of her trance, however, she opened up to them just as Myrtis had earlier in the day. "I'm just so upset about Meagan having to spend the holidays with me. . . . I mean, she pretends she's okay, but I can tell she misses her parents. . . . I worry about her so . . . and then I worry about her parents, too . . . particularly my daughter, April. . . . What did I do wrong? . . . Is this my fault?"

Laurie and Powell exchanged puzzled glances and then Laurie said, "Is what your fault? I'm not sure what you're getting at."

Wittsie fidgeted on the sofa, looking down into her lap as she spoke. "What I mean is . . . well, why is it that my April isn't around for Meagan any more than she is? . . . She and my son-in-law, Pace, are always traveling. . . . They just don't stay put, and they're always leaving Meagan behind with relatives . . . mostly me . . . and don't get me wrong, I don't mind in the least. . . . I was happy to have her this summer, and I'm happy to have her now. . . . She's really a darling girl and no trouble at all. . . . "

"Oh, she's adorable," Laurie added. "She was the perfect maid of honor in my wedding this summer—I thought the two of you were the fashion smash of the Piggly Wiggly in your matching dresses."

"Yes, I thought we pulled that off quite nicely," Wittsie continued. "But that's not the point. . . . I wondered if there was something I did to make April abandon her family the way she does at times. . . . I mean, she only seems to be thinking of herself. . . . I was never like that . . . neither was Carleton. . . .

We emphasized family all the time. . . . So, I just don't understand. . . . Why doesn't April pay more attention to Meagan? . . . Sometimes it just breaks my heart. . . . It's not enough just to leave a bunch of presents behind."

Laurie rose immediately and moved to sit beside Wittsie on the sofa, taking the time to pat her hand gently before she spoke. "I know the kind of sweet, gentle person you are, Wittsie, and I'm quite certain you and Carleton gave April good values. But you can't live her life for her and tell her what to do. If there's one thing all of us Second Creekers know, it's that people have their own agendas, and there's no accounting for the whys and wherefores. The best advice I can give you is to keep on doing what you're doing now. Just continue to be there for Meagan, no matter what your daughter and son-in-law do. She'll remember that as time goes on. I think you might be taking on too much to try and figure out what's going on with her parents right now. Meanwhile, aren't you glad Meagan has you?"

Wittsie looked greatly relieved and managed a smile. "That makes sense. . . . Good thing, too, since it would definitely drive me crazy to try and figure it all out. . . . My powers of concentration aren't the greatest. . . . How I muddle through at times, I'll never know."

"Listen," Laurie added, inching a bit closer to her friend. "Why don't you and Meagan drop by Christmas evening for some eggnog and cookies? Powell and I are starting a new openhouse tradition this year. I've invited all the other girls, so I insist you come and bring Meagan with you."

Powell patted her shoulder and said, "We won't take no for an answer."

"Okay. It's a deal, then," Wittsie replied, brightening considerably.

"Great!" Powell said. "As for the radio spot, I'll give you a call about the production date down at the radio station, but it looks like we'll get to it right after Christmas. You'll soon be hearing yourself over the air."

The excitement in Wittsie's voice was quite evident. "I'll look forward to that. . . . Oh, I hope I can make a difference for Mr. Choppy. . . . You know, I've always thought he was the dearest soul. . . . Oh, and be sure and give me enough notice to get to the beauty parlor so I can look my best for my audience. Maybe I'll even try a new hairdo."

Laurie laughed good-naturedly. "You can do just as you please, Wittsie, but it's radio, remember?"

"Oh, that's right. . . . So it is. . . . What was I thinking? . . . Well, there's further proof I needed to turn the Nitwitts over to you when I did."

★

The copy session with Novie at the breakfast table the following morning was well under way. Of all the Nitwitts who had embraced Laurie's radio brainstorm, Novie had been the most positive from the outset. She had stood up before the others during their meeting and unflinchingly declared her age as sixty-six, and now she was losing no time in ironing out the specifics with Powell.

"For starters, I think my spot should center around my travels," she was saying after her last bite of the eggs Benedict that Laurie had so expertly prepared. "Taking on new things, exciting adventures — that's exactly what Mr. Choppy is trying to do with his campaign. He's zeroed in on the true Second Creek spirit, and I think I should mention that to the voters, don't you, Powell? I didn't see that anywhere in the other two spots you've shown me."

"You took the words right out of my mouth," he replied, shoving back a bit from the table and letting his breakfast settle. "Go ahead, then. Suggest a phrase or two—you seem to know what you want here."

Novie considered at some length, silently mouthing words before perking up for the payoff. "I'll leave it up to you to embellish this, but I was thinking of something along the lines of, 'Change is vital. You can travel to find it, of course, but the truly imaginative people make it happen in their own backyard. Hale Dunbar Junior has embarked upon just such a mission—much as I have routinely embarked upon my world travels to get a different perspective on things. Won't you join us both in voting for a new political outlook in Second Creek?'"

Powell picked up his notepad from the table, arched his brows, and shot her an approving glance. "Very impressive. You've essentially done my job for me. I'll be able to whip something up for your approval in practically no time."

An almost cocky expression broke across Novie's face as she said, "I guess I'm just full of myself and Laurie's wonderful eggs and hollandaise this morning. Everything seems to be going my way, and I think I'm going to have a very special Christmas for the first time in a long while."

"I'm reading between the lines here," Laurie replied, eyeing her shrewdly. "But does this have anything to do with your son, Marc? Oh, and I did take the liberty of telling Powell about your situation there. You said you wouldn't mind."

"Not at all. Glad you did. In fact, I feel positively liberated about it these days. I took your advice and got on the phone with Marc and invited him and his friend Michael to spend Christmas here with me. You can't imagine how thrilled I was when he accepted. They're flying into Memphis tomorrow and then driving down. They'll be spending almost a week with me, and I can't wait. This is the greatest Christmas present in the world — getting my son back after this long period of estrangement. That's why I feel so strongly about going out on a limb for Mr. Choppy. Everyone should know this feeling that I have now, this feeling of starting over and putting the past behind you."

"It's like our slogan says, Hale Dunbar Junior — A New Beginning with a Trusted Friend," Powell replied. "And congratulations on working things out with your son."

"I've extended this same invitation to all the other Nitwitts, so I'll extend it to you as well now," Laurie added. "Powell and I are having an open house Christmas evening, and we'd love for you to come by and bring Marc and his friend with you. The whole gang will be here, it looks like. Just think of it as an extended family outing."

Novie laughed heartily and said, "Outing! There were times in the past that that word would have made me cringe — but no longer!"

"Oh, I guess I made a pun without meaning to." Laurie grinned.

"No more running away for me. I'm going to accept my son and his friend for who they are and not worry about what other people think. That's where Geoffrey and I got off track — there we were worrying about conventionality in a place that puts a premium on being who you are no matter what. That's just not the Second Creek way, and I had no business taking this amount of time to realize it."

Laurie rose from her chair and started clearing the table. "Better late than never. Hmm . . . I wonder if that ought to be on the sign welcoming people to our fair town. I'll run it past Mr. Choppy when he gets elected."

"I like the way you put that, Laurie," Novie replied. "When, not if. Maybe our campaign and our radio spots are a bit offbeat by the usual political standards, but I have a good feeling about all of it. I think we're going to come from behind and win this thing outright."

★

Laurie had not miscalculated concerning the radio spot recalcitrants. Word soon got back to Renza and Denver Lee about how much fun the others had had working out their copy with Powell, as well as how flattering and tasteful the finished spots were going to be. It was an unwritten rule of Nitwitt behavior that what any one of them did with a flourish, all the others had to do as well. The competition among them was subtle but very real. In no time at all, both holdouts were on the phone with Powell, begging for and pinning down a session for themselves, and he and Laurie were able to accommodate them on Christmas Eve.

Renza was scheduled for late morning, having declined Laurie's gracious invitation to arrive in time for breakfast. Renza's servant situation had taken a turn for the worse, she had explained rather cryptically, and there was the matter of an early interview with a replacement that she simply must negotiate. True to form, she provided a blow-by-blow as soon as she had removed her trademark fox fur and settled in on the living-room sofa just past ten thirty.

"I gave that little Vidalia Williams every chance to prove herself," Renza began, dramatically shrugging her shoulders with her palms outstretched. "You remember I hired her back in September, Laurie."

"Oh, yes. The one from out in the county?"

Renza fairly pounced upon the remark. "Exactly. The child seemed sweet enough to start with, but as the weeks went by, she began to complain about the strangest things. Frankly, I refuse to see anything political in where I kept her apron and the feather duster, but she apparently objected to the fact that they were both hanging on the wall in the kitchen closet next to the trash can. She made such a to-do about it one morning that I thought my coffee was going to go down the wrong pipe. 'What are you talking about, Vidalia?' I said to her. 'What difference does it make where I keep those things?' And she says, 'I'm not ashamed to be cleaning your house. It's an honest day's work.' Of course, I still had no idea what she was getting at, so I had to pursue it. 'Yes, of course, it's honest work,' I said. Well, to cut to the chase, it turns out that she'd taken up with a young man who'd convinced her that housekeeping was beneath her and that she was somehow being exploited. 'You don't need the money?' I said to her then. Well, she really had no answer for that, but I could see that she'd suddenly developed an attitude and probably wanted to pick a fight so I'd let her go and she could please her boyfriend, so I accommodated her. Honestly, at my age, I don't have the time and energy to deal with such nitpicky horse apples!"

Powell and Laurie exchanged bewildered glances while Renza caught her breath. They would both certainly have agreed that her reputation as the most high maintenance of all the Nitwitts was in no danger of disappearing anytime soon.

"So how did the interview go this morning?" Laurie finally ventured when she felt the coast was clear, and her head would not be bitten off.

"Oh, it was grievous!" Renza exclaimed. "I agreed to see this Hispanic woman named Lunez something or other that Mary Fred Goodlett had heard about, but we could hardly communicate. I think I last studied Spanish when Queen Isabella commissioned Christopher Columbus, and this woman's English seemed to be limited to 'You casa berry big—you rooms have so many of.' We both did a lot of that obvious, cheesy smiling and eyebrow arching, and I told her I would call her back, but I don't even think she understood that much." Renza broke off for one of her more histrionic poses and sighs. "It was just another dead end, I'm afraid. If I hired her, I'd never be able to explain such things as doing the baseboards and fetching furballs from under the beds—especially in my casa berry big with my rooms have so many of."

"Perhaps you'll find someone after the holidays," Laurie replied, more amused by Renza's diatribe than anything else. "This isn't the best time to be looking, you know."

"At any rate," Powell put in, determined to put the subject to bed, "why don't we get started on your copy? That'll at least take your mind off your servant dilemma for a little while."

Renza shot him a skeptical glance. "Very well, but I want to say at the outset that I have no intention of revealing my age. That's still beyond the pale, in my book."

"That won't be necessary," Powell replied with a reassuring grin. "We'll do it entirely your way."

Though it was clear that Renza had arrived loaded for bear, Powell's remark seemed to have caught her off guard, and her customary hauteur quickly melted away. "Then let's get started.

What are your suggestions? Myrtis called up to say you had worked wonders with her image, if that's the proper way to look at it. I'm sure you can appreciate the fact that I have to keep my image in mind as well, since I'll be taking over from Myrtis as president of the Nitwitts in a couple of months. Not long after the election, in fact. So even if Mr. Choppy doesn't win, there will be at least one changing of the guard around here."

Powell glanced down at the notes he'd made while questioning Laurie earlier—notes entitled "Renza Belford Tactics." He promptly proceeded with his wife's suggestions. "Laurie told me all about your shared presidency. Congratulations! I know you're looking forward to it. Now, if you would, I'd like for you to give me a bit of background about your position in the community."

The ploy had the desired effect. Renza puffed up proudly. "Oh, well, of course. I'd be more than happy to do that. As you may or may not know, I was married to Lewis Belford for nearly forty-two years, and he was the third generation of his family to play the real-estate game here in town. The old adage among the Belfords was that if a piece of dirt rested inside the city limits of Second Creek, it very likely had been bought and sold at least three times over by a Belford family member. Belford Realty endured it all over the years—fire, hail, ice, tornadoes, straight-line winds. You name it, they lived through it. And a Belford was always there to help people pick up the pieces and get things started again—much like the Dunbar family with their Piggly Wiggly. I confess that's why I have such a soft spot for Mr. Choppy with this campaign of his. Lewis and his entire family always spoke so highly of the Dunbars."

Powell shuffled his notes a bit further and then started writing things down. "Give me a moment or two. I think I'm onto something you'll be very pleased with."

"Oh, already? My, but you're a fast worker," Renza said, her voice full of curiosity.

A few minutes later, the efficient Powell unveiled his handiwork. "Hello, Second Creek voters. I'm Mrs. Renza Belford and—"

"I prefer Mrs. Lewis Belford, if you don't mind," Renza interrupted. "I don't much cotton to the notion that you forget where you've been just because your husband has bought the farm. And I didn't just make that up either. It was one of Lewis's inside realtor jokes. He was always saying to me, 'Please remember me after I've bought the farm.'"

"Mrs. Lewis Belford it shall be, then." Powell made a quick revision, smiled pleasantly, and started over. "Hello, Second Creek voters. I'm Mrs. Lewis Belford, and I'd like to talk with you today about Hale Dunbar Junior and his mayoral campaign. As some of you may know, the Belford family has bought and sold real estate here in Second Creek for many generations. As such, I feel I have a vital stake in the economic health of this community, and I want to see the right kind of progress made here, one that takes into account the treasures of the past and orderly growth for the future. Upholding Second Creek zoning laws and architectural ordinances is something that Hale Dunbar Junior is committed to, coming under the heading of doing business the right way. As a mature and intelligent woman with a clear sense of history, I urge each of you to vote with me on February fifth, 2002, to preserve the best of Second Creek while ensuring for it a bright future. Hale Dunbar Junior—a new beginning with a trusted friend."

"Oh, I adore the way that makes me sound!" Renza exclaimed. "Myrtis didn't exaggerate about you in the least. You

see, Laurie, there was no need to go into numbers. That was my
big objection to your idea from the start."

"Perhaps you were right," Laurie replied, electing to take the
high road and eager to preserve Renza's pleasant mood—something of a rarity in itself. "At any rate, I'm glad you're pleased
with Powell's approach. We've covered a lot of different bases
with these spots so far. I think the overall effect will be positive
for the campaign and give Mr. Choppy some momentum once
they get on the air."

Powell offered a variation or two on his latest theme before
Renza approved the final version, and then the three of them
moved to the kitchen table, where Laurie offered everyone a
choice of coffee or mulled cider.

"You really did make this rather effortless, Powell," Renza
was saying as she poured a bit of cream into her coffee. "In fact,
I feel rather giddy about the whole thing. I'm not really very
good at letting my hair down, as Laurie can tell you. But for
some reason, I feel like doing just that this morning with the
two of you."

Laurie's eyes widened with surprise, but she nonetheless
remained composed. "Yes, well, we've been privy to a revelation
or two over the past couple of days."

Renza fidgeted a bit and spoke slowly. "I think . . . I may have
painted too rosy a picture of the Belfords a bit earlier. Lewis's
brother, Paul, is running the business now all by himself, since
my son, Cole, wanted nothing to do with it and moved to Atlanta
after he got married. I hardly ever see him or my daughter, Meta,
who's down in Florida doing God knows what. I think I have an
inkling of why they've chosen not to stay here in Second Creek,
though."

"That seems to have been the trend among the next generation — to move away, I mean," Laurie interjected. "The fact is,
Second Creek is getting older and more eccentric by the
minute. I wonder what the town will be like twenty years from
now."

"That's why this election is so important," Powell added. "I
think we're definitely at a crossroads. The town will look and act
one way under Mr. Choppy and quite another if Mr. Floyce continues in office."

Renza nodded and blew across her coffee before taking a sip.
"I think we all agree on that. At any rate, back to my inkling.
What I neglected to say previously regarding the Belfords was
that my mother-in-law, Mamie, was a harridan of the highest
order. She never thought I was good enough for her Lewis. I
was a Garrison from Rolling Fork, and that just wouldn't do.
She made life difficult for me, always criticizing everything I did,
especially regarding the children, and they eventually saw what
was going on. I think they wanted to get away from all the tension as soon as they could."

"I had no idea," Laurie replied. "The only dealings my mother
and I ever had with Mamie Belford were at garden club meetings, and she was always the picture of good manners on those
occasions."

"Oh, yes, once she was out the door and all gussied up to the
extent her wizened little buzzard of a frame could be, she was on
her best behavior. But behind the scenes, she never let up on me.
Lewis did his best to confront her and plead my case, but after a
while, he just gave up and concentrated on the family business. I
think he felt guilty about the whole thing, and that's why he
insisted I spend as much of his money as I possibly could." Then

Renza put down her coffee cup and indulged a genuine laugh. "I got my revenge of sorts. It's lying out there on your sofa, Laurie."

Laurie blinked, and Powell looked equally confused.

"I'm talking about my fox fur," Renza explained. "Mamie despised animals of any kind. She never let Lewis or Paul have any pets growing up, not even a goldfish. Then one Christmas, Lewis gave me a fox fur, and Mamie declared that it was positively the ugliest thing she'd ever seen in her life with all those little stuffed heads sticking out from my shoulders. From that moment on, I vowed that I would never be without those little faces in public — especially whenever I was in the presence of my mother-in-law. It drove her absolutely nuts until the day she died, particularly after Lewis gave me several more as the years went by. I think he got a little kick out of it, too — knowing that it bugged her."

"I would never have guessed," Laurie said with a little chuckle. "I wonder just how many people's quirks can be chalked up to in-law problems."

"Or being a frustrated actress — in the case of Lady Roth," Powell added.

Renza took a generous swig of her coffee and said, "I've never told anyone what I just told the two of you. I was brought up never to air the family's dirty laundry, and I suppose I still sub-scribe to that in the main. You'll keep this little revelation in strictest confidence, won't you?"

"Of course we will," Laurie replied. "Though in a sense I regret all the mystery being taken out of your vast collection of furry foxes."

"I know what you mean," Renza said. "It's great fun being mis-understood and memorable at the same time. But then that's par for the course here in Second Creek."

★

"I was toying with ideas for my radio spot last night," Denver Lee was saying to Powell and Laurie later that day. They were all seated around the kitchen table enjoying a midafternoon snack of raw carrots, celery, and cauliflower with a fat-free artichoke and ranch dressing dip—all in deference to Denver Lee's struggle to diet-manage her impending diabetes. "And I was wondering if you thought there might be enough people out there with diabetes to make that the theme of my spot. Novie called up to rave about how you built her spot around her interests in travel. Could you maybe personalize mine in a similar way?"

Powell stopped crunching on his celery long enough to think on his feet. Whatever he had anticipated from Denver Lee, it was not this. "Of course, I have no idea what the diabetes statistics are for Second Creek, Denver Lee. I'm wondering if that's a strong enough theme to put out there for the voters."

Denver Lee's face dropped noticeably. "Then you don't think it's a good idea? I've been reading up on diabetes, you know, and it's becoming a very serious problem these days. More and more children are even developing it."

"I don't doubt that," Powell continued, trying to sound as diplomatic as possible. "But I wonder if there's something else, some other topic that you could possibly speak to."

"I was afraid you were going to say that," Denver Lee replied, taking out her frustration on the piece of carrot she was chewing to shreds. "Only two things came to mind last night. One was Diabetics for Mr. Choppy and the other was Oil Painters for Mr. Choppy. As you know, I've finally given up trying to force my still-life efforts down people's throats, and I readily admit that Oil Painters for Mr. Choppy sounds positively silly. So, I'm at a loss."

Powell briefly glanced at Laurie, but he could tell from the quizzical expression on her face that she had nothing for him. So he fell back on what had worked with the others. "Why don't you start by giving us a bit on your family life? Maybe something about your husband. I think I can work that up into a winner for you in no time."

Denver Lee looked incredulous. "You want me to talk about Eustice McQueen? I don't think so. Euss was the wheeler-dealer and schemer-dreamer of all time. My husband was always looking for that pot of gold at the end of the rainbow, but he really never made so much as a plugged nickel. He tried inventing things like a miniature pecan hull cracker, drilling for oil in the most unlikely places, even restoring antique cars, but he just wasn't very good at any of it. I loved him dearly, of course, and I have to give him credit for brushing himself off and getting to his feet every time he got knocked down, but nearly all the money I have now I inherited from my family. I was a Rainwater from over in Bolivar County, and my father made his money off of—what else?—soybeans. So I'm afraid there's not much to talk about there."

Powell screwed up his face, searching for an angle that would work. Surely he could latch onto something. Then it hit him. "I'm going to have to disagree with you there, Denver Lee. Don't you see that your Eustice embodied the spirit of Second Creek in his own way? There he was—taking chances all those years, hunting and pecking for something that would work without worrying what other people thought, fighting the good fight, still on the prowl for the big breakthrough. So it never worked out for him. At least he never gave up. I even see a similarity between your husband and our Mr. Choppy that we could emphasize."

"In what way? Mr. Choppy stuck with managing his Piggly Wiggly for decades, and he'd probably still be doing so if not for the MegaMart."

"No, that's not what I meant." Powell explained, "I'm referring to the fact that Mr. Choppy embodies the spirit of starting over and trying something new no matter what adversity life deals you. It sounds like your Eustice was that kind of man, too."

Denver Lee smiled pleasantly for the first time that morning and said, "Yes, he was. You're right. I definitely see your point now."

"Then let me go to work on that angle right this instant," Powell said. And over the next five minutes or so, he did just that—scribbling on his notepad with such speed and intensity that it appeared his pen might snap in two. Only the noisy crunching of raw veggies altered the mood of concentrated effort.

"I think I've got it now," Powell said finally. "Try this on: 'Hello, I'm Mrs. Denver Lee McQueen, and I'd like to talk to you Second Creek voters today about Hale Dunbar Junior and his mayoral campaign. My husband, Eustice McQueen, embodied the entrepreneurial, never-give-up spirit that our town is so famous for. He would certainly have appreciated Mr. Dunbar's efforts to begin a new career in public service after such an outstanding run as a local small-business man. We Second Creekers have always admired those who take chances and follow their dreams, no matter how long the journey takes or what sacrifices it requires. That's the sort of energy and spirit Hale Dunbar Junior will bring to the office. He already has the civic-minded know-how in his résumé. As a mature and intelligent woman, I'm proud to support him for mayor, and I invite you to join me in voting for him on February fifth, 2002. Hale Dunbar Junior — a new beginning with a trusted friend.'"

Denver Lee actually began to tear up during the brief silence that ensued. "Oh, that was inspirational, Powell," she said, dabbing at her eyes with her napkin. "I really needed to hear that about Euss. I think he went to his grave believing he had failed me, but I never once thought that about him. I only wish I had told him so outright. This sort of sets things right and promotes Mr. Choppy at the same time."

"Out of all the Nitwitt spots, I like this one best," Laurie chimed in. "Many people should recognize themselves in it if they do a little soul-searching."

Powell put his pad down and struck a jaunty pose. "Then it looks like we're all set — except for the production session at the station. That'll just be a matter of going into the booth and recording — one after the other. It might require a few takes, but we'll get the job done. In the end, I'll make sure that each one of you sounds like a pro."

Denver Lee looked positively enthralled, clasping her hands together over her head in a victory gesture. "How marvelous! I really think this will be our best Nitwitt project ever — especially if it makes the difference between Mr. Choppy getting elected or not."

"Never underestimate the power of the Nitwitts," Laurie replied with an impish grin and a wink.

"Or the spirit of the true Second Creeker," Powell added. "We've got them all on our side — Lady Roth as Susan B. Anthony, Lovita Grubbs as the Book Sheriff, and Hunter and Mary Fred Goodlett as ... well, themselves — just to name a few.

And just this morning, Vester Morrow of the Victorian Tea Room called up to sign on, offering to prepare free box lunches for our campaign workers once things get going full speed in January. He says Mr. Choppy supplied the restaurant with the best cuts of meat for years, and now it's important to have the troops well fed in the heat of battle."

Denver Lee pushed away from the table and rose from her chair. "Indeed, it is. Well, this has been delightful, but I must be going. On the way home I think I'll drop by the Victorian Tea Room and advise Vester and Mal on some diabetic-friendly choices they can fix for those lunches. Oh dear, I'm afraid I've become as big a pest about that as I was about those terrible oil paintings of mine. I realize now just how pushy I was."

"Nonsense," Laurie said. "I like the way you've embraced this health challenge of yours. We want you around as a Nitwitt for many years to come."

"Oh, yes. I can crunch crudités with the best of them, as you surely heard this morning."

And on that convivial note, the creation of the ageless radio appeals of the Nitwitts came to a successful end.

10.

ROMEO AND JULIET
AT THE PEABODY

M r. Choppy drove his Dodge through the valet entrance of
the Peabody Hotel in downtown Memphis for the second
time since his arrival. My, but he was doing it up fancy for this
two-day rendezvous with his long-lost but recently rediscovered
Gaylie Girl! Heretofore, he had never had the occasion to use
valet service during his seventy-one years, but on this particular
afternoon he wanted to sample the feeling of living large with
every move he made. After all, he and his Gaylie Girl were sharing one of the hotel's multilevel Romeo and Juliet suites on the
eleventh-floor Peabody Club Level—complete with stairway
leading to bedroom balcony, a delightful Shakespearean conceit.
At Gaylie Girl's insistence, they would also be choosing from
such succulent fare as shellfish fricassee or boneless lamb shank
with miso-braised cauliflower couscous that evening in the
Peabody's signature restaurant—Chez Philippe. True, the menu

was a bit rich for Mr. Choppy's tastes, but above all this was a weekend to splurge and see where it led him.

Meanwhile, he had been sent out on the spur of the moment to a liquor store for a bottle of Cristal. Gaylie Girl had discovered to her dismay that a recent convention had exhausted the hotel's customary supply. Mr. Choppy had returned from the hunt with the prescribed bubbly in hand, however, after tipping some earnest young man for fawning over his weather-beaten vehicle as if it were a celebrity's stretch limo. That amused him no end.

Once inside the sprawling atrium lobby, Mr. Choppy headed toward the elevators, clutching his brown bag tightly to his side and marveling once again at the hotel Christmas tree, which was bedazzling guests from every angle. It was the most impressive he'd ever seen indoors—at least three stories tall and exquisitely trimmed in white lights, gold ornaments, and red bows—and it complemented perfectly the elaborate garland draped all around the mezzanine railing.

Unbeknownst to him, however, he had chosen the five o'clock hour to return to the hotel with his champagne. It was precisely the time the red-jacketed Duckmaster always escorted the five famous Peabody ducks from their lobby fountain to their rooftop Royal Duck Palace. The routine included marching the mallards along a red carpet that had been rolled straight up to one of the elevators, whereupon the birds were whisked to the top to retire for the day. A substantial throng had gathered to witness the trademark daily ritual, and Mr. Choppy decided to join them cheerfully rather than stress out over the inevitable delay. In fact, he had great fun watching the whole waddling production, especially since the ducks acted as if they somehow knew they were the only game in town at that moment.

On the ride up to the eleventh floor a bit later, Mr. Choppy's thoughts once again turned full force to the glamorous and wealthy widow who eagerly awaited his return. The years had been more than kind to his Gaylie Girl—they'd been substantially reversed by the skill of the plastic surgeon's knife, as she had readily admitted to him during her summer visit. The Lyons Insole fortune she'd inherited from her tycoon husband, Peter, had more than taken care of that. She looked nowhere near her chronological age of seventy-four, and the contrast between her appearance and his had indeed been the incentive for his recent quest to trim down and spruce himself up a bit. It had not been merely a matter of the fifteen pounds he'd told Powell he'd lost either. He'd looked himself in the mirror and done some sobering stock-taking. A new haircut and cologne, a sportier wardrobe, even those teeth-whitening strips had all been part of his regimen to look better not only for her but also for the home stretch of the campaign itself.

"You look so handsome in your three-piece suit!" she had told him when he'd walked through the door of their suite a couple of hours earlier. "What have you done to yourself?"

He'd beaten around the bush and insisted that it all had solely to do with looking his professional best for the upcoming election, but she was having none of it.

"I'm flattered," she had continued, standing before him immaculately coiffed and wearing a shimmering gold gown that accented her still youthful figure. "But you had my vote all along."

Then she had leaned in and given him a sweet little kiss on the cheek, and he thought he was going to swoon. Perhaps it was her perfume, or maybe it was her flawless smile, but echoes of the teenage emotions he'd felt for her more than half a century ago settled somewhere beneath his sternum in the form of adrenaline spurts. Somehow, he had managed to sound both composed and amused, though his legs had turned to oatmeal. "I wish you really could vote in the election. You never know. It might make the difference."

Upon his return at quarter past five, she took the Cristal out of the bag and put it in the minifridge to chill. Then they picked up where they had left off regarding the campaign, settling in together on one of the sumptuously appointed sofas.

"Do you think you can close the gap between you and Mr. Floyce after the holidays?" she began, gesturing toward the iced shrimp cocktail she'd ordered up in his absence. "Fifteen percentage points seems like an awfully big hurdle to me. Not that I'm doubting your ability to overcome it."

"Our best is yet to come," he replied. "Our radio campaign starts up soon, and I expect to catch Mr. Floyce off guard with the points we'll make. He's tried to use my inexperience and even my age against me indirectly, but my brilliant campaign managers want us to throw it right back at him and see what happens. We've got some mighty powerful women on our side, and I think they'll make the difference in the end."

Gaylie Girl winked—unhooking a shrimp from the rim of the platter, dipping it in cocktail sauce, and posing smartly with it. "I'm sure you've heard there's at least one powerful woman behind every good man, and I'm very proud to have contributed the seed money for your campaign." Then she took a generous bite of her shrimp and ran her tongue across her lips. "Mmmm. Delicious. Won't you have one, Hale?"

"In case you hadn't noticed, I'm a bit nervous right now," he replied, his smile decidedly on the strained side. "You . . . you have no idea how beautiful you look. All of this, the suite, the time we'll be spendin' together—it's a lot to take in for an ordinary guy like me."

She finished off her shrimp and turned to lock eyes with him. "And you have no idea how adorable you are at this moment. Believe it or not, you just ooze that same irresistible innocence you had when you were sixteen and I was nineteen, and we had our little fling at the Second Creek Hotel. I am slightly disappointed about one thing, though." She paused for effect and held out her hand, causing him to straighten up with a look of bewilderment. "Where are my zinnias, Hale?"

He thought for a moment, and then it came rushing back all too vividly. How could he have forgotten the makeshift bouquets he had made for her two nights running, plucking zinnias out of his mother's front yard garden and presenting them to his Gaylie Girl at the door of her hotel room? "You're absolutely right. I shoulda remembered and brought you some for old times' sake." He relaxed, laughing in spite of himself. "Didn't those zinnias have a bug or two crawlin' around on 'em? That's bound to happen when you don't go through a florist."

"There were a few disoriented ladybugs, I believe," she answered, matching his laughter. "Nothing life-threatening, though. No spiders or anything creepy-crawly like that. At any rate, those zinnias did the trick. You melted my heart."

He went silent and solemn on her for a while. Should he dredge it all up again or not? Over the summer, reuniting after more than fifty years, they'd completely rehashed the way she'd run out on him when she found out he was only sixteen. They'd even touched upon it now and then in their many phone calls since, trying to drain it of its power to affect them in the here and now. In the end, he decided to put it to bed for good and try for a new chapter in their relationship. After all, they had the perfect setting for it.

"So, what do you make of that balcony up there by the bedroom?" he said, changing the subject and returning the smile to his face. "Should I stand down here like I'm Romeo and serenade you like you're Juliet or somethin'? First, let me warn you—I can't carry a tune."

"Never mind that. How's your dancing these days? I seem to recall that my cousin Polly said you stepped all over her toes that night at the Piggly Wiggly. She may have even said something about three left feet. But I'm quite sure it was just another of her bitchy exaggerations. When you and I danced together right after that, I can assure you that it was a very pleasant experience. That was when I first became interested in you."

Her response made him feel slightly self-conscious again. It was one thing to work through emotional baggage with her long-distance but quite another face-to-face. Then he remembered Larry Lorrison and His Big Bad Swing Band, appearing nightly in the Continental Ballroom downstairs, and he brightened immediately. "You'll find out tonight about my dancin' when we go down to catch that band that's playin'. Maybe we'll even get to dance to some of the tunes we listened to over the radio back then."

"Oh, I'm sure we will—in fact, I just can't wait. Shall we go before or after dinner?"

"Before, I think. Let's work up an appetite." For some reason he found himself blushing at what he had just said. "I meant for dinner, of course."

"No reason to exclude other things, however," she replied, refusing to let him off the hook.

He read between the lines and that seemed to vanquish his lingering doubts about the evening ahead of them. He decided he could handle a boiled shrimp after all, and she joined him. After polishing off a second with gusto, he said, "I'm just curious. You haven't talked much about your family's reaction to your trip down here. Only that they thought you were crazy. Have you ever let them know about me at all?"

She fell back against the sofa cushions and sighed. "Not yet. They mostly think I'm attending a reunion of people I met during that War Bonds Tour that brought me to Second Creek. But my daughter, Amanda, has been the most vocal about my little junket. She's been saying things like, 'Mother, what in God's name do you have in common with people you haven't seen for over fifty years? What in hell will you talk about?' Then she's been making a big to-do about my not being home around Christmastime, but she should be the one to talk. With all the money she and her siblings were left by their father—somewhat unwisely, I might add—they're never around except when it pleases them. They're always off on excursions all over the world. They're never there for me anymore. Why should I be there for them? I sometimes wonder if any of them would even manage to get home for my funeral."

"I see," he replied, his voice tinged with disappointment.

"Hale, I've gone back and forth about telling them what I'm really up to, and maybe I should have said something by now. You have to understand that it's a different world up there in Lake Forest, but it's the one I chose long after our fling. The bottom line is, I hooked up with Peter Lyons and settled for being his pampered trophy wife and all that goes with it, and I've had to deal with the consequences ever since—both pro and con."

Mr. Choppy thought for a moment, wincing mentally at what he had just heard. Had his Gaylie Girl indirectly answered the big question he would have for her at the end of their tryst? For the time being, he would put it out of his mind, concentrating on big-band music and gourmet cuisine. After that, he would simply have to take his chances.

★

Larry Lorrison and His Big Bad Swing Band had a limited but very popular repertoire that covered most of the hits Tommy Dorsey and his orchestra had originally introduced in the forties. The slim, rangy Lorrison even bore a superficial resemblance to the legendary trombone player himself, though his own role in the retro orchestra consisted of arranging and conducting rather than playing an instrument. The massive Continental Ballroom was packed to the rafters later that evening, mostly with older couples in search of their salad days, but there was a sprinkling of young people who obviously enjoyed the music as well. All of it was being played out onstage against an enormous shell backdrop that lent further nostalgia to the period proceedings.

Mr. Choppy lost no time in threading his way through the crowd with Gaylie Girl in tow once they'd paid the cover charge. The tuxedoed orchestra had just struck up their rendition of "Once in a While," and Mr. Choppy found himself dwelling on the lyrics as they began slow-dancing to the sound of muted trombones and trumpets.

"Remember this one?" he said, being especially careful not to even come close to stepping on her toes. There wasn't much room to maneuver with the crowd pressing in all around them—a sea of immaculately dressed couples moving in slow motion lockstep.

"Of course. I have all the Tommy Dorsey hits on CD at home. I imagine we'll hear everything that made the hit parade all those years if we just stick around long enough."

And stick around they did—enjoying the rest of a first set consisting of "Song of India," "I'm Getting Sentimental Over You," "I'll Never Smile Again," "Opus One," and "On the Sunny Side of the Street." Mr. Choppy dug deep throughout, trying to place exactly where he was and what he was doing when he'd first heard each of those classics. In nearly every instance, however, the answer was that he was listening over his father's office radio on his breaks at the Piggly Wiggly. It was during those precious stolen moments that he had grown almost as obsessed with wartime swing music as he'd always been with the hundreds of movies he'd plunked down all his spending money to see at the now-demolished Grande Theater.

"I was so naïve back when we first met," he said, raising his voice over the music as they continued to dance. "Imagine me thinkin' I could be the next Humphrey Bogart at one of the big Hollywood studios."

"Let's not go there tonight, Hale," she replied in somewhat hushed tones. "I still feel guilty that I exploited your dreams to get you into bed with me. Don't get me wrong, though. You gave me two incredible nights, but my coming down this time is all about new beginnings."

He pulled back slightly and gave her his brightest smile. "That almost sounds like part of my campaign slogan, you know. It's—"

"Wait, don't say it," she interrupted. "You've told me enough times over the phone. I ought to know it by now. A new beginning with a trusted friend, right?"

"Right." He pressed close to her once again, feeling better by the minute about this latest stage of their unorthodox friendship.

By the time the band had announced their first break, Mr. Choppy noted that the workout on the dance floor had produced the desired effect of hunger pangs. "Are you ready for dinner at Chez Philippe now? I think we've paid our respects to the past."

"Lead the way, my dear Hale," she replied. "I'm famished."

★

After their superb dinner of seafood fricassee, Greek salad, and Grand Marnier soufflé had been leisurely dispatched at Chez Philippe, Romeo and Juliet ascended to their suite to continue their evening over chilled Cristal.

"Will you do the honors?" Gaylie Girl said, pulling the bottle out of the minifridge and handing it to Mr. Choppy.

He worked the cork to perfection at the wet bar, filling a couple of wineglasses and handing hers over as he proposed a toast. "To new beginnings."

She repeated his words, and then they clinked rims and sipped.

"You found us a good one here," she continued. "You must know champagne."

"I have to confess I really don't. I think I just got lucky today—in more ways than one."

"I would agree."

Mr. Choppy suddenly realized they had veered into small talk, and he was surprised. His Gaylie Girl had been warm and pliant in his arms on the dance floor, and their conversation over dinner had been suggestive and peppered with laughter. Now, however, they seemed a bit nervous in each other's presence.

He took another sip of his champagne and eyed her shrewdly. After all, he'd just defined the moment as a new beginning. Might as well make good on it or have a good laugh trying. "Methinks thee should climb to the balcony above and looketh down upon me as I speaketh."

She quickly fell to, embracing his idiom with delight. "And what, pray tell, will I heareth when I looketh down?"

"Goeth up and findeth out."

He watched with some degree of trepidation as she made her way up the stairs with glass in hand, finally striking a dramatic pose at the railing. What in God's name was he going to say next? It was one thing to conjure up a few clever lines in faux Shakespearean, Monty Pythonese, or whatever the hell he was attempting to imitate. So he wisely switched gears and somehow found inspiration in his Second Creek vernacular.

"In all seriousness," he began, enunciating as slowly and evenly as Powell had coached him to do for his campaign appearances, "you are every bit the vision you were over fifty years ago. You never left my dreams, you know."

She let out a little gasp. True, it was barely audible, but nonetheless, it was there.

"Oh, Hale, that's absolutely beautiful." She paused briefly, not bothering to disguise the fact that she was tearing up. "And as I said before, you've never lost that wonderful innocent quality you had as a boy of sixteen. That's quite an achievement, in my book. It's not easy to hold on to that sort of thing, given the way of the world. Second Creek truly seems to have preserved you intact."

He blushed, momentarily hanging his head and then gazing upward with stars in his eyes. "Then I spoke good?"

"Shakespeare couldn't have written better dialogue. Now, you get your adorable Second Creek rear end up here this instant. I don't like doing balconies solo. Or bedrooms, for that matter."

Mr. Choppy dutifully climbed the stairs with a spring to his step that belied his age, heading toward a session of lovemaking that he'd been dreaming of for well over fifty years.

★

Room service had just cleared away the refreshing breakfast of freshly cubed honeydew, cereal, coffee, and juice that Mr. Choppy and Gaylie Girl had ordered up and quickly finished off. At the moment they were snuggling together on the sofa in their robes, still sorting out the remarkable events of the previous evening. They had taken their time in bed, and though their efforts were nowhere near as raw and lust driven as that first time so many decades ago, they were satisfying nonetheless. This time, there were sweet nothings whispered at the outset by the both of them, the pace gentle and completely devoid of the frantic experimentation that had overwhelmed them way back when.

Gaylie Girl was the first to put words to their profound sense of contentment. "That was quite an early Christmas present we gave each other last night. I loved falling asleep in your arms. We never got to do that at the Second Creek Hotel. You always had to run off so we wouldn't be discovered."

Mr. Choppy turned his head, giving her his most earnest look. "We were both teenage idiots—no two ways about it. But that was then. This is now. And that's what I'd like to talk about."

She snuggled even closer, hooking her arm through his. "I was thinking that myself. I mean, what do we make of all this? I have to admit I came down here not quite knowing what to expect, but I hoped we could put a few things to rest for good. And I think we did just that last night. You were so affectionate from start to finish. A woman my age really appreciates that. What the hell am I saying? All women appreciate that."

Mr. Choppy liked what he was hearing so far and was growing more emboldened by the minute. "You mentioned you weren't getting much attention from your family up there in Lake Forest, and you've told me more than once how lonely you've been since your husband died."

"Yes, I have been," Gaylie Girl replied. "And I think Peter would be very disappointed that his money hasn't done much more than give me a sense of security. Other than that, I feel completely stymied by my family and friends—by my entire routine, if you want to know the truth. I'm bored to tears."

Mr. Choppy braced himself, deciding to go for it no holds barred. "Would you ever consider changing your marital status?"

She shot him a skeptical glance at first, but it soon softened into a smile. "Is that a proposal?"

Strangely, Mr. Choppy felt a profound sense of relief sweeping through him. There, she had uttered the actual word. It somehow made it easier for him to explore things further. "Let's just say I'm testin' the waters. Of course, I realize Second Creek, Mississippi, isn't the great metropolis of Chicago. If you're bored up there, maybe you'd die on the muscadine vine down here."

"That's an amusing way to put it, but I'm so entrenched up there. I'm entangled in so many things. There's that enormous mansion I ramble around in all by myself, except for Harriet, my secretary. And then there's all the property Peter left me. I just keep collecting my share of the profits. But I can assure you there's very little human warmth in a bank balance."

Mr. Choppy could not get a reliable read on her. One minute she sounded like she couldn't wait to escape her privileged but boring life on the shores of Lake Michigan, and the next she seemed to be going out of her way to justify the status quo. Nonetheless, he decided to press on. "I don't have a ring or anything like that to offer you right now — I'm not even officially suggestin' marriage at this point. I was just wonderin' if you'd consider First Lady of Second Creek as somethin' worthy of your time and energy."

Gaylie Girl perked up noticeably. "I like the way you put that. A woman always wants that kind of confidence in a man. That was the thing that attracted me to Peter, other than his money, of course. I'm not going to lie to you about that."

"So what exactly are you sayin' to me?"

She thought it over for a while, then leaned in and gave him a peck on the cheek. "I'm saying that I'll keep an open mind about things at this point. I won't rule anything out, no matter how much my family might howl down the line. Meanwhile, I have something I need to ask you, too."

"Shoot."

She took his hand, warming it between the two of hers. "Despite all that wonderful confidence you're exuding aside, would you still want me to be your wife if you should lose the election?"

Mr. Choppy found himself at a loss for words as the full impact of her question registered with him. Was he living in a fool's paradise? Moving from Lake Forest to Second Creek would be a significant sea change for his Gaylie Girl in itself, but without the incentive of helping him run the town, what would she do with herself all day? He suddenly realized that he had gotten so caught up in their romantic reunion that he had momentarily dismissed the possibility of defeat. Somehow, he was able to strike a hopeful note.

"I'd be proud to have you as my wife under any circumstances," he replied. "But I gather you think maybe we shouldn't decide anything so important just yet."

"That might be best. You know I fully support you in your bid to become mayor. I've certainly put my money where my mouth is. But perhaps we ought to wait and see how things turn out first before we commit to each other any further."

Somewhere deep inside, a part of Mr. Choppy shuddered slightly. Would she run out on him again—fiftysomething years later?

"Please don't panic," Gaylie Girl added, almost as if she were reading his mind. "I know we've been here before. But this time, I can assure you that I'm going to be taking a different approach. I'm a good deal older and wiser—we both are—and I'm going to let you in on the New Year's resolution I've decided to make this very instant."

Mr. Choppy leaned in expectantly, taking a deep breath for the payoff.

"I promise you that sometime next week when 2002 rolls around, I'll round up my daughter, Amanda, and my son, Petey, and finally tell them all about you. Any decision I'd be making about our future together would have to start there. How does that sound?"

He exhaled what could have passed for over half a century of air and found the perfect reply. "Like a new beginning . . . with a trusted friend."

11.

CHRISTMAS GIFTS

The guests had begun to arrive for Laurie and Powell's Christmas open house. The evening had developed a bone-chilling bite after a bright, crystal clear day, but the cozy cottage was toasty warm and inviting, overflowing with the aromas of holiday food and drink laced with cinnamon, cloves, and nutmeg.

Laurie had put on her best red dress and her little reindeer antlers and stationed herself in the foyer, greeting each visitor at the door with her mother's most enduring Christmas tradition. "Christmas Gift!"—Laurie and her siblings had been taught to blurt out upon first glimpse of another family member on Christmas morning. It was always an amusing little contest to see who could get the words out first, but there were never any losers—only lots of laughter and playful finger-pointing until the entire household had been accounted for.

"Christmas Gift!" Laurie exclaimed for the umpteenth time, as Novie walked through the door, bundled up to the point of near disguise. Two additional greetings rang out as her son, Marc, and his friend Michael Peeler queued up next.

What a study in contrasts the young men were, Laurie noted. Marc was short in stature like his mother—with dark, curly hair and a somberness that seemed to shade his delicate features; Michael, on the other hand, was a tall, freckled-faced redhead with a broad, square face dominated by arresting green eyes and a quick smile.

After Novie had made the introductions, Laurie greeted the newcomers. "Welcome to my home. I'm so pleased to meet you at last!"

"Same here," Marc replied. "Mother's kept me posted from time to time on the Nitwitts these past few years, and all I ever seem to remember her saying was how everything began and ended with Laurie Lepanto."

"It's Hampton now. But good grief," Laurie added with a little giggle, "you make me sound like something out of Genesis there. I assure you I'm just an ordinary Southern belle—twice married but none the worse for wear, according to my husband. But enough of that. Give me your coats and join the fun." She began pointing in this direction and that, running through her spiel as efficiently as any flight attendant before takeoff. "We've got plenty of food on the buffet table over there, and in the kitchen right through there, you can help yourself to mulled cider, eggnog, hot chocolate, or mix yourself something stronger. Powell was bartending for a while, but I think he's been kidnapped by one or more of the Nitwitts. They're around here somewhere, discussing the upcoming mayoral election. That's all anyone in town is talking about these days."

"I'd like to talk with your husband about that, too, if I can," Marc added, handing over his coat. "I did a gig awhile back in FM radio, and Mother says he's going to be producing some spots for the campaign this week. I'd like to help out in any way I can. Mother's told me all about this Mr. Choppy, and I can tell you right here and now that I've always admired people who have the guts to go out on a limb. Is Mr. Choppy here tonight, by any chance?"

"I'm afraid not. I'm told he's up in Memphis taking a little time off from the campaign. The calm before the storm, so to speak. But I'm sure you'll meet him later this week, especially if you're going to be involved with the radio spots. I know my husband will take any help he can get. Just keep moving around from room to room, and you'll spot Powell sooner or later. He'll be the tall guy with the reindeer antlers growing out of his head and all the women hanging on his every word."

With that, Marc and Michael proceeded to mingle, but Novie remained behind while Laurie hung up their coats in the hall closet. "I just wanted to thank you again for helping me deal with Marc," Novie said.

Laurie shut the closet door and smiled. "Nonsense. I didn't really do anything you wouldn't have done eventually as a good mother. Then it's going well, I take it?"

"Oh, I positively adore Michael. He put me at ease the moment he walked in the door, almost like I was his mother instead of Marc's. He's so warm and funny—he just talks up a storm, and I can see how he's brought Marc out of his shell so much. Geoffrey and I never knew what to do about Marc's constant moodiness, but then we never knew what was really going on. Anyway, I think Marc and Michael were made for each other."

Laurie embraced her friend warmly and then pulled back. "I'm so happy for you. After all, this is the time of year for families to get together, isn't it?"

★

Michael Peeler had always been a very sociable creature, equally at ease with old friends and new acquaintances alike. As Novie and many others had remarked, he was the sort of person who could walk into a room and start up a conversation with anyone, then walk away at the end and make the other person feel as if they'd known him forever. He also had an extraordinary gift for homing in on people in trouble. It was that particular faculty that had drawn him to Marc Mims when they'd first been introduced by a mutual friend out in San Francisco. At the moment, his gift had kicked in once again. After losing track of Marc, he'd wandered down the hallway and poked his head into a small study that smelled of leather and old books. Inside, a very pretty teenage girl with freckles and red hair sat on a sofa by herself, staring out into space.

"Hello, there," he said, standing in the doorway and draining the last of the cup of cider he was holding. "Why aren't you out there having fun with the rest of us?"

The girl caught his gaze and shrugged. "Don't much feel like it. There's no one my age. This is the worst Christmas ever."

Michael moved to the sofa and put his cup down on the nearby end table. "Would you like to talk about it? I'm a really good listener."

"Who are you? I've never seen you before. Do you belong to one of the Nitwitts?"

He sat down beside her, giving her his full attention. "Indirectly, I suppose I do. Do you know Novie Mims?"

"Miz Novie?" the girl replied as the first hint of a smile crept into her face. "Sure. I know them all by heart. I was in a wedding with them this summer. They were the matrons of honor, and I was the maid of honor. I didn't think it would be cool at first—but it was. I hope I'm as much fun as they are when I'm old like that."

"Good point. That is something to shoot for," he added, extending his hand. "Well, I'm Michael Peeler, and I belong to Marc Mims. He's Novie's son."

She shook his hand and said: "I'm Meagan Thurman, and I belong to Wittsie Chadwick. She's my grandmother, but I call her Gran-Gran."

He gave her a playful wink and flashed that ingratiating smile of his. "You're also a dues-paying member of The League."

"Paying dues? League? What are you talking about?"

"I'm talking about The League of Redheads. We're a very special group, you know. We're the most misunderstood minority on the face of the planet, no matter what anybody says otherwise."

Meagan's face lit up immediately. "Yeah. When I was younger, I got teased all the time about it. This group of mean boys used to call me a redheaded, freckle-faced woodpecker at recess. I hated that."

"And look how wrong they were. Look how you turned out."

"You're cool, you know that?"

"Everyone likes hearing that," he replied. "But I'd like to hear why this is your worst Christmas ever. What's going on?"

She hesitated at first, shaking her head with a disgusted expression. "It's my parents. They went to London for Christmas and dropped me off here in Second Creek with my grandmother. Again. Not that I mind being with Gran-Gran. She's kind of a trip, even if she forgets where she puts things and makes burned cookies for me and can't work the remote no matter how many times I show her. She's really a sweetie, though, and she lets me do pretty much anything I want."

He thought for a moment, cocking his head. "That doesn't sound so bad."

"No, that part's not. But my parents are always running off without me—they keep saying it's business, but I know different. You know what they gave me for Christmas before they left? A three-hundred-dollar gift certificate to spend at the mall back home. But they're not even here to see what I bought. It just doesn't seem very much like Christmas to me."

"It won't always be like that. They'll probably come around. Trust me—things could be worse," Michael responded, reaching over to pat her hand. "Your family hasn't disowned you completely, the way mine did."

Meagan looked surprised at first, but that was soon replaced by dismay. "Why would they do a thing like that? Did you do something wrong?"

Michael shook his head and gave an ironic little chuckle. "No. I just showed up as who I am, that's all."

"I don't understand."

"I'm gay," he explained further, deciding at that very instant that she was old enough to handle the revelation. "I've known it ever since I was a very young boy. That's the way I arrived on this planet, and that's the way I'll go out. But my parents couldn't accept that. It didn't mesh with their religious beliefs, so they kicked me out of the house right after high school graduation. I'm glad I at least waited until then to tell them, or I might not have been able to stay with them even that long."

Meagan gasped, briefly covering her mouth with her hand. "Are you really gay? You don't act gay."

He laughed. "You don't think so?"

"I'm only going by what the kids at school say. Especially some of the boys. But I guess I don't really know, huh?"

"Don't worry about it," he replied, careful to keep the casual tone in his voice. "Let's just say that I act the way I act, and you act the way you act, and that's what makes us both unique."

"I can't believe you came in here and told me all this."

He leaned in with that smile of his. "I hope you feel a little better about things now."

There was still a bit of hesitation in her voice, but she nonetheless managed a smile. "Maybe a little. But can I ask you a question?"

"Sure."

"What did you do after your parents kicked you out of the house? I don't know what I'd do if my parents did that to me."

He sat up a bit straighter and gently cleared his throat. "Well, I found a job doing whatever I could and kept at it. I saved a little money, got a student loan, and put myself through college. Got a degree in landscape architecture and ended up doing what I do now. I work for a nursery out in Sausalito. I like to see things grow. It makes me feel good about my life."

"Wow! So, do you have one of those green thumbs?"

"I like to think I do," he told her. "Now, how about joining the party with me? Let's go find my friend Marc. I assume you haven't met him yet."

Meagan said she hadn't.

"Well then, we can head back to the kitchen together, and maybe we'll spot him on the way. I want some more of this wonderful cider. Have you tried it yet?"

They rose from the sofa together. "I like eggnog better," Meagan said. "But Gran-Gran won't let me spike it yet, even though I'm nearly sixteen, and she and the other Nitwitts are always drinking up a storm. You should see how crocked they get sometimes. It's a hoot and a half."

Just then, Marc appeared in the doorway. "Ah, there you are. I was wondering where you'd gone. I've been having a very interesting talk in the kitchen with Powell Hampton about those radio spots, and he's asked me to sit in on the session at the station later this week. I think I can offer some constructive suggestions from a production standpoint."

"Once a radio man, always a radio man," Michael observed, winking at his friend.

Then Marc focused on Meagan. "And who is this pretty young lady?"

Michael quickly made the introductions, being careful not to leave out all the Nitwitt connections, and Meagan suddenly seemed like a brand-new person.

"Would it be okay if I hung out with you guys for a while?"

"Why not?" Michael said, offering her his arm. "You can just think of us as your date. Two for the price of one."

"Cool!" she said, hooking her arm through his. Then the unlikely trio headed off to enjoy the remainder of the festivities.

★

Across town, Mr. Floyce and Eljay were huddling in the tacky, moose-head-lined conference room of Jeffers and Jeffers, having cut short their Christmas celebrations in order to put out an unexpected constituent brushfire. Both their wives had been miffed by all the cell phoning back and forth on such an important family day and issued them strict orders to return as soon as possible. But rushing critical behind-the-scenes machinations to soothe ruffled female feathers was the last thing on their minds.

At the moment, Mr. Floyce was flashing on his longtime accomplice while pouring neat bourbon into a couple of tumblers. "I still don't see how the hell this happened, Eljay. And why today of all days? Couldn't it have waited until tomorrow?"

"There's always been hell to pay when these black churches start competin' with each other, Floyce. What one does, the other has to do. What one gets, the other has to get. The way it was put to me, Brother Thompson's cousin, Sister Lula or Lola or somethin' like that, left Hanging Grapes in a huff last year over God knows what and joined Rock of Ages Baptist on the other side of Ward Six. Apparently, back when they were still on speakin' terms, Brother Thompson made the mistake of braggin' to this pissed-off cousin a' his about some of our extra contributions to Hanging Grapes. Now she and her new link to salvation, Pastor Harris, want a little somethin' extra for Rock of Ages to keep their mouths shut and deliver the vote."

Mr. Floyce slammed back his bourbon and poured another. "The friggin' nerve of Rock of Ages dictatin' to us like I'm supposed to be Santa Claus or somethin'—and on Christmas Day, no less."

Eljay leaned back in his chair, downed his bourbon, and blew out all the air from his enormous chest. "Fact of the matter is, Santa Claus is just about who you are by now, Floyce. I told you there might be a downside when you said you wanted to sweeten their pots for a little extra insurance. Now we can't go back. At least not until this election's over and you're safely in again. Then I suggest we nix these church handouts—you've created a monster."

"You know damn good and well how crucial Ward Six is—and please deep-six the 'I told you so' speech." Mr. Floyce looked at his Rolex and made a face. "They're late. They were supposed to be here five minutes ago." Just then, the back door buzzer sounded, and Mr. Floyce started in his seat. "That must be them now. I'll go let 'em in. You got everything?"

Eljay sat up straight and patted the pocket of his overcoat. "We're all set."

A few minutes later Pastor Waymon Harris and Sister Lula Mayes had settled in around the conference table, staring ahead expectantly. They provided an almost comical contrast—he was short, scrawny, and garbed in clergyman black, while she was big-boned, bosomy, and fairly bursting out of a blinding frock that looked as if it might have been stitched together from bits of tinsel and aluminum foil.

Mr. Floyce spoke first, doing his best to disguise his irritation. "Let's get down to business, shall we? Mr. Jeffers here and I need to know exactly what urgent new church project you need assistance with." He cleared his throat pointedly. "We need to know for our records, you understand."

Interestingly enough, it was Sister Lula who answered. "We been talkin' 'bout that very thing. And we decided that the church needs a daycare room for some of the ladies that work all day. That way, they got their babysittin' taken care of."

"And you agree with this, Pastor Harris?"

"Yes, I do, Mr. Floyce," he replied. "And Rock of Ages Baptist and myself appreciate whatever you can do in this matter. Sister Lula pointed out this worthy project when she first came to us from Hanging Grapes. She says the church needs to take care of all the little children who come unto us."

Mr. Floyce nodded to Eljay, who dug into his pocket and handed over a blue bank bag to Pastor Harris. "I think you'll find the amount you discussed with Mr. Jeffers inside. That should take care of all the little children nicely—and some of their elders, too, I imagine."

Pastor Harris accepted the bag without unzipping it, tucking it away in his coat pocket. "Yes, indeed. And Rock of Ages Baptist and myself surely thank you on this Christmas Day."

"Praise the Lord!" Sister Lula chimed in.

Then they all got to their feet, more or less at the same time. "I trust we can count on you and your congregation come February fifth?" Mr. Floyce said.

Pastor Harris nodded enthusiastically. "Yes, indeed, you can. Sister Lula and me, we'll see to it personally."

"I'll be pickin' up the ones that don't have cars and carryin' 'em to the polls myself," she added. "You don't have to worry 'bout a thing now."

"And I trust we don't need to have any more church project discussions between now and then?"

"Yessir, Mr. Floyce," Pastor Harris put in. "This Christmas gift wraps it all up with a nice big bow."

Mr. Floyce managed a wry smile. "More like with a nice big bank bag, but, yes, it is the season for givin' it up, no?"

"That's right. 'Tis the season. Y'all have a Merry Christmas now," Pastor Harris said. Then he sailed out the door with Sister Lula on his tail like a great silver battleship.

★

It had been more than ten minutes since Pastor Harris and Sister Lula had left with their loot, but Mr. Floyce was still in the mood for some serious drinking and grousing. To hell with getting back to the wives! At the moment he was on his fifth shot of bourbon and beginning to feel no pain, his thought processes and enunciation stopping and starting under the influence.

"Do you . . . do you she any more . . . fires we need to put out, Eljay . . . or have we suffishly . . . no, wait . . . suff-ish-unt-ly . . . covered our . . . ashes . . . uh, our asses?" He cackled to himself in high-pitched fashion and pointed at his friend sitting across the table. "Of course . . . it's damn near impossible . . . to cover your big ass."

Eljay, who had had less to drink—but only slightly less—took no offense, finding his own peculiar amusement in the remark. "It is . . . a very big ass! True enough!" he replied, raising his voice while shifting his great bulk in his chair. "Sometimes . . . I can't even get up off it!"

Both men howled.

"Hell," Mr. Floyce continued, "they couldn't . . . lift you with a . . . crane!"

There was more howling. But eventually it stopped, and Mr. Floyce drifted into the heavy-lidded, head-bobbing body language of intoxication. "Tell me this . . . uh, Eljay . . . why is it . . .

no, wait . . . why am I runnin' for this office again . . . is . . . is this what I really want?"

"Is this what you . . . really want?" Eljay answered, mindlessly parroting him.

"That's just what I said," Mr. Floyce continued. There was a long silence with both men smiling at each other, but Mr. Floyce eventually broke the drunken stalemate. "What . . . what was I sayin'?"

"I dunno," Eljay replied. "Should we . . . go home to the wives?"

"Do we . . . have to?"

Both men howled again.

"Jo Nelle . . . thinks I drink too much," Mr. Floyce added when they were no longer amused with themselves. "Says I need to move on . . . we need to move on . . . do you think . . . I drink too much . . . uh, Eljay? . . . do you think I need to . . . move on?"

"No . . . I don't."

"You don't . . . what?"

"What?"

"What what?"

The two men eyed each other shrewdly and then burst into gales of laughter once again. When they were finally spent, Mr. Floyce rose from his chair and said: "Let's go home . . . to the wives, okay?"

"Sure," Eljay replied, struggling to get up out of his chair but eventually managing it. "Let's do it."

Just before they reached the doorway, Mr. Floyce paused and patted Eljay on the shoulder. "We're . . . we're gonna win this damned election, rrrright?"

"Rrrright."

"No question?"

"No question."

Mr. Floyce squared his shoulders and took a deep breath. "But first . . . there's somethin' we just gotta do."

"Wazzat? Hit the head?"

Mr. Floyce guffawed. "Naw. We gotta call a cab. I'm too crocked to drive . . . and so are you."

COUNTING DOWN

M r. Choppy's campaign kicked into another gear shortly after Second Creek had rung in the New Year. A few days after Christmas, Powell had carefully overseen the production of the Nitwitt radio testimonials as promised, while Marc Mims had sat in and contributed his professional expertise as well, making helpful suggestions for appropriate background music. They had settled on "Hail to the Chief," potted down low to add that certain commander-in-chief oomph.

Amazingly, the sessions had not required all that many takes— each and every one of the ladies had quickly settled down at the radio station and cooperated fully with Powell's instructions. Only Wittsie seemed to be a tad bit befuddled by the procedure, but no one really minded. Even her spot was put to bed with relative ease, and the ads hit the airwaves in earnest the first week of January 2002.

It wasn't long before Powell received a pair of interesting phone calls—one each from Renza and Wittsie—and he handled them in his usual diplomatic fashion.

"When will we know if our spots are having the proper effect?" Renza began. "Are there any reactions yet? I don't want to have done all that for nothing."

"Give it a little time," Powell answered. "It's early yet. There's a new poll due out from *The Citizen* at the end of the week. Something might register by then."

But Renza was not about to let him off the hook so easily. "Why do I sound so different now? I don't remember sounding like that when you played it back for me at the radio station. Have they been fooling around with my voice?"

Powell steeled himself, taking a deep breath and not missing a beat. "As if anyone would dare tamper with that very special sound of yours, Renza. Everything's exactly the same as it was when you left the radio station. Have you been listening at home or while you've been driving around town?"

"Mainly in the car, I suppose."

"Well, there's your answer. Power lines and transformers can affect your reception, of course. They're probably causing a bit of static. The signal can fade in and out on you."

There was a brief silence on the line. "Oh, I didn't think of that. But how can you avoid power lines? They're everywhere."

Powell had a smile on his face in spite of himself. "Just listen at home. And don't turn the car radio on when you're out running errands."

"Oh, I suppose that would work, wouldn't it?"

And with that, Renza appeared to be mollified, at least for the time being—although she signed off with a promise to call back if she detected any further slippage in the quality of her voice.

"You do that," Powell replied, not wishing to prolong the conversation. "And thanks for calling."

The conversation with Wittsie, however, proved to be somewhat of a puzzle.

"I wanted to ask you something, Powell," she began. "I wanted to know when we're finally going to finish up with those radio spots. . . . I keep waiting for your call. . . . Oh, I've been out shopping now and then. . . . But I've left the answering machine on. . . . Maybe it's not working. . . . I've had it since before Carleton died, you know. . . . It's probably time I got a new one anyway. . . . Those things aren't made to last, I've heard. . . ."

Powell was frowning at his end. "But, Wittsie, we've already finished up with the spots. We've got them all running in the morning and evenings—six a day, five days a week. Just tune in your radio. You'll catch one of yours sooner or later."

An uncomfortable amount of time passed before Wittsie answered. "Oh . . . I see."

"Wittsie? Are you all right?"

This time she appeared to have a ready answer, and her tone switched dramatically from confused to cheerful. "Oh, don't mind me. . . . I'm just missing my little Meagan after spending so much time with her over the holidays. . . . You get used to having someone around the house again and doing for them. . . . Oh, Powell, I feel so silly. . . . Of course we finished the spots. . . . I remember now. . . . You know me."

"Your spot turned out to be one of the most effective, I think. You just keep listening for it, and you can call me back anytime and let me know what you think."

Powell was keeping Laurie updated on any new contact with the Nitwitts, and she in turn was keeping him posted on her shifts with the phone bank volunteers at headquarters. They usually found time to touch on both subjects at the dinner table, offering suggestions and insights to each other.

"I see we're both having a bit of trouble with Renza," Laurie was saying in between bites of the grilled catfish she had prepared for them. "I saw her with the most exasperated expression on her face while she was working her way through the D's this afternoon. So I went over to her station and asked if anything was wrong. She said she didn't want to call Juanita Dobbs because they hadn't been on speaking terms since Juanita got plastered at some cocktail party in the midsixties and criticized her for 'killing all those little foxes,' as she put it. I said, 'Renza, you just can't skip over people because you had an argument with them back when Lady Bird Johnson was beautifying highways. We need to get as many people as possible to show up on Mr. Choppy's behalf for the Town Hall debate.' I reminded her that Mr. Floyce will try to pack the audience with his people for effect, and we just can't let that happen. We have to have some sort of balance in that room."

Powell stabbed a piece of catfish and smirked. "And what did Renza have to say to that?"

"She said Juanita would interpret the call as waving the white flag on the fur-wearing issue, and she had no intention of giving her that sort of satisfaction. She absolutely insisted that someone else handle the call. So I gave Juanita to Myrtis, who has responsibility for A through C in the phone book. But that wasn't the end of it, no sir."

"Oh? Is Myrtis feuding with Juanita, too? Maybe going back to Truman?"

Laurie rolled her eyes and took a sip of her muscadine wine. "No, Myrtis had no objections to calling. She's too professional to get into personalities. But a little while later Renza called me over and said she'd found someone else she couldn't phone. She didn't want to talk to Nonnie D'Amico because she says she once caught her flirting outrageously with her husband, Lewis, and still doesn't know to this day whether they had an affair or not. I tell you, Renza sure knows how to hold a grudge."

"Maybe you should try giving her another part of the alphabet," Powell replied with an impish grin on his face. "She seems to have made too many enemies in the D's."

"To be honest with you, I don't think any letter is safe." Laurie giggled and then took another bite of her dinner. Then her mood grew more thoughtful. "I don't quite know what to make of Wittsie's call, though. It seems a bit strange, even for her. But maybe she was a bit distracted by her granddaughter leaving. Has she called you back about the spot?"

"Not so far. How's she been doing at headquarters? Not refusing to call people, I assume?"

Laurie reviewed the last couple of days in her head. "I don't recall anything out of the ordinary with Wittsie. She has G through I, and she's had no complaints. Nothing from Denver Lee, Novie, and Myrtis either, although I think I'm going to have to separate them all soon. They insisted on sitting together on the back row, but I'm thinking they might get more done if they're spread out. There's an awful lot of gossiping and other foolishness going on. You know how they can get."

Powell started laughing and couldn't seem to stop, putting down his fork and going all pink in the face. "I know you were president of the Nitwitts for a long time, but you sounded exactly like Sister Mary Maurice just then."

Laurie blinked and drew back. "Who is Sister Mary Maurice?"

"Was," he replied, calming down somewhat. "She's gone to her eternal reward, which I trust was a huge disappointment to her. Sister Mary Maurice was only the strictest nun to patrol the parochial school yards since the Christians were fed to the lions. She was the holy terror of the Catholic school I attended as a teenager. Being the casual Episcopalian I was at the time, I was totally unprepared for both her bark and her bite."

"Good heavens!" Laurie exclaimed, trying her best to take offense at his remark but unable to remove the smile from her lips. "I'm not anywhere near that bad. So you think I should just leave the girls alone and let them stay where they are?"

He nodded vigorously and gave her a reassuring wink. "Yeah, I think so. They all mean well, and we know for a fact they're devoted to Mr. Choppy. And who knows? Those spots we concocted could end up making all the difference."

★

The next election poll published by *The Citizen* at the end of the week contained some encouraging news for Mr. Choppy's campaign. Mr. Floyce's percentage had fallen to forty-eight percent, Mr. Choppy's had risen to forty percent, while the ranks of the undecided had shrunk to twelve percent. What had been a fifteen-point lead for Mr. Floyce a little before Christmas had basically been cut in half, and the Hale Dunbar Jr. campaign was ecstatic. Mr. Choppy conferred with Powell and Laurie, and the three of them agreed that it would be a smart move to gather

the troops as soon as possible and give them a rah-rah halftime
pep talk. After all, they were basically one week away from the
Town Hall debate on January 15.

Headquarters wasn't quite standing room only when the
rally convened on Monday morning of the following week, but
there was a healthy, buzzing crowd nonetheless. Dressed in a
gray three-piece suit and silver power tie, Mr. Choppy
marched resolutely out of his office to their cheers and
applause and surveyed the faithful from his makeshift podium
beneath the big blowup. He saw many familiar faces smiling
back at him, as well as Laurie and Powell off to one side. All
the Nitwitts were there in a pack—including a sprinkling of
their family members. Then he spotted the Hunter Goodlett
family; Lovita Grubbs, the Book Sheriff; Lady Roth, still in
her Susan B. Anthony drag; and several former employees of
the Piggly Wiggly—including his longtime cashier, Lucy Faye
Stiers, and his favorite teenage bag boys, Jake Andersen and
Kenyatta Warner. In addition, there was that young reporter
from *The Citizen*, Rankin Lynch, and a camera crew from
WHBQ in Memphis. The hubbub from the spontaneous demonstration took some time to die down, but eventually Mr.
Choppy gained their full attention and started in on his spiel,
careful to use the studied delivery techniques that Powell had
drilled into him.

"Good morning, ladies and gentlemen. Your enthusiasm
overwhelms me today. But you and I have good reason to be
enthusiastic, don't we?" He quickly picked up the front page
of *The Citizen* and brandished it high above his head. "How about
this latest poll? We're gaining ground, and Second Creekers are
getting our message!"

The crowd responded immediately with more cheering, applause, and flourishing of campaign slogan placards, and again it took some time for all the commotion to die out.

"But let's not rest on our laurels," Mr. Choppy resumed. "Let's make this last week leading up to the debate really count. Let's stay on those phones and call everyone we can and talk up this campaign to everyone we run into around Second Creek. Whether you're shopping, out at the movies, or just out and about enjoying The Square, mention the Hale Dunbar Junior campaign to somebody. Tell them why you're supporting it and why you think they should join you. Don't let up. Tell them to tune in their radios and listen to what other distinguished citizens are saying about us. Let's see if we can move those poll numbers even more in our favor. We've cut Floyce Hammontree's lead in half in less than two weeks. Imagine what we can do in another two weeks!"

The faithful flared up again, and Mr. Choppy smiled patiently throughout it all, acknowledging their support with an occasional nod of his head and wave of his hand.

"Let me also urge you to help us get our supporters into those Town Hall seats on January fifteenth. You never know how many undecideds will be there, and our enthusiasm could help them make up their minds in the end. So what do you say, folks? Can I have your best efforts in the home stretch?"

There was an explosion of agreement, and this demonstration was the longest yet. After it had finally petered out, Mr. Choppy took a deep breath and scanned the audience with his biggest smile yet. "And now, ladies and gentlemen, it is my distinct pleasure to turn the floor over to someone well known to many of you. He first made himself known to us last summer when he was working for WHBQ up in Memphis and covered all our dancing antics here at the Piggly Wiggly. But he soon moved on to bigger and better things at CNN in Atlanta as a correspondent and gave us national publicity as well. Now he's here today with us with some very exciting news. Please welcome back to Second Creek — Ronnie Leyton!"

Ronnie then emerged from Mr. Choppy's office to the healthy applause and cheers of the crowd, taking big, crisp strides to the podium and waving all the way. Working at CNN seemed to be agreeing with him — he had discarded the jeans and polo shirt look of the local market field reporter for the button-down three-piece approach favored by all the network anchors. He also appeared to have acquired a tan and a new hairstyle as well — everything about him now fairly oozed national news personality.

"Thank you for that wonderful introduction, Mr. Dunbar," Ronnie began. "It's a pleasure to be back here in Second Creek for this exciting new chapter in your life. I've taken the liberty of getting in touch with WHBQ in Memphis and asked them to send down a crew for the occasion. They're here now with us shooting some footage for what could be another CNN story down the line. I know some of you have been waving at the camera, and I do hope you were smiling because you might end up as a part of that segment."

Here the crowd began to ooh and aah a bit, and Ronnie paused to let them soak up the significance of what he had just said. "Now, I need to make it clear at the outset that I've haven't been able to get the green light yet on the mayoral election as a broadcast piece, but I'm taking a little downtime with you today to lay the groundwork. I've asked the WHBQ crew to return for the upcoming Town Hall debate and assemble the raw footage for me, and I'll take it from there. My idea is to try to get it on the air in between the debate and the actual election date on February fifth. How does that sound to you folks?"

The crowd's response was predictably raucous and positive, and then Ronnie wrapped it all up. "One additional caveat here. In all fairness, I must get some footage of Mr. Hammontree's campaign, too, and try to put the showdown in perspective. As usual, my mission will be to stay as objective as possible in presenting this unique story to the public. So I do need to cover the Hammontree rally scheduled for Rock of Ages Baptist this afternoon. But I'd be lying to you if I said I didn't have a soft spot in my heart for Mr. Dunbar and his Piggly Wiggly here—oops, I meant to say campaign headquarters here. After all, it was his story this past summer that helped me land my job at CNN, and for that I shall be forever grateful."

"And we're grateful for your continued interest in our very special little town," Mr. Choppy declared after Ronnie had stepped away from the podium to one final round of cheering and applause. "The world was watching us before. Maybe they will be again."

★

Two days later, *The Citizen* announced that its society columnist, Erlene Gossaler, would be moderating the forthcoming Town Hall debate, citing her track record of objectivity and devotion to the principles of good reporting as the impetus for their decision. That statement was met with utter disbelief by Laurie and Powell at the breakfast table. No one had fudged the facts more consistently over the years than the Gossiper, as she had come to be called by most Second Creekers.

Laurie poured herself a second cup of coffee and briefly reflected on the announcement. "Who do you think this favors? Mr. Floyce or Mr. Choppy? The Gossiper did a very poor job last summer in disguising her disdain for our Piggly Wiggly wedding. She got pretty catty in her write-up."

Powell downed a generous spoonful of his oatmeal. "I honestly don't think it matters. She'll be forced to follow the formula for debate, no matter what her personal opinions are. For once, she won't be able to trot out any of those asides that always seem to be dripping from her snippy little columns."

"I can hardly picture her doing anything in a straightforward manner," Laurie said. "But you make a very good point. This will be politics, not wedding fashion. Perhaps we'll be pleasantly surprised."

"I think Mr. Choppy is the only one we need to be concerned about, and so far, our mock debates have been going smoothly. His confidence seems to have soared to new heights following that trip to Memphis to see his Gaylie Girl."

As Laurie slathered her toast with orange marmalade, she wrinkled up her nose, her voice almost girlish with excitement. "Ooh, I just think that's the sweetest thing ever. Imagine the two of them getting together after all these years. Wouldn't it be too perfect for words if Mr. Choppy won the election and got the girl at the same time? Is that the stuff Hollywood is made of or what?"

Powell stirred more cream into his oatmeal. "I'm wondering which he'd choose if he could only have one of them, though — the political office or the girl? My gut instinct is he'd settle for the romance at this stage in his life. I know it's made all the difference to me."

She reached across the table and grasped his hand. "No complaints here either." She went back to her toast, taking a bite, and reviewed the upcoming day's activities. She would be supervising the phone banks at campaign headquarters throughout most of the morning, and Powell would be spelling her after lunch.

Lunch. The word jogged her memory. Oh, yes. She would not be coming home for a cup of soup and a sandwich today as usual. Instead, she would be meeting Denver Lee beneath the white ceiling fans of the Victorian Tea Room. There was something they needed to discuss, Denver Lee had told her over the phone yesterday. Laurie had asked why they couldn't just talk about whatever it was right then and there.

"No," Denver Lee had replied. "I want to talk to you in person, Laurie. You'll understand when we get together tomorrow."

Laurie shrugged, finished off her toast, and pushed away from the table, eager to get started on another productive day for the up and coming Hale Dunbar Jr. campaign.

★

Laurie and Denver Lee had just finished ordering Caesar salads and bowls of chicken gumbo at their corner table flanked by ferns, and at first Denver Lee seemed preoccupied with justifying her choices.

"There's really nothing I need to avoid in any of that," she began. "Except I have to monitor the rice in the gumbo. I can only have so much. Turns to sugar, you know."

Laurie winced ever so slightly. Practically every sentence Denver Lee uttered these days ended with the phrase "Turns to sugar, you know!" But Laurie had decided some time ago to cut her friend some slack. Denver Lee had never been able to do anything halfway, whether it was painting a still-life or sticking her finger to monitor her health.

"Yes, I'd heard that about rice," Laurie replied, trying to sound as matter-of-fact as possible. Actually, she hadn't heard that, but she didn't want to encourage another one of Denver Lee's long-winded nutrition lectures. Then she squeezed lemon into her ice water and stirred it in. "So. What was it you wanted to discuss with me today?"

Denver Lee cut her eyes to the side as if checking to see if someone might be eavesdropping. "I feel a little bit awkward about this because I'm just not sure what's going on. But I think maybe this is one of those times that an intervention is called for."

Laurie straightened up in her chair, reacting to Denver Lee's serious tone. "For heaven's sake, what is it? You've got me on the edge of my seat."

"It's Wittsie," she replied. "I'm very worried about her. She doesn't seem to be making much sense these days."

Laurie pursed her lips and frowned. "As opposed to when she did?"

"Yes, I know. She's always seemed to be at sea with the English language. But something is different now." Denver Lee leaned in further, her face clearly full of concern. "Maybe I should back up a tad. I've already discussed this with Myrtis, Renza, and Novie, and they elected me to broach the subject with you. It seems everyone now regards me as the medical expert because of my condition, and, well, you see, I've been doing some research at the library. The Book Sheriff helped me out, and what I've come up with has me worried."

"Denver Lee, will you stop beating around the bush and get to the point here?"

Denver Lee heaved her bosom and finally blurted it out. "Alzheimer's. I really do think there's a chance that Wittsie's developing it. I think she may need some help."

Laurie's immediate reaction was to block the words from penetrating her brain. What Denver Lee was saying was absolute nonsense. If everyone who forgot details every now and then or who was a less-than-sparkling conversationalist had Alzheimer's, then most of the world had it. Then she remembered the phone call from Wittsie that Powell had told her about, and she suddenly became more receptive to what Denver Lee was saying.

"All right, then. You certainly have my attention. Tell me why you think Wittsie may have it."

"Well, it's an accumulation of things, but the other day something happened while we were all down at headquarters on the phones. Myrtis and I were sitting on either side of Wittsie calling people up, and all of a sudden, Wittsie turned to me and said, 'Denver Lee, why are we calling these people? Is it for a party?' Well, of course, I thought she was kidding, so I said, 'Yes, it's for Mr. Choppy's inauguration party, if things go our way.' Okay—so far, so good. Then she turned to Myrtis and said, 'Why are we throwing an inauguration party for Mr. Choppy?'"

"Oh, dear," Laurie murmured.

"Of course, Myrtis also thought she was joking and basically just laughed it off. But Wittsie kept questioning both of us. She wanted to know when the party was so she could give people the specific date and time when she called them up. We suddenly realized she was serious about everything and reminded her about the Town Hall debate. She didn't seem to have any more trouble the rest of her shift, but it was like she was fading in and out at times."

"Why didn't somebody say something to me? I was just telling Powell the other day that Wittsie was doing just fine. He'd described this weird phone call he'd gotten from her regarding the radio spots. It seems she'd forgotten they'd finished them up and wanted to know when that was going to happen. Powell thought it was strange at the time, and it seems even stranger in light of what you've just told me."

Denver Lee glanced down at the table in guilty fashion. "We didn't say anything because we wanted to discuss it amongst ourselves first. So we've been calling back and forth, and the girls decided to have me go and do the research and then report back to you."

"Did the research clear anything up for you?"

"Yes and no. She has symptoms typical of the disease in that her memory has gone to hell in a handbasket, and she can't seem to think logically. Her language skills seem to have been impaired—I certainly can't remember a time when she's been able to utter a complete sentence. The research has got me thinking that all this time we've known her maybe she's had early-onset Alzheimer's. It said that most patients have symptoms that progress slowly over a number of years. That certainly fits in Wittsie's case."

Laurie took a sip of her water and sighed thoughtfully. "You said yes and no, though. Is there a possibility that she doesn't have Alzheimer's?"

"Yes," Denver Lee replied, brightening a bit. "My research indicated that her symptoms could be typical of other medical conditions and that only a doctor could determine what's what.

That's why I think an intervention might be in order. I think all of us should go to Wittsie and insist she go to a doctor to be evaluated. If we all go together, I think she'll listen to us, especially if you're the ringleader."

Just then Vester Morrow, himself—a rangy and fastidious man with an Adam's apple the size of a lemon—approached their table, his hand extended in a solicitous manner. "So pleased to have both of you ladies lunching with us today. Mal and I always appreciate your patronage. Your orders will be here shortly." Everyone politely shook hands, and then Vester tugged at his vest, bent near, and cleared his throat as if he were about to announce the daily specials. "I do hope you approve of those box lunches we've been sending down to headquarters, Miz McQueen. We followed your diabetic-friendly suggestions to the letter."

Denver Lee adopted a coquettish pose. "Oh, I didn't really expect you to go to all that trouble, Vester. But it's most appreciated, I can assure you. It goes without saying you've gone the extra mile for Mr. Choppy and his campaign, keeping all of us down at headquarters in fighting shape."

Vester straightened up, clasped his hands together, and executed a strange little snort, obviously very pleased with himself. "Well, I have even more good news for you, then. Mal and I have been conducting a straw vote of our diners regarding the election, and the latest count is twenty-nine votes for Mr. Choppy and twenty-one votes for Mr. Floyce. Now, that's not everyone who's been in the last few days, mind you. Just the ones who didn't mind telling. But it seems to be somewhat of a reversal of the percentages in *The Citizen*'s latest poll, where Mr. Floyce is still ahead. I wonder if it's a townwide trend or just the folks who

crave our gumbo and sinful desserts." Vester continued to ramble on in that fussy way of his, gesticulating broadly every now
and then. "Oh, that's right. You probably can't have any of our
desserts, can you, Miz McQueen? Our warm brownie à la mode
and bourbon bread pudding are both naughty with sugar."

"I've enjoyed them in the past, though," Denver Lee replied,
sounding slightly guilty. "But those days are over, I'm afraid."

At that moment the waiter arrived with their salads and
gumbo, and Vester stepped aside as the food was placed on the
table. "I'll let you enjoy your lunches now," he continued. "Mal
and I are pleased as punch to be able to help Mr. Choppy out."

"And in such a delicious way, too," Laurie added.

After Vester had left to tend to other duties and the two
women had dug into their salads, Denver Lee said, "What do
you make of that Tea Room poll? Do you think it really might
be part of a bigger trend or just limited to a certain class of
people?"

Laurie blew across a spoonful of gumbo before cautiously
swallowing. "Possibly the latter. After all, this is one of the
favorite haunts of our generation of women, and many of us reg-
ularly pushed those Piggly Wiggly carts along the aisles in search
of groceries and a little gossip. No doubt Mr. Choppy's the sentimental pick here. At any rate, I'll pass along the good news to
him. It'll make him feel even more confident heading into the big
debate."

They enjoyed a few more bites in silence, and then Denver
Lee heaved a little sigh. "But back to Wittsie. What do you think
about our intervention idea? The girls think she'd listen to just
about anything you say. And I really am worried, Laurie. I
noticed a big red spot on her hand the other day, and she

brushed it off as a little burn she got taking something out of the oven. Do you see my point? If she really does have Alzheimer's, she could be a real danger to herself down the line."

"I do see your point," Laurie replied, the worry clearly evident on her face. "I'll have all of you over for dinner, and we'll address it then. I'm sure we'll all feel better once Wittsie's seen a doctor."

Denver Lee managed a weak smile and then looked suddenly distraught. "I feel bad about this in a way, Laurie. Some of us have tended to make fun of Wittsie over the years, and she's been nothing but good-natured about it. Why, she even let us name the club after her—or at least after her gift for being slow on the uptake. What if it turns out she just couldn't help it? I'll feel awful."

"You shouldn't feel that way. This isn't Renza we're talking about here. Wittsie could never hold a grudge against anybody about anything. Whatever the outcome of this, she'll do her best and keep on going with a smile on her face. I can't picture it any other way, can you?"

Denver Lee looked somewhat relieved as she got in the last word. "No, I can't. Wittsie's a sweetheart, through and through. She's always been on the side of the angels, even if it turns out her wings are missing a few feathers."

★

Having just taken a long, hot shower, Mr. Choppy was perched on the edge of his bed in his bathrobe, waiting for the phone to ring. It was nearly eight o'clock the evening before the Town Hall debate, and Gaylie Girl had promised to call up, wish him luck, and—most important—maybe give him the answer to only the

most pressing question he had ever asked anyone in his life. Never
mind that her children had not taken her revelation about his exis-
tence and their recent reunion very well. Actually, they had over-
reacted badly, even going so far as to threaten to have her mental
faculties evaluated if she didn't cease and desist at once.

"What are you gonna do?" Mr. Choppy had asked near the
end of that stressful and disappointing phone call.

Gaylie Girl had not hesitated, her tone full of indignation.
"Ignore them as usual. They ignore me. They have their money.
I have mine. And at this stage in my life, there's no way in hell
they're going to tell me what I can and cannot do."

But when Mr. Choppy decided to pop the big question in the
next breath, she had equivocated, saying she needed more time
to make up her mind. "It's a terribly big decision for me," she
had continued. "Life-changing for both of us, as I'm sure you can
appreciate."

Mr. Choppy had pressed further, hoping to pin her down. "So
when do you think you'll be able to decide one way or the other?
I'd like to get some idea before the big debate, if I could."

If nothing else, she had accepted his deadline. "Well, let me
work on it, and I'll call you the evening before. Maybe I'll even
have an answer for you then."

After he'd hung up, he realized he couldn't have set up worse
timing for her answer. The eve of the big debate? What if she
said no? He'd be going into his showdown with Mr. Floyce all
down in the dumps about his personal life, and no amount of
coaching by Powell would be able to snap him out of it. Why
had he forced the issue so soon?

The phone rang, and Mr. Choppy started so badly, he slipped
off the quilt. He let it ring two more times, running his hands

through his damp hair, before he gathered up the courage to answer. When he finally picked up the receiver and said hello, he was every bit as nervous as that first night he had appeared at Gaylie Girl's hotel room door with a bouquet of hand-plucked zinnias.

"Hale? It's me, your one-woman cheerleading squad—and right on time," she said. Her voice sounded steady and cheerful—possibly a good omen?

"I've been countin' down the hours to your call almost as much as to the debate tomorrow." He took a deep breath. "I bet I sound like some foolish teenager to you, huh?"

"Not at all. You sound just fine." There was a very pregnant pause. "But I want you to pay close attention. You may not like what I'm going to say to you."

Mr. Choppy winced. Was he going to be ditched all over again by the same woman half a century later?

"I want you to hear me out, Hale. What I'm going to say makes the most sense for both of us, so don't panic until I finish. First of all, I want to assure you that this has very little to do with Amanda and Petey's reaction to my finally telling them about you. If they can't handle it, that's their problem. They can drown their sorrows in all that money Peter left them. As a matter of fact, I expressed to them in no uncertain terms what they could do with their suggestion that I go to the doctor and get a checkup. I just had one, and I'm in remarkable health for someone my age, thank you very much."

"Well, that's good news—about your health, I mean," Mr. Choppy interjected, feeling a little bit better about things.

"Yes, it is. So I don't want you to worry about my children one way or the other. What I do think we need to consider is the outcome of this election. I brought it up before at the Peabody, and you just shrugged it off like it was no big deal. But it is a big deal, Hale, it really is. I need to know how you'll feel about me after the results of the election are in, whether you win or lose. Either way, your life will change, and I need to know where I stand before I agree to change my life so drastically, too."

Mr. Choppy sifted through everything quickly. "But if I tell you it won't matter to me one way or the other, can't you believe me?"

"You say that now, but to some extent I think you're still drifting in the clouds after our little Romeo and Juliet bedroom scene at the Peabody. Please don't misunderstand. It meant a great deal to me, of course. But you may feel very differently about things if you should end up losing. You may not want me around to watch you lick your wounds. Maybe this time, you'll be the one who runs away from our relationship."

Mr. Choppy glanced at the sepia-toned picture sitting over on the night table beneath the lamp—the one of him at the age of sixteen. The one that captured so well the essence of the innocent teenager who had been mesmerized by a manipulative, slightly older woman. Was she trying to manipulate her way out of further involvement again? He was growing more impatient by the second.

"I don't understand," he said. "I might need you more than ever if I lose. Are you trying to tell me somethin'?"

The silence that intruded lasted so long that Mr. Choppy wondered if they'd somehow been disconnected. "Hello? You still there?"

"I'm sorry," she finally replied. "I'm afraid I've been bluffing a bit and sounding a bit braver and more in control than I actually am. My family's reaction has thrown me more than I expected.

Even my secretary, Harriet, thinks my mind has gone south. If I'm going to consider saying yes to you, I'm going to need your strength and absolute commitment no matter what happens, and I'll need it up front. I want to know you're strong enough to block the doorway if I get down there and chicken out again. Do I make any sense?"

Mr. Choppy could feel something easing up in the core of him. He hadn't realized how much he'd tensed up throughout their conversation, and the phone nearly slipped out of his hand. It also suddenly dawned on him that in a roundabout way she was giving him the go-ahead. All he had to do was be decisive and close the deal.

"You have my promise that I won't let you go, if that's what you're worried about. I'm welcomin' you with open arms, and once you're here, I won't let you run away again. This is a classic case of better late than never."

Thankfully, she did not keep him in suspense any longer. "I know you mean what you say. So to hell with Lake Forest and this Tudor mansion and all the rest of it. I'm coming down to the sunny South to be your wife, win or lose. Let them all think I'm crazy—Amanda, Petey, Harriet, my grandchildren—I don't care!"

"Hot damn!" he exclaimed, leaping to his feet and doing a little happy dance. "She said yes, she said yes, she said yes!"

Gaylie Girl began laughing uncontrollably at the other end. "Yes, she said yes! She had no idea she would actually say yes to you tonight, but she said it, she said it, she said it!"

After that, they kept on talking back and forth about the monumental decision they'd just made together, continuing to take a stab at ironing out the details. "You've got too much on your plate right now," she was saying. "I think it's best we do it after the election is over. Something simple, I think—a civil ceremony, perhaps down there. I don't have the strength to deal with wedding planners and caterers at my age. I spent a truckload of Peter's money doing all that for my daughter and vowed never again. It's a very expensive racket—that, and burying people."

"Let's don't go there just yet," Mr. Choppy replied, taking her to task seriously. He was finally going to have the woman of his dreams after a lifetime of resigning himself to being alone. The last thing he wanted to do was contemplate it being all over even before it had really begun. Then he moderated his tone, putting the smile back into his voice. "We've let so many years pass us by. Let's just enjoy what we have now."

After they'd hung up, Mr. Choppy picked up his teenage picture and started talking to it as if it had come to life, clamoring to celebrate with him. "See there? You did it, kid, you did it. It took damn near forever, but you did it. There's no way in hell you're gonna lose this election now. That debate is yours to lose tomorrow."

When Mr. Choppy's head hit the pillow later that night, the smile on his face duplicated exactly the one in the picture. To his way of thinking, the past and the present had been morphed and merged, leaving only a bright future for the taking.

13.

ONE-ON-ONE

At long last, the big showdown had arrived. It was high noon—January 15, 2002—and Town Hall on the ground floor of the white-columned courthouse was overflowing with the partisans of both camps. Based on the number of signs, T-shirts, and other campaign paraphernalia, it appeared that Mr. Floyce's troops outnumbered Mr. Choppy's. The proof would be in the noise each contingent could make in response to their candidate's remarks, however. Every seat in the house was occupied— including the sprawling upper gallery designed to accommodate slaves before the Civil War. There was a perceptible tension in the air as Erlene Gossaler, the moderator, stepped to her podium beneath a proscenium draped in red, white, and blue bunting.

"Welcome, ladies and gentlemen, to the 2002 mayoral campaign debate, sponsored by *The Citizen*, your Second Creek newspaper of record," she began, tugging at the formless frock that hid her enormous bulk. She was also sporting her trademark hairdo, a mound of cotton candy bleached to within an inch of its life and adding a good five inches to her already impressive height. "I'm Erlene Gossaler, and I'm pleased to be your moderator today."

There was restrained applause, and then the Gossiper introduced the two candidates, who stood behind their own podiums, flanking her on both sides. The incumbent was announced first, and the not-so-spontaneous demonstration that ensued for Mr. Floyce lasted for several minutes. When Mr. Choppy's name was announced—as Hale Dunbar Jr., of course—the commotion was healthy but not nearly so pronounced, nor did it last nearly as long. As Laurie and Powell had speculated, the Hammontree campaign had managed to stack the deck in their favor. Several signs reading Hanging Grapes A.M.E. for Hammontree, and Rock of Ages Baptist for Hammontree, left no doubt as to their allegiance.

Mr. Choppy's supporters were grouped together mostly all along the left third of the auditorium—not a terrible showing by any means—but their work as supporting cast was clearly cut out for them. "I really thought there'd be more of us here based on the response we've been getting on the phone banks the past few weeks," Laurie whispered to Powell from their vantage point of one of the shorter rows nearer the front. She turned around in her seat to count heads, and in the process, many familiar faces smiled back at her.

Among them were the Nitwitts with some of their friends and selected family members, of course; the Book Sheriff and a sprinkling of her library staff; the Hunter Goodletts; Lady Roth, ever faithful to her interpretation of Susan B. Anthony; more than a

few of Mr. Choppy's former Piggly Wiggly employees and customers; and Vester Morrow and Mal Davis, who had shut down
their restaurant temporarily for the event. Somewhere near the
center of the group sat a strange woman, provocatively dressed
in a sequined gold gown and matching gold wig. In her right
hand was what appeared to be a papier-mâché torch bearing a
striking resemblance to that hoisted on high by the Statue of
Liberty, and in her left hand was a small sign on a stick that read
The Spirit of Second Creek Supports Hale Dunbar Jr.

Laurie turned back to Powell and continued in hushed tones.
"Who is that woman back there? I've never seen her before, have
you? I mean, the golden girl."

He craned his neck for a quick peek and shrugged. "I have
no idea. I would say Lady Roth if she weren't sitting over there
in her Susan B. Anthony getup. There can't be two Lady Roths
in this town, can there?"

Laurie gave him a little nudge and chuckled. "Anything's possible in Second Creek. Perhaps it's Lady Roth's twin."

Meanwhile, the Gossiper finished up with the preliminaries.
"Before I proceed further, I wanted to acknowledge the outstanding media coverage we are receiving today for this event —
our local, of course, but also the newspaper and television
coverage from Jackson and Memphis. We've even been informed
that there is some preliminary interest from CNN, so I ask each
of you to remember that and conduct yourselves accordingly."

That caused a slight stir and manipulation of signs and placards throughout the audience, and Erlene waited a few moments
for it to subside.

"Yes, it is exciting, isn't it? Now, as many of you surely know,
The Citizen has been soliciting pertinent questions over the past

few weeks from you, the voters, to ask of our two candidates here, and we at the paper have selected what we feel are the ten best. I will announce each question, and each candidate in turn will have one minute in which to respond. There will be no rebuttal period, but following the end of the questioning, each candidate will then have a final two-minute summation. In the interest of time, I will ask audience members to hold their applause until the end of each final summation. The two candidates will alternate who addresses each question first, and a coin toss a few minutes ago determined that Mayor Hammontree will open the proceedings, as well as take the first summation."

Laurie continued her whispering. "I hope that's not a bad omen."

"To the contrary," Powell whispered back. "We'll end up having the last word. I've always thought that was the stronger position in any debate."

"Mr. Choppy sure seemed pumped and ready to go."

"That he did," Powell replied, "and I think talking with Gaylie Girl last night has him going for the gold."

Laurie turned around in her seat once again to glance at the mysterious woman with the golden torch and garb. "You don't suppose that's Gaylie Girl, do you? Can you get down here from Lake Forest that fast?"

Powell shook his head emphatically. "Nah. He told me there was no way she could make it, even though she wanted to. We'll meet her in good time, though."

Finally, it was time to address the public's concerns. The two men moved toward each other to shake hands, and the Gossiper quickly glanced down at her notes and threw out the first question.

"Mayor Hammontree, this voter asks, 'Why have zoning laws around The Square been enforced so lackadaisically in recent years?'"

Laurie gave a little gasp and nudged Powell excitedly. "That was the question I submitted. I can't believe it made the cut."

"Nice," Powell whispered back. "Hardball all the way. So far, it appears *The Citizen* is not stacking the deck."

Mr. Floyce gathered his thoughts for a few moments and began. "I don't think our zoning laws have been relaxed arbitrarily. We've made some exceptions from time to time for reasons which we felt were in the community's best interests. Last summer, for instance, we viewed the condemnation of the Grande Theater—grand as it was over the years—as necessary for health reasons. It was just too far gone to consider salvaging it, and as the saying goes, they just don't build buildings like that anymore. No matter what we put in its place, it wasn't going to live up to the elegance of the Grande. That's unfortunate. But we now have a thriving business bringing in tax revenue where before there was only an eyesore contributing nothing to the community but memories, fond as those may be. Governing a town such as ours is no easy task, it goes without saying. But it's necessary to view the overall picture when making tough decisions. I think the Hammontree administration has done so regarding our zoning laws."

There was a brief attempt at applause from the black congregations, but the Gossiper nipped it in the bud with a few emphatic hand signals, and then she put the same question to Mr. Choppy.

Laurie crossed her fingers and whispered once again out of the side of her mouth. "Come on, Mr. Choppy, knock it out of the ballpark. He's given you the perfect pitch."

"I agree with Mr. Hammontree that governing a town such as ours is no easy task," Mr. Choppy began after a short deliberation. "That's why it's so important to consider why our zoning laws were passed in the first place. If we had no historic structures here and nothing of interest to protect, zoning wouldn't matter all that much. But Second Creek has been around since before the Civil War, and we have a lot to be proud of in and around The Square and throughout the town as a whole. As to the Grand Theater matter, let me say that the fact that the roof had caved in did not mean the building was unsalvageable. True, it would have taken a lot of work to save it from the wrecking ball, but the comment that nothing would have lived up to the grandeur of the Grande is beside the point. More to the point is why a service station which could just as easily have been approved for a Bypass location was allowed to set up shop in the midst of the historic buildings on The Square. The effect has been jarring to the downtown area, to say the least. This is only one example of the Hammontree administration failing to protect the unique nature of Second Creek."

This time, Erlene had to stifle an attempt by Mr. Choppy's following to applaud the rhetoric. It was quite clear that she intended to make everyone play by the rules.

"Home run!" Powell whispered, noting that Laurie seemed about to jump out of her seat. "I couldn't have put it any better myself."

"On to the next question," Erlene continued, turning slightly toward Mr. Choppy. "Mr. Dunbar, this voter asks: 'What do you think should be done to further promote tourism in Second Creek?'"

Powell felt a little spurt of adrenaline beneath his chest. He and Mr. Choppy had concentrated particularly on that issue during their exhaustive rehearsals. "Home run number two," he whispered as Laurie reached over and patted his hand.

"I have a very constructive proposal in mind," Mr. Choppy began. "First, I think we should establish an official tourism bureau to promote special events like the Miss Delta Floozie Contest in June to the media and the general public. I think this bureau should have a full-time director and staff and should work in conjunction with the Second Creek Hotel and our motels to block rooms and offer special rates to tourists for that and other events such as the Springtime in Second Creek Historic Homes and Cottages Tours. Over the years we have been content to use word of mouth about our fair city, but this is the new millennium, and it's high time we got with it and out of the horse-and-buggy days of self-promotion. The way I see it, this is the right kind of progress for us to pursue, rather than tearing things down willy-nilly without considering the lasting effect on the charm of our town. We have a product to sell, and in today's world, we need to be a bit more savvy about our salesmanship. Nothing less will keep us competitive with all the other tourist attractions in Mississippi and elsewhere throughout the South."

When Mr. Floyce addressed the question, there was a noticeable change in his tone of voice. To anyone listening closely, a definite note of sarcasm had crept in, and the omnipresent politician's smile had also disappeared. "I would have to ask Mr. Dunbar how he proposes to pay for this new bureau and all those staff positions. Our Second Creek municipal budget is allocated down to the penny. Is he actually proposing a tax hike to all you hardworking folks out there? Think about it carefully, ladies and gentlemen. If you've never tackled the nuts-and-bolts issues of paying municipal salaries and paving roads and keeping up the streets and maintaining the parks and making sure your police and fire departments are solvent to protect people's lives and property, it's easy to make pie-in-the-sky proposals without the revenue to pay for them. What my opponent says may have merit, but there's a practical side to governing that he has not experienced, quite frankly. Down the road, it may be possible to entertain such a notion as a tourism bureau but right now, Second Creek simply cannot afford it. The Hammontree administration has done a credible job with the media regarding tourist promotion, and events such as the Miss Delta Floozie Contest have grown in popularity and attendance every year. Without any additional cost to taxpayers, I might add!"

Laurie and Powell continued their hushed appraisals. "That sounded like a rebuttal to me. He really didn't offer anything new," she said.

"Agreed. Although the tax hike thing was a good lick on his part."

The third and fourth questions were rather unremarkable — the former concerning expansion of the city limits, and the latter lengthening the Springtime in Second Creek Historic Homes and Cottages Tours by a week. Both candidates were in favor of expanding and lengthening, and no advantage appeared to be gained by either in the exchange.

Then came the fifth question, and Laurie beamed when she heard it, briefly turning around in her seat to give a thumbs-up to the Book Sheriff two rows behind her. "This ought to be good," she told Powell. "Lovita to the rescue."

"Mayor Hammontree," Erlene began, "this voter asks: 'What kind of priority should library funding be given by any Second Creek administration?'"

Mr. Floyce appeared to be uncomfortable as he deliberated, but finally said: "Every municipal department probably regards itself as the most important in the scheme of things. I happen to believe that some things such as police and fire protection should come first. Fixing potholes and making sure folks can get back and forth to work from their homes on all the farm-to-market roads should also be near the top of the list. Buying extra library books to cater to the reading tastes of certain patrons seems to me to be a lesser priority. If it can be accommodated financially without harming those other departments, then fine, I say let's help out all we can. That's what I mean when I say that municipal governance requires some tough decision-making, and this is one of those instances. I say people's lives and property come first, no matter what. Second Creek can survive if today's best sellers arrive a little late, but it cannot survive if its police officers and firemen arrive late."

"I certainly can't disagree with the mayor about the critical services the police and fire departments provide us here in Second Creek," Mr. Choppy began moments later. "But I don't see this as an either-or situation. The public library is a vital educational resource for the community. School library hours are limited. Therefore, our students need to have access to research materials provided by the public library and its expanded hours of operation. People who are out of work frequently use the public library for help with résumés and information about job openings. Our library director, Lovita Grubbs, informs me that public use of computer terminals for Internet access continues to soar.

Libraries, too, have entered the new millennium. They are not just places to check out best sellers and read newspapers and magazines for free on your lunch hour, and I don't think they should be shoved to the bottom of the list when it comes to funding. I see nothing wrong with having a community that is safe and well informed at the same time."

Despite the Gossiper's previous admonitions, Lovita Grubbs got carried away by the moment, shooting up from her seat and bursting into solitary applause.

"Please!" Erlene exclaimed, wagging her finger. "There'll be time for that later."

Questions six through nine veered once again into the mundane. Both candidates essentially agreed on the issues of the need for adding a turning lane to the Bypass; making Cypress Avenue one-way leading into The Square, and Pond Street one-way leading out; installing additional lighting in Downtown Park; and adding youth soccer leagues to Second Creek's Summer Recreation Program. The lack of controversy even lent an air of polite boredom to the proceedings. Then came the tenth and final question.

"Mr. Dunbar," the Gossiper said, "this voter asks: 'Why do you think you're the most qualified candidate for mayor of Second Creek?'"

Laurie and Powell smiled at each other, confident that their man would shine on this one. Powell had given a great deal of thought directing Mr. Choppy along those lines during their numerous rehearsals.

"I believe that I can bring something extra to this job," Mr. Choppy began without hesitation. "It's true that I have the dollars-and-cents background to know what makes Second

Creek business tick. It's also true that I've lived here all my life and know the town and its citizens like the back of my hand. But the something extra I can bring to this job is a visionary approach. Second Creek is not just any town. It relies upon the unconventional and the unexpected to make it work, and that's where I think I can provide a different kind of leadership. I want to do what's best for all of Second Creek, not just a select few who happen to have the ear of certain elected officials. The bottom line is this: mayors come and go, but the town itself is the constant that must be nurtured and protected. I do not take this town for granted, and I think it's way past time Second Creek elected someone who holds it in such high esteem."

At last, Mr. Choppy's contingent could show their appreciation for what could objectively be termed a solid performance, and they all rose with their signs and applause, demonstrating enthusiastically for nearly five minutes. The mysterious woman in gold was especially vigorous in her show of support, towering over the others and hoisting both her torch and sign to the rafters.

It took some effort for the Gossiper to bring their outburst to an end, but eventually she prevailed, and Mr. Floyce took his turn.

"Ladies and gentlemen, I do think my qualifications speak for themselves. I'm no novice running for this position—I've been hard at work for all of you for over fifteen years. I've helped bring new businesses to town, improve your streets and roads, make everyday life a little better for each of you. I understand fully the kind of pride we all take in Second Creek because I've been on the job listening to you all these years. I don't have to guess what being mayor is all about—I know what it's all about, and evidently most of you agree because you've elected me to this office several times over. I don't think you would have done that if you hadn't been reasonably satisfied with my performance. So I think it bears repeating: I do think my qualifications speak for themselves, and I ask you to bear that in mind come February fifth."

Now it was Mr. Floyce's flock doing all the shouting—and *shouting* was the appropriate word. Their decibel level easily exceeded that of Mr. Choppy's crowd, outlasting them by a couple of minutes as well.

"And now for the summations," Erlene said after order had finally been restored. "Mayor Hammontree will go first."

Mr. Floyce was evidently feeling his oats because his summation basically consisted of rehashing his answer to the question about his qualifications, adding several extra sentences for good measure. "In conclusion, I'd like to say that it has been a privilege to serve you, the people of Second Creek, all these years. Rest assured, I do not take the trust you have placed in me lightly. It is well placed, and I urge you not to opt for the unknown and unproven on Election Day."

During the second vociferous demonstration on Mr. Floyce's behalf, Laurie had to raise her voice to Powell to be heard over the din. "Well, that was a bit of negative selling there at the end! Think it worked?"

"Don't know!" Powell shouted back. "But Mr. Choppy will take the high road regardless!"

Indeed, Mr. Choppy appeared unperturbed as he began his summation. "Ladies and gentlemen, I'd like to share with you today something my father, Hale Dunbar Senior, once told me as a boy when I first started working for him in the Piggly

Wiggly, which was my livelihood throughout my entire adult life. He told me to always give my best effort to anything I did but to never be afraid of moving on when something better appeared on the horizon. 'Never be afraid to take chances,' he told me. 'All great accomplishment starts with a dream.' At the end of last summer, I realized that it was time to move on to greater things in my life. Some instinct, some benevolent force guided me to the decision I made to run for this office. It led me along the back roads and across the soybean fields of the county to a dried-up cattle pond, where I saw for myself where the gold-plated hand pointing to heaven on the First Presbyterian Church had been deposited many decades ago by one of our unpredictable Second Creek storms. I took that discovery to be a sign that I had a mission ahead of me to undertake, and now I'm seeing that through to the end. I believe that I am in tune with and completely understand the Spirit of Second Creek that dwells within all of us, and I therefore ask for your vote on February fifth."

"Where did that come from?" Laurie asked Powell after the ensuing demonstration had languished somewhat. "He not only took the high road, he took the high road to heaven!"

Powell shrugged. "Beats me. We never discussed anything like that during our mock debates. He must have come up with that at the last minute. But I think it was effective."

"Was it ever! I still have goose bumps!"

Backstage a few minutes later, Laurie warmly embraced Mr. Choppy, and Powell gave him a firm handshake, while the Nitwitts and several other supporters crowded around.

"Did I do good?" Mr. Choppy said. But there was a rhetorical shading to his voice, and the smile on his face clearly indicated how satisfied he was with his performance.

"You know you did," Laurie replied. "Advantage Hale Dunbar Junior all the way!"

"Congratulations, Mr. Choppy!" Myrtis exclaimed, hugging him with great fanfare. "That's an official Nitwitts' hug from the outgoing president herself. And you weren't just mayoral, you were absolutely presidential. We're talking Oval Office here. I think that 'Hail to the Chief' music we used in our radio spots did the trick!"

Renza stepped up next. "And here's another hug, from the incoming president of the Nitwitts. Now, I absolutely insist you drive me out to that cattle pond and show me that gold-plated hand!" Renza added. "I can't believe you've kept that to yourself all this time!"

Mr. Choppy was about to reply, when the mysterious woman in gold made her way through the crowd, torch still in hand, and confronted him with a devilish look on her face. "That was a perfectly marvelous performance, Mr. Choppy. I couldn't believe you closed with those inspirational words about the Spirit of Second Creek." She paused to lift up her homemade sign. "I felt as if you were zeroing in on me and my message here, and it was quite a rush."

"As a matter of fact, that's exactly what happened," Mr. Choppy explained. "At the last minute, I ditched the summation Mr. Hampton and I had rehearsed so many times and just let your sign inspire me. I went with the flow, as they say. I was hopin' you'd come up and introduce yourself so I'd have the chance to tell you that."

The golden woman tucked in her chin coyly and said: "No introduction needed, Mr. Choppy. We've been there and done that before." It was truly déjà vu as the woman removed her wig, lowered her voice an octave, and added: "It's me, Mr. Choppy. Gary Greene, Esquire—last year's winner of the Miss Delta

Floozie Contest. I had such an unforgettable time in your Piggly Wiggly last summer dancing with Mr. Hampton as Miss Emerald Greene that I wanted to do everything I could to support you in this campaign."

"I'll be damned. Fooled again! Well, all I can say is that I'm happy you're on my side, Mr. Greene!" Mr. Choppy exclaimed, offering a handshake while all the other supporters began laughing and talking amongst themselves.

In the midst of it all, Lady Roth as Susan B. Anthony made her presence known, sidling up to Mr. Choppy and obviously determined to get in her two cents. "What about me? Didn't I inspire you sitting out there, too?"

"Why, of course you did, Lady Roth!" he exclaimed, thinking quickly on his feet. The difference is, you've been inspirin' me all along on a daily basis."

Lady Roth seemed placated for the time being. "Well, I'm certainly glad to hear it, considering all the trouble I've gone to. You have no idea how much I detest dressing up in black this way. I've felt like I've been in mourning for weeks."

"You're just dressin' for the part. And to perfection, I might add," Mr. Choppy replied. "Many of our women supporters have come up to me at headquarters and told me how much they've appreciated the thought that's obviously gone into your portrayal. Very original, most of them say."

"I have to admit I've gotten nice little notes from some of them, and one adorable little girl even asked me if I would be willing to help her with her social studies project."

"If Second Creek gave out its version of the Oscars, you'd win hands down!" Mr. Choppy added, putting an exclamation point on the exchange.

"I think we can all agree on that," Myrtis interjected. "But a quick reminder, everyone—I'm expecting all of you at Evening Shadows for a little postdebate cocktail celebration in about an hour. I won't take no for an answer. And Lady Roth—please feel free to run on home and change into something more comfortable, if you'd like. I'm sure no one would mind if you gave Susan B. the evening off."

14.

MY DARLING MEMANTINE

Wittsie rose from her sofa perch in Laurie's parlor and moved gingerly to the middle of the room. There she politely cleared her throat, clasped her hands together neatly, and began singing in a bright, clear voice in front of all the other Nitwitts.

"In a cavern, in a canyon,
Excavating for a mine,
Dwelt a miner, forty-niner,
And his daughter, Memantine.
Oh my darling, oh my darling
Oh my darling, Memantine,
Thou art lost and gone forever,
Dreadful sorry, Memantine."

She paused, further increasing the bewilderment of her friends. "I like this song so much. . . . I think it sums me up perfectly, girls . . . lost and gone forever. . . ."

Wittsie executed a dainty curtsy and quickly resumed her seat, leaving each of her friends speechless. It was Laurie who finally gathered her wits about her and broke the silence.

"That was charming, Wittsie. I had no idea you had such a sweet voice. I never could carry a tune. Now, tell us what it all means. I'll ask you again what the verdict from your doctor was. You've had us all on the edge of our seats and worried to death since you got here."

"Yes," Renza added with her usual air of aggravation. "Stop playing games and tell us what the doctor said. Then we can all have our toddies and some lunch. I'm starved."

Wittsie's behavior had been evasive since they'd all arrived for Laurie's luncheon, and now the delicious aromas drifting in from the kitchen were making them even more impatient. "Please, Wittsie," Laurie began. "I threw all this together at the last minute because we were so concerned about you. Tell us what all the test results showed before we bust out of our panty hose."

Finally, Wittsie relented and blurted it out. "I'm sorry, girls. . . . Unfortunately, the diagnosis was that I do have Alzheimer's. . . . It's gone past early onset to moderate now . . . or at least I think that's the way Doctor Mandrell put it. . . . There, I've said it. . . . I know I've been dawdling . . . but I was looking for a clever way to let you all know. . . . I came up with the song and rehearsed it several times last night. . . . Maybe I didn't do such a good job. . . . Oh, dear, I'm always muddling things up, aren't I? . . ."

Myrtis and Denver Lee, who were sitting on either side of her, reacted immediately by gently stroking Wittsie's arms, while the others around the room offered up their most solicitous expressions.

"Oh, you didn't muddle up anything, Wittsie," Laurie replied. "You were just your usual adorable self. But can you maybe give us more details? This is distressing for all of us to hear, as you can imagine."

"Take your time, sweetie," Myrtis added, still stroking. "We're here for you."

"I know," Wittsie began. "You are all my dearest friends in the world. . . . I mean, I suppose that's why I came up with that silly song. . . . It was silly, wasn't it? . . . Something we all grew up with and sang as children. . . . 'My Darling Clementine' . . . I just reworked it a bit. . . . " She paused for the sweetest of sighs. "How simple things were when we were all children singing to our dolls. . . . That seems light-years away now, of course. . . . "

"What was that word you substituted?" Novie interjected. "Meman-something?"

Wittsie was staring straight ahead in that disarming way of hers, working her fingers into a nervous jumble. "Memantine? . . . Oh, she's my new friend . . . my new medication, actually. . . . Doctor Mandrell says it's the latest thing for treating moderate Alzheimer's patients. . . . That's me, it appears. . . . He said my brain signals are constantly being disrupted . . . probably have been for years . . . but then I guess you girls knew that already, didn't you?" She laughed so gently that it was somehow strangely reassuring. "Now, don't pretend you all don't know what I'm talking about. . . . I've sensed something might be wrong all these years but just never had the incentive to do anything about it. . . . I wanted to thank all of you again for coming to me the way you did last week and insisting I get help. . . . I mean, it turns out you were all right on target with your concerns. . . . "

"Oh, it was the least we could do," Denver Lee replied. "What are friends for? You would have done the same for any of us."

"What's the long-term prognosis, Wittsie?" Laurie said.

The gentle smile on Wittsie's face began fading away. "Not so good, I'm afraid. . . . I mean, there is no cure . . . at least not right now, Doctor Mandrell says. . . . Oh, they're working on things all the time . . . but meanwhile, my faculties will only get worse over time. . . . My darling Memantine will help delay things, of course . . . put things off until a later date, I should say . . . postpone the inevitable. . . . "

Denver Lee was shaking her head. "I feel a bit ashamed to be complaining about all my food restrictions the way I have."

"No, no, no," Wittsie replied. "We all have different things to deal with. . . . That's yours, this is mine. . . . I mean, it's not as bad as it sounds, girls. . . . I've been functioning reasonably well all these years without even being diagnosed. . . . Now that it's all out in the open, maybe I can concentrate on things a little better . . . with a little help from my darling, of course. . . . I was thinking on the way over today how we all made those radio spots for Mr. Choppy's campaign . . . how we all stepped up and found something positive to say about the advantages of maturity. . . . We didn't pull our punches, did we? . . . Of course, we kind of ignored the downside of getting on up there, didn't we? . . . I mean, we are all doing just that, you know. . . . "

Laurie sat back in her chair with a look of astonishment. "Are you sure you have Alzheimer's? What you just said is absolutely brilliant, Wittsie!"

The remark seemed to ease the tension in the air a bit, and everyone managed a tentative laugh.

"Oh, I'm afraid there's no two ways about it," Wittsie continued. "I'll have my good days and bad days . . . and then later maybe it'll just be good moments and bad moments, the doctor says . . . and maybe the Memantine is helping me think things through a little better right now. . . . But, girls, I also have the most wonderful news to share with you. . . . I mean, it's like the old adage about God never shutting a door without opening a window for you somewhere . . . or is it the other way around . . . I forget? . . ."

There was more polite laughter, as the roomful of faces changed from concerned to expectant. "You see, when I called up my daughter, April, to let her know what was going on, she reacted the way I'd hoped she would . . . actually, the way I've been praying she would act toward me all these years. . . . I've always felt like they've been running away from me as fast and as often as they can. . . . You already know how that's affected my precious Meagan. . . . But anyway, April says she wants to come down and spend some time with me. . . . There's so much we have to talk about. . . . Mark my words, girls, I intend to give her a piece of my mind—what's left of it, of course—about Meagan. . . . I should have taken them to task about that a long time ago. . . . This diagnosis gives me the perfect platform now. . . . "

Laurie nodded. "You make so much sense, I still can't help but wonder if Doctor Mandrell knows what he's talking about. Of course, I'm thrilled for you about April and what this could mean for Meagan, too."

"It's funny," Wittsie added. "You lose some, and then you win some . . . or at least that's how it feels to me right now. . . . "

Myrtis gently patted her shoulder. "You definitely won this one, sweetie."

Laurie sniffed the air and shot up from her chair. "Good heavens! The rolls! That's the one thing I never could seem to manage in my many years of cooking for Roy, my girls, and now Powell. They all said I could give a class in how to burn bread every time out."

Wittsie raised her hand tentatively. "If you need an assistant, I'm available."

Laurie laughed as she headed toward the kitchen to see about salvaging the rolls and putting the final touches on her impromptu little luncheon.

★

Despite the seriousness of the conversation that had preceded lunch, the Nitwitts brought healthy appetites to the dining-room table. They eagerly dug into the shrimp and wild rice casserole and garden salads that Laurie served up, minus the rolls that were just too burned even to scrape off. Interestingly enough, Wittsie's diagnosis was moved to the back burner momentarily to accommodate a lively discussion of *The Citizen*'s latest poll. One week out from the election, the numbers had moved once again in Mr. Choppy's favor. Though Mr. Floyce had continued to hold steady at forty-nine percent, Mr. Choppy had gained two more points and now stood at forty-seven percent with only four percent still undecided.

"We've almost caught him!" Laurie exclaimed. "In another week we could pull even or possibly go ahead. Powell's down at headquarters right now plotting last-minute strategies. He says you never know what Mr. Floyce might decide to do or say when we're just about to cross the finish line."

Myrtis gave her a skeptical glance. "What could he possibly do at this stage of the campaign except more of the same? More kissing babies out at the MegaMart? Hasn't that gotten a little old by now? We're not even doing much of that anymore at headquarters, are we?"

"We took a picture one afternoon with my little grandson, Christopher," Denver Lee pointed out. "He had a wonderful time, and so did my daughter, Nita."

"Oh, yes. It worked out just fine for what it was," Laurie said. "But Powell and Mr. Choppy both took a long, hard look at the kissing babies at the Piggly Wiggly ploy and decided it was putting the campaign in too much of a copycat mode. We needed to be more substantive—which I think we accomplished with those wonderful radio spots. Besides, there was no way Mr. Choppy could possibly duplicate Mr. Floyce's ability to kiss up to men, women, and children of all ages in general. But Powell also thinks we still need to stay alert up until the end. Considering how tight the race is getting, we can't afford to underestimate the opposition."

"I know Marc was thrilled to work with Powell on the spots," Novie added. "Anyway, we have just one more week to go. This is getting very exciting."

Over dessert, the conversation returned to Wittsie's condition, but Wittsie herself seemed determined not to let the topic become too maudlin. "I'm really not worried about what the future holds," she was saying over coffee and caramel custard. "After all, I have all of you to check in on me. . . . That's nothing new. . . . I mean, we've all been sticking our noses in each other's business all these years. . . . Why, with my Memantine to give me a boost, I'm apt to be the one checking up on all of you most of the time. . . ."

"Don't you lose that thought," Laurie replied with a wink. "We'll hold you to it. Somebody's got to keep us Nitwitts out of trouble, you know."

★

Laurie was sitting across from Renza in the living room, sipping her second cup of coffee and wondering what was coming next. Renza had found a moment in the midst of helping clear the table to reveal that she wanted to talk about something important after the others had left. So there they were, just the two of them, and Laurie could sense that she was in for another of her frequent counseling sessions with one of her friends.

"Laurie, I feel just awful," Renza began, putting her cup down on the coffee table in front of her. "I'm getting my comeuppance, I suppose."

"What on earth are you talking about?"

"I'm talking about Wittsie. All these years I've known her as a Nitwitt, I've been the one who's poked fun at her most of all. I've been the one who's complained the most about how slow she always was taking the notes of all our meetings. I look back on it all, and I see how unkind I've been, and I feel just awful about it now that I know she couldn't help any of it."

Laurie put her cup aside and gave Renza her most reassuring smile. "Now, why should you single yourself out? We've all had a laugh now and then at Wittsie's expense. But the telling thing here is that Wittsie's always gone along with it. She was the one who thought the name Nitwitts was the funniest thing ever, and I think she still routinely brushes aside any remarks we make about her behavior."

Renza sat back and briefly reflected on Laurie's comments. "So you're going to let me off the hook that easily?"

"I don't understand."

"What I'm saying to you is that I don't think the comments you and the others have made were uttered in the same tone of derision that I've always used. I don't think any of the rest of you meant anything by what you said. I, on the other hand, seem to be devoid of the milk of human kindness. Maybe it has to do with all the trouble I had with my mother-in-law, or maybe it's just something I've indulged without thinking about it. But the truth is, I know where my heart's come down on this one in the past, and now I can feel my heart breaking about what will eventually happen to Wittsie. She's just beginning a long downhill slide, and this guilt I'm feeling right now—well, I think that's my comeuppance."

Laurie took her time to reply, but when she did, there was an unmistakably triumphant expression on her face. "I have to disagree with what you just said, Renza. Particularly the part about the milk of human kindness. Don't you see that if what you're saying about yourself was true, your heart wouldn't be breaking right now? If you didn't really care—and if you hadn't really cared all along—you wouldn't be feeling like this."

Renza eyed her shrewdly, finally allowing herself the suggestion of a smirk. "I suppose you have a point. But still—I just wish there was a way I could somehow make it up to Wittsie."

"You can. We all can. We can agree to be there for her and be especially diligent about checking up on her and doing things for her that she won't be able to do for herself when the time comes. Without making a big to-do about it and without letting her know up front, we'll just make her our next ongoing Nitwitts project. She's going to need us down the road. Think about it that way, and you should be able to let go of all that guilt."

"Well, you've done it again," Renza replied, offering up a genuine smile. "You've made me see things in the right light. I don't know how you do it. It makes me feel a bit apprehensive about taking over the presidency from Myrtis in a couple of weeks. How can I possibly live up to the precedent you've both set? I realize I put on airs all the time, but that doesn't mean I necessarily think I'm worthy of them. Underneath it all, I guess I'm a fraud in fox furs."

Laurie leaned in and caught her gaze. "I don't want to hear that kind of talk. You keep all of us on our toes."

"Perhaps. But I don't think I'm even-tempered enough to be president. I've been toying with the idea of telling Myrtis I want her to continue. She's been doing a wonderful job, and she has all the social skills I lack. I'm just as likely to tell someone off as to listen to what they have to say."

"I think you'll have to take that up with the others at your next meeting. You and Myrtis agreed to split this year, and the club agreed to it, too," Laurie replied. "If you want my opinion, I think you should just leave things as they are and step up to your duties when the time comes. You might surprise yourself."

Renza picked up her cup and finished off her coffee. "The truth is, Myrtis and I are still figureheads. You're still the driving force behind the Nitwitts, even if you have stepped down as president. Everyone still looks to you for advice and counsel, and you're always good for it."

Laurie tried to wave her off, but the gesture lacked conviction. If anything, her involvement with the Nitwitts had increased since she'd voluntarily resigned. "I guess I'm my mother's daughter. Martha Jane Prather was the ultimate family arbiter when I was growing up. She kept all of us on the straight and narrow, and I probably learned by osmosis. This past summer when Lizzie came down for the wedding, she found time to tell me how thankful she was that I'd prepared her so well for married life with Barry. It meant the world to me to hear that from her, particularly on the verge of my hooking up with Powell. I'd worried a bit that she might view it as turning my back on her father."

Renza sighed poignantly. "Everything you touch turns to gold, Laurie, and that includes Mr. Choppy's campaign. You and Powell have got him well within striking distance, and I can remember last fall how most people weren't even giving him a whisper of a chance. I know I didn't. Just between us, I thought it was the silliest thing I'd ever heard of. Imagine—a grocery store owner making the leap to mayor of Second Creek. But now I'd be crushed if Mr. Choppy isn't able to pull it off, and I'm happy to have contributed my radio spot to the cause."

"We've all done our part," Laurie added. "And in one short week we'll know the results."

15.

THE EVE OF JUDGMENT

The Reverend Quintus Payne of the Marblestone Alley Church
of Holiness walked crisply into Mr. Choppy's campaign headquarters, accompanied by Kenyatta Warner. It was just past noon
on Election Eve, and Mr. Choppy quickly ushered the pair into
his office with a broad smile, shutting the door behind him.

"I was delighted to get your call, Reverend Payne," Mr.
Choppy began as everyone settled into their chairs. "My campaign needs all the help it can get here at the last minute. Every
vote counts."

The rangy, imposing Reverend Payne drew himself up, nodding thoughtfully for a few seconds before he spoke. "Well,
Mr. Dunbar, you have one big fan here in Kenyatta. He kinda
clinched the deal for you, if you wanna know the truth. I had
some notions of my own, but this fine young churchgoer put
everything in perspective."

Mr. Choppy gazed fondly at his former bag boy. He still thought of Kenyatta almost as a son, and now it was clear that the boy still thought of him somewhat as a father figure. "We always worked well together in the store, didn't we, Kenyatta? I could always count on you."

Kenyatta looked slightly embarrassed but quickly recovered. "Mr. Choppy, you were always good to me and Jake. The extra money always came in handy, gotta tell ya. Helped me and my momma and my aunties make ends meet."

"You worked hard 'round the clock. You never shirked your duties."

"I learned all 'bout work and responsibility at the Piggly Wiggly, Mr. Choppy. When it shut down, I had no trouble findin' me another job at one a' the department stores. That's why I went to Reverend Payne and asked him could he maybe think about supportin' you in this election. I know some a' them other churches are on Mr. Floyce's side. I saw how they carried on at that debate."

Reverend Payne cleared his throat and leaned in. "I want you to know, Mr. Dunbar, that I usually stay out of politics. But I'm gonna make an exception this time around. I don't cotton to Mr. Floyce's act. He's come around to my church over the years, makin' all kinda noises 'bout doin' things for me and my congregation and winkin' all the while. But I wasn't buyin'. I don't care for that approach. The Lord's work is not for sale."

"Amen," Mr. Choppy replied solemnly.

"So I wanted you to know that I did make this election the point of my sermon this past Sunday. I told my congregation that I believed it was time for a change, and I wanted to take the time to let you know that. I won't go any further than that from the pulpit. I'll leave it up to each voter. But I can tell from Kenyatta's testimony that you're a good and godly man. I don't mind revealin' that you certainly have my vote."

Mr. Choppy reached across and shook hands firmly. "I appreciate that more than you know. It's not just the churches, you know. Mr. Floyce has all those good ole boy building contractors and asphalt road pavers on the take, too. I've had to fight hard for every vote, black or white."

Reverend Payne stood up and squared his shoulders. "Don't you give up now. The good people of this community'll figure it out for themselves. I've always believed in the good fight. After all, it's my life's work."

At the front door, Mr. Choppy again thanked Reverend Payne for his support and then turned to Kenyatta. "Don't you be a stranger, son. I'd like to know how you're gettin' along in that new job."

Kenyatta gave his former employer a quick pat on the shoulder. "I got my eyes on a scholarship to Delta State down the road, Mr. Choppy. I'll keep you posted."

★

Later that evening, Mr. Choppy collapsed on the tattered living-room sofa in his Pond Street bungalow. It was just past eight o'clock, and he couldn't seem to get *The Citizen*'s final poll numbers and the sidebar that had appeared beside it out of his head. "Dunbar Campaign Fails to Close the Gap," by Rankin Lynch, the early afternoon edition had trumpeted shortly after Reverend Payne and Kenyatta had left. It was downright depressing, that's what it was. After more than a month of steadily inching up on Mr. Floyce, the Hale Dunbar Jr. campaign had seemingly reached an impasse during the critical final week, failing to pull even and essentially leaving the election as Mr. Floyce's to lose. As a result, everyone at headquarters had appeared to be merely going through the motions on the final afternoon of phone solicitation and electioneering. This, despite the pep talks that Mr. Choppy and Powell continually conjured up to boost morale, including news of the promising, last-minute support from the Marblestone Alley Church of Holiness.

Furthermore, Mr. Choppy had received a disheartening phone call from Gaylie Girl shortly after opening up the morning paper and digging into his bacon and eggs over easy. She had revealed that her impulsive decision to fly down from Chicago to be with him on Election Day would not come to pass.

"My flight to Memphis has been canceled. In fact, all the flights out of here have been canceled," she had explained, her voice filled with disappointment. "This massive winter storm has just swooped down on us from Alberta. Both Midway and O'Hare are buried under ice. I'm afraid your number-one cheerleader is just going to have to check in with you long distance for those results tomorrow. But don't worry, Hale. If my being there in spirit counts for anything, you've already won hands down."

It was a huge emotional blow for him. He had been looking forward so much to showing her off to Laurie and Powell, the Nitwitts, and all the rest of his friends and supporters, giving them a sneak preview of the next First Lady of Second Creek, if the vote went his way. There was a part of him that still couldn't quite believe she had said yes to him, and getting her here to confirm it in person would be the ultimate proof. Earlier in the week, he'd suffered more discouraging news in another long-distance call at headquarters—this one coming through while he munched on a tuna sandwich during lunch break.

"I'm so sorry to have to tell you that I couldn't talk my boss into okaying the Second Creek election story," Ronnie Leyton had explained from his office at CNN. "I had most of the footage lined up and ready to go, but he was adamant about it."

Mr. Choppy had sounded placid, though his guts were churning. "I understand, Mr. Leyton. Don't worry about it. You've already done more than enough for us here."

Perhaps the national publicity from CNN would not have had any appreciable effect on the outcome of the election, particularly at this late date, but the conventional wisdom was that the challenger always needed more help—and sometimes an extra little spark—to unseat a legendary incumbent. To some extent, Mr. Choppy had hoped against hope that the CNN coverage would provide the media slingshot to slay Goliath.

How had things managed to go south so fast in the space of one week, especially when everyone's spirits had been soaring following the Town Hall debate and Myrtis's little to-do out at Evening Shadows? The radio spots had continued to run and draw favorable comment everywhere he went. He had faithfully appeared before all the civic and social clubs and recited Powell's carefully crafted rhetoric to perfection. He had had scores of pictures taken with parents and children at headquarters and at outlying shopping centers. Here and there, he'd even reverted to kissing a baby or two at headquarters when coaxed by a devoted supporter.

He'd even called up on an impulse and made an appearance all by his lonesome at that Hanging Grapes A.M.E. potluck dinner this past Wednesday evening to shake a few hands and break bread with the faithful. The reception from Brother Willyus Thompson over the phone had been polite but reserved.

"Here at Hanging Grapes, all God's people are welcome, Mr. Dunbar, but it's the first time we've ever heard from you out this way. We didn't know you knew our address."

"I want to represent all Second Creekers, Brother Thompson, not just a select few," Mr. Choppy had said later in person over fried chicken and potato salad, well aware that he was trespassing on Mr. Floyce's territory.

So where had all the momentum gone? Would it end like this—a game but nonetheless failed effort? Had he come this far and spent all this money just to learn how to enunciate and think on his feet a little bit better?

The doorbell rang, and Mr. Choppy started. He wasn't expecting anyone, and the way he was feeling right now, he was certainly not in the mood for guests of any kind. Somehow, he managed to trudge to the door and opened it to find Laurie, Powell, and the Nitwitts gathered en masse on his front porch.

"Surprise!" they all shouted at once, bundled up against the sharp wind whistling around them.

Powell brandished a large brown bag above his head and flashed a smile. "We brought you some last-minute courage of the bubbly variety. We figured you might be able to use it along about now!"

Mr. Choppy quickly recovered his manners. "Please, come in, all of you. The wind chill must be somethin' awful out there!"

"Unfit for Eskimos," Powell replied, shivering while leading the way to warmth. "The temperature's been dropping all day. I heard Rick Wentworth on WSCM say that one of those Alberta clippers is on the way."

Once everyone had taken off their coats and settled around Mr. Choppy's modest little living room, the impromptu celebration began. Several of the Nitwitts had brought hors d'oeuvres of various kinds in their Tupperware, and there was no shortage of the idle chitchat trotted out when people were trying to avoid a difficult topic—in this case, the campaign's last-minute flameout.

Finally, however, Mr. Choppy broached the subject himself, aided by his second glass of champagne. "Folks, I appreciate all the forced frivolity. But it really wasn't necessary for you to come out in this raw, nasty weather to hold my hand."

"Well, to tell the truth, it wasn't just for you," Laurie explained, working on a second glass of the bubbly herself. "I think we were all a little depressed by the final poll, and it just seemed like we walked out of headquarters this evening like a bunch of zombies. Our rah-rah-rah was MIA today. That was a pathetic excuse for a final rally. So when Powell and I got home, I told him we ought to get off our rear ends, stop feeling sorry for ourselves, and keep our chins up. After all, polls aren't always the final say. The race is still close, and there's still important work to do."

"Yes, we've all got our assignments driving voters to the polls tomorrow," Myrtis interjected. "It's not over until it's over, and when Laurie called all of us up to remind us of that, we just rallied from our housecoats, rustled up a few things in our kitchens, put on our faces, and headed over here pronto. It was our bounden duty as Nitwitts to support this project of ours to the very end. We're not quitters, you know."

Laurie hoisted her glass and the others followed suit. "Well said, President Myrtis!"

"We've all got a busy day coming up," Myrtis added, pointing to her glass. "So we'd best not tie one on tonight. Moderation, girls. I've promised four people rides to the polls, and I'll have to make at least two trips to keep my word."

"Oh, I think we've got Ward Four covered, Myrtis and myself," Denver Lee said. "I'm making a few trips back and forth, too. I always got a wonderful response from voters on the east side of town, where we both live."

Myrtis put down her glass and struck a triumphant pose. "I confess I've been Queen of the Yard Signs all the way out to Evening Shadows. After every shift here at headquarters, I'd pick a street and knock on every door to ask if I could plant one for the cause. No one could get within five miles of my house without getting our message, and I gave out those 'new beginning' campaign buttons at the front door like Halloween candy. I tell you, I practically made it a trick-or-treat proposition for everyone from the UPS driver to the meter reader. Even had a couple of Jehovah's Witnesses running for cover."

"You've more than held your own out there, Myrtis. Ward Four is definitely friendly to our cause," Powell pointed out, thoroughly amused. "And our phone bank records indicate we got many positive responses everywhere else except for Ward Six. The demographics just didn't favor us there."

Mr. Choppy shrugged his shoulders and swallowed the rest of the egg roll he was enjoying. "What can you do? Mr. Floyce has several influential black churches eatin' out of his hand. As I told you all Thursday mornin', my little excursion to that potluck affair at Hanging Grapes on Wednesday didn't net me much more'n a roomful of fake smiles and a touch of indigestion. I doubt Mr. Floyce has every black voter wrapped up, though. The Marblestone Alley Church of Holiness endorsement gives us some real hope."

"That's good news, of course, but there's something else worrying me now," Laurie added while passing around the plate of raw veggies and ranch dip she'd thrown together at the last minute. "WSCM wasn't the only one with the grim weather report. When Powell and I got home from headquarters tonight, all the Memphis TV stations were saying they're not exactly sure when or how fast that nasty front will move through here. But if this bad weather keeps even a few of our supporters from voting, we don't stand a chance of springing that Election Day surprise. We just don't have a vote to spare."

Mr. Choppy was nodding pensively, staring off into a corner of the room. "I haven't had the opportunity to tell any of you this yet, but the weather's already thrown a wrench in the works for me. My Gaylie Girl, my wonderful wife-to-be, was all set to fly down here to be with us for the returns. I was hopin' to be able to introduce her to all of you as your new First Lady, but that same winter storm that's on its way down here has her trapped up in Chicago at this very moment. I wanted to surprise all of you and maybe put an exclamation point on our victory there at the end. Or at least that was my dream right up until yesterday."

"Oh, we would have adored that!" Myrtis exclaimed. "Ever since you told us about her accepting your proposal, we've all been phoning back and forth plotting parties like mad for the both of you, haven't we, ladies?"

Each of the Nitwitts was smiling and nodding enthusiastically. "We'll put your Gaylie Girl through an absolute whirlwind once she gets down here, Mr. Choppy," Novie said. "When the time comes, we'll make her feel like one of the girls."

"That reminds me," Renza added, finishing off her champagne. "I was thinking of proposing something when I took over as president in a week or so, and this seems as good a time as any to bring it up. Mr. Choppy, could you track down a pen and pad for Wittsie so she can take notes?"

"No need for that," Wittsie said. "I have those things right here in my purse. . . . I mean, I've gotten better about thinking ahead. . . . Credit my darling Memantine, if you like. . . . Or maybe I'm trying harder. . . ."

With Wittsie at the ready a few seconds later, Renza continued. "I think we should consider changing the bylaws of the club to allow those who aren't widows to join us. That way we can invite Mr. Choppy's Gaylie Girl to become a Nitwitt. Right now she's a widow and perfectly eligible, but as soon as she and Mr. Choppy get married, her status will change. We should have changed everything when Laurie and Powell got married so she could stay in the club and not have to resign the presidency. What does everyone think?"

The Nitwitts exchanged inquisitive glances, but Powell took the plunge immediately. "I know I don't have a vote, but I think it's a splendid idea. Laurie has spent even more time with all of you since she stepped down. Of course, I realize the election campaign has had a lot to do with that, but once a Nitwitt, always a Nitwitt."

Mr. Choppy's eyes widened as he nodded enthusiastically. "And I'm sure my Gaylie Girl would appreciate the invitation. She won't know a soul when she moves down here. In fact, the culture shock has been one of my biggest worries about all that. Why, if you Nitwitt ladies took her under your wing, I'm sure it'd make the transition a lot easier for her."

Myrtis surveyed the sea of smiles around the room. "Everybody seems to like your idea, Renza. For the record, ladies, are there any opposing opinions?" There was not so much as a no, only the universal shaking of heads. "Good. Then may I see a show of hands? All in favor of Renza's proposal, raise them, please."

Five hands shot up immediately. "Unanimous," Wittsie said.

"All opposed?" Myrtis added quickly. There was only silence.

"Good. Then as president of the Nitwitts, I hereby declare Laurie Beth Prather Lepanto Hampton to be an official member of the club once again."

Laurie giggled and placed her hand over her heart as if she were pledging allegiance. "Thank you, thank you, thank you. But I'm sure you all realize I never really left you here where it counts."

"And I want to thank you on behalf of my Gaylie Girl," Mr. Choppy added. "I know she'll fit right in from the moment she orders a bowl of gumbo with y'all at the Victorian Tea Room. Maybe it's not Lake Forest, but our little town has its charms, too."

Laurie flashed a smile in Renza's general direction. "If that's any example of the leadership we can expect from you during your tenure as president, Mrs. Lewis Belford, I think we're in good shape. Well done!"

Uncharacteristically, Renza looked as if she were about to melt into a puddle. "I've always had an eye for the practical underneath all my posing, you know."

Then Myrtis took the floor again. "Now, is everyone straight about tomorrow? I'm expecting you all around six out at Evening Shadows for the returns. No need to bring a thing— I'll have plenty of food and booze—just bring yourselves and your most positive attitude. I, for one, still think we can pull this thing off!"

"God willin' and the creek don't rise!" Mr. Choppy added with a gleam in his eye. "And I wanna thank all of you again for comin' out on a night like this to lift my spirits. I'm afraid I wasn't much of a leader today at headquarters, but they say a good leader surrounds himself with good people and knows how to delegate. Tonight at least proves I've done a good job of that."

"Laurie and I have known that all along," Powell said. "And what say you, Nitwitts?"

Powell definitely knew how to work a room, and everyone was soon chattering away, exchanging pleasantries and sampling more of the hors d'oeuvres and wine.

Over her second glass of champagne, Renza said, "I'm not letting you off the hook about showing me where you found that gold-plated hand, Mr. Choppy. That's been intriguing me no end ever since you mentioned it in your summation at the debate."

Mr. Choppy suddenly frowned. "You know, Miz Belford, I would have no earthly idea how to get back out there. All I know is that it was in the middle of some dried-up cattle pond in someone's pasture way out in the county somewhere. I remember a pecan orchard, too, but not much else. If you really wanna know the truth, I just seemed to end up there after drivin' for miles and miles. It was almost like someone else was drivin' the car— a weird sort of remote control."

"Oh, now, that gives me chill bumps," Renza replied, absentmindedly fingering her fox fur.

"Yeah, I know what you mean," Mr. Choppy said. "There's really no way to explain it, except that maybe Mr. Gary Greene had it right at the debate with that sign of his. You know, the one about the Spirit of Second Creek?"

Moments later, there was a rapid-fire succession of tapping sounds at the windows and front door, almost—but not quite— like someone knocking insistently.

"What the hell is that?" Powell said, jumping up from his seat to investigate, with Mr. Choppy, Laurie, and a couple of the others close behind.

At the front door, they all peered out and Powell marveled at the opaque, gravelly bits landing near his feet with a subtle popping, hissing sound. "I'll be damned! That's sleet coming down out there. Folks, we're in the middle of an ice storm!"

16.

SLIP SLIDIN' AWAY

That capricious river of wind known as the Northern Jet decided it had ignored the mid-South long enough during the winter of 2002. Now it steered a doozy of an Arctic storm southward into the warm air that always hung around the Gulf. The result was an atmospheric clash the likes of which the region had not seen in decades.

All of Arkansas, much of West Tennessee, and the northern third of Mississippi bore the brunt—with the upper westernmost part of the Mississippi Delta particularly hard hit. Traffic—what there was of it when the storm first began bulldozing its way throughout the night—was virtually frozen in place on the back roads and state and interstate highways, and Second Creek awoke to an eye-searing, crystalline landscape.

After rushing home from Mr. Choppy's to avoid the storm, Laurie and Powell had spent a rather restless night listening to the ice pellets steadily attacking their house. Although they were rightfully concerned about property damage, they still found time for a round of spirited lovemaking, a little fire in the midst of so much ice. They also couldn't help thinking out loud about how the storm might affect the election.

"If a smaller percentage of the voters can actually get to the polls," Powell suggested at one point during his tossing-and-turning sessions, "it stands to reason this will be a brand-new ball game. You can throw the records out the window, as they say."

Whatever reality they had imagined or dreamed in their fitful sleep, it paled in comparison to the sight that greeted them when they groggily arose, pulled back the bedroom curtains, and gazed out into the morning.

"Oh my God!" Powell exclaimed, wiping the sleep out of his eyes. "I may be considered a traitor for saying so, but that's the most beautiful thing I've ever seen in my life!"

Laurie nudged him aside slightly, gasped, and agreed with his evaluation. "It's like some kind of painting."

Indeed, it was. Bare branches of every shape and size had been transformed into drooping magic wands, fanciful necklaces, and bracelets; azaleas and camellias had taken on the identity of plump little gnomes stationed like sentries throughout the glazed landscape; everywhere, the sun glinted off eaves and fences with such unrelenting intensity that it was like staring into an eclipse. That human instinct for self-preservation somehow kicked in, warning the fond gazer to turn away or risk damage to his eyesight. Above the sheer undisturbed purity of it all, a deep blue sky gave no hint of the blustery turbulence that had struck and lingered so long under cover of darkness the night before.

"Can we drive around on that stuff?" Laurie asked, trying her best to collect her thoughts while gazing out onto the street.

Powell turned away from the mesmerizing scene and arched his brows. "If we can't, it's not all that far to walk to our polling place at First Presbyterian."

Laurie was frowning now. "That may be okay for us, but what about the rest of Second Creek? I have a bad feeling about this, Powell. I think this may be our worst-case scenario, don't you?"

He was getting ready to agree with her when something Mr. Choppy had said to him months ago flashed into his head. A chance comment that he had so readily dismissed about their notorious Second Creek weather having more to do with the outcome of the election than anything either of the candidates did or said. Was that coming to pass?

"Let's just wait and see," Powell replied instead. "Who knows how it'll turn out now?"

Laurie walked to the bathroom and flipped on the light switch. "At least we still have power. I wonder if all the rest of the girls do."

Powell picked up the phone beside Laurie's plantation spool bed and grinned. "Got a dial tone here. I guess you and the Nitwitts will be talking all morning."

★

Across town, Sister Lula Mayes had swathed herself in several layers of clothing to keep warm. They'd been without heat for several hours now, and it was working on her last nerve. All the power lines were down in her neighborhood, and neither she nor her husband, LeRon, had cell phones. She was pacing around her kitchen like some caged animal, casting frustrated glances at the clock on the wall. "Here it is, way past nine, and I cain't even get outta this house, much less pick all them people up and carry 'em in to vote. I promised Mr. Floyce—he won't like this one bit! We got two trucks already blockin' the street right out in front!"

LeRon, a hulking, even-tempered fellow who took a rather dim view of church matters and politics alike, shrugged and shoved his hands into the parka he had put on over his bathrobe. "Now, you listen to me, Lula—what that Mr. Floyce likes is the last thing on my mind this mornin'. We're freezin' to death and you're still worried 'bout all that political mess. I only got one thing to say to you and Mr. Floyce and the Lord and anybody else today, and that's to gimme some heat!"

"You're such a blasphemer, LeRon! I hope the Lord don't look down and strike you dead!"

LeRon managed an ironic little smirk. "He already took a pretty good shot at both of us with that storm last night."

"How'm I gonna get to our pollin' place today? How those other folks gettin' to it? Might as well be a skatin' rink out there."

"Maybe we won't, and maybe they won't. Would it be the end of the world?"

Sister Lula collapsed at the kitchen table and exhaled forcefully. "Maybe not. But it might be the end of that extra money Mr. Floyce sends our church every now and then."

"The way I look at it, my vote's not for sale. Mr. Floyce might as well be a modern-day carpetbagger. I betcha some a' the folks in the congregation feel the same way if you got 'em to tell the truth."

Sister Lula turned up her nose and made a contemptuous little noise. "So now you're gonna put on airs? You never set foot in the church, LeRon Mayes. Don't you lecture me. We put the money to good use. I can tell you this much. I'll be castin' my vote today for Mr. Floyce if I have to walk to the pollin' place on foot."

"Well, you know what, Miz Lula? I just might go with you to cancel out your vote. How 'bout that?"

"You heathen!"

LeRon pointed to the window and laughed. "Hey, I'm only doin' my civic duty!"

★

The good news was that New Vista Acres still had power. The bad news was that Charley Franklin Forbes was in the midst of the worst row ever with his wife, and she showed no signs of coming to her senses anytime soon. It was that damned sense of loyalty Minnie doggedly maintained where Mr. Floyce was concerned. That pipe dream she had about that raise he kept dangling in front of her—the old carrot-in-front-of-the-workhorse trick. Just another broken promise, as far as Charley was concerned. He still regretted not having put his foot down and made her quit long ago, but then, what would they have done for money? They still needed the income from both their jobs to make ends meet.

"Minnie, I've just hung up with the highway patrol, and it's pretty glazed over out there. They recommend we wait until the roads get salted before we head in to do anything today. It'll take a little while for the town to get all their equipment up and runnin'. They say we should wait until later in the day. According to their reports, it's like bumper cars all over Second Creek, and we should stay off the streets for now. It's just not safe—there are power lines and trees down all over the place."

"But I need to get to the courthouse to see what I can do to help," she replied, fidgeting at the kitchen table. "I just can't let Mr. Floyce down—he's countin' on me."

Charley felt like ramming his fist through the kitchen wall. He was not about to let her go out there by herself, so he decided not to pull his punches. "We'll just cancel each other out, you know. Our votes, I mean."

Minnie appeared unmoved, stubbornly shaking her head. "It's your right to vote against my job if you think that's a wise thing to do."

"All right, then, you asked for it. Here's how much I think of your Mr. Floyce," Charley continued, going for broke. "I thumbed through all your notes from your meetings with him and Mr. Jeffers, and I saw to it that Mr. Choppy got the gist of 'em."

Minnie just sat there in jaw-dropping amazement, saying nothing.

"Yeah, you can look shocked all you want. I spied for Mr. Choppy, and I'm glad I did. I wanted him to have every damned advantage he could have to beat that bastard you've been workin' for all these years, and it shouldn't come as no surprise to you that I did it. All we ever do is argue about your job up at that damned courthouse, and I'm good 'n sick to death of it!"

Minnie drew herself up, the very picture of indignation. "I had no idea I was married to a secret agent. And what do we do if your Mr. Choppy wins? You think he'll hire me as his secretary? Not likely."

"Mr. Choppy's promised me a position in his administration— that's what we'll do for a job. And you can sit back and take some time off at last."

But Minnie would not budge. "And if your Mr. Choppy loses? Where are we then? I'll tell you where. I'll still have my job, and we'll still have our money comin' in, that's where. Maybe a little extra, if that raise comes through."

"Don't hold your breath on that."

"If I have to, I'll drive myself in," Minnie replied, keeping the pressure on her husband.

"The hell you will. If you're bound and determined to do this, I'll drive us both in. But I want you to know right here and now that I'll be doin' it with gritted teeth."

Minnie made a little snorting noise. "Good. At least you won't be able to go on and on about how much you hate Mr. Floyce. That temper of yours will be the death of me yet!"

★

Ward Four was one of the first areas of the town to get salted, but it was past noon before most of the people living there dared to venture out. Myrtis was among those taking her time, content to let her fears about driving on ice slowly melt away while the road salt and the sun worked their magic. She had also come to a decision about the returns party she was supposed to host at Evening Shadows following the six o'clock closing of the polls. What with travel being as treacherous as it was, she had called it off, suggesting that everyone stay at home for safety's sake — after doing their best to vote, that is.

In the meantime, she had pulled out a few of Raymond's favorite records from her treasure trove in the hall closet, spinning them on his old turntable out on the glassed-in back porch and sipping a Bloody Mary to help her pass the time. At the moment she was mouthing the lyrics of "Slip Slidin' Away" from Raymond's Paul

Simon phase, the last he had indulged before his death. It almost seemed to her that the song had been written specifically for this tempestuous morning by a very prescient Paul Simon, although she was reasonably certain he had never come anywhere near Second Creek.

The phone rang for the umpteenth time that morning, but Myrtis still jumped. Four of the five other Nitwitts—everyone but Renza, in fact—had already checked in with her. Denver Lee's tale of woe was that she was safe but hardly warm, since she didn't have power yet. Laurie explained that she had power, but Powell kept insisting it wasn't safe to venture out in the car yet. Novie couldn't stand the smell of the space heater she'd been forced to drag down out of the attic because her central heat was acting strange. And Wittsie couldn't seem to stop sneezing for some reason but suggested in her rambling fashion that it might have something to do with her new medication, considering she hadn't had so much as a head cold in years.

The conversations had then centered around the party being called off and who should pick up whom on the way to vote. That had triggered in turn the age-old Nitwittian debate about who was a god-awful driver and who wasn't. Myrtis had always thought that honor belonged to Novie but tactfully refused to get into it with her on such an unsettling morning. Denver Lee, however, was not reluctant in the least to go into a diatribe about Renza's behind-the-wheel tactics. At one point, Myrtis simply put the phone in her lap, picking it up occasionally to say uh-huh. Of course, no one dared attack Wittsie these days, but Wittsie made up for that by running down her own driving skills in a striking display of honesty. The whole sequence had eventually driven Myrtis to drink, but she didn't allow it to get to her as much as she might have otherwise. She had her just-past-noon liquid courage in hand now, along with her memories of Raymond and his favorite music to console her and help her cope.

After letting the phone ring a couple more times, Myrtis picked it up and decided to play the odds. "Renza?"

"How did you know it was me?"

"You're the only one I haven't heard from. Process of elimination. How are things out your way?"

There was a plaintive sigh on the other end. "Just awful. I'm calling you on my cell, but I have no heat, and I don't think I want to go out in that mess. I can see people sliding around from my window. What are the others doing? I assume you haven't gone in to vote yet."

"No, I haven't, and I'm not going to rush things. The radio station says all the polls are open now despite everything—if you can get to them, that is. Light turnout so far, as you can imagine. I'm just lounging around my porch listening to some of Raymond's music and looking out on my wonderful ice-covered maze. It's actually a thing of beauty. I've already taken some pictures."

"My God, you're getting to be as bad as Novie."

"I don't admit the comparison," Myrtis replied, taking a generous swig of her drink.

"When are you going in to vote?"

"I told Laurie and Powell to come pick me up around two. By that time I trust everything will be good and thawed out. Laurie says her street is open now, but Powell says they're not going to rush out to vote either. I've never driven on ice in my entire life, and I don't think Raymond did either, now that I think about it. Ordinarily, I don't think a soul would be venturing out in this unholy mess, but it is Election Day, so there's your conflict. So

I'm just putting my feet up out here and having a little dressed-up tomato juice. I suggest you do the same."

There was a brief silence. "I think I'll give Laurie a call and ask her to pick me up, too. I'd feel a lot safer with Powell driving. . . . Oh, has anyone checked up on Wittsie?"

"Don't worry about her," Myrtis replied with a chuckle. "She was the first one I heard from, and she certainly sounded like she had her wits about her. She didn't lose her power like I did either—although I'm back on now. It's spotty around town, apparently. No rhyme or reason. Just a matter of which trees fell where. Wittsie did say a couple of pines in her backyard were snapped off like matchsticks."

"Have you heard from Mr. Choppy?"

"He's fine, too," Myrtis said. "He called me up early. Didn't lose his power."

"Some people have all the luck, I suppose." Renza paused so long that Myrtis thought she had lost the connection.

"Renza? You still there?"

"Oh . . . sorry. I just remembered I didn't have any more vodka or tomato juice in the house. I don't suppose you could pour me a Bloody Mary through the phone?"

★

Mr. Floyce had been riding herd on Second Creek Street and Sanitation all morning, giving Lance Walkley, the supervisor, an earful. The two of them had been in constant contact via their cells, but no matter what progress was made on salting and clearing the streets and roads, it was never fast enough to suit His Honor, the incumbent.

"Dammit, man! I've got an election to win today! I've got

people to get to the damn polls down in Ward Six. Speed it up, man—no excuses!" he had shouted through the phone every fifteen minutes, once he'd settled into his courthouse office.

He'd gotten up at the crack of dawn and roused all the movers and shakers at Second Creek Street and Sanitation with him, after putting them all on alert the evening before. Even before any of the crews had been able to get out and start shoveling salt onto the omnipresent glaze, he had nearly mummified himself in sweaters and coats, warmed up the SUV, and somehow managed to creep along to The Square without incident. Jo Nelle had howled long and loud while he dressed in between his phone calls to the various municipal-department heads.

"It's not worth riskin' your life to go out there, Floyce!" she had proclaimed. "I vote that you stay right here until it's safer!"

"It's not just about the election," he had replied, greatly annoyed by her nagging. "It's about my duties as mayor right now. I've got to get this town goin' again. Second Creek Utilities says half the people are without their power."

"I think this storm might just be a sign we've overstayed our welcome," she added, trying to get in the last word.

He had refused to answer, leaving her behind in her sulking mood and determined to put out all the fires on this icy morning. It was just too bad this hadn't happened a week earlier. His leadership qualities would clearly have emerged in time to impress those last few fence-sitters and perhaps put the election to bed in a decisive manner. Now the effect the weather might have on the turnout was beginning to worry him.

Once ensconced safely behind his office desk, he was forced to become a makeshift one-man Crisis Central, since he'd been unable to reach the always trusty Minnie Forbes. Eljay had phoned earlier to say that a tree had fallen across their driveway and essentially imprisoned them inside their own house.

"Maybe you should get in touch with Judge Moreton and see if he'll issue a temporary injunction. We could get the whole damned election postponed," Eljay continued. "It's worth a try, isn't it?"

"Nah. Moreton won't go for it. That old fart walks the straight and narrow path. He'll just say this isn't enough of a catastrophe, and we should just proceed with clearin' the roads. The ice isn't all that thick. We've got enough bulk salt out at the maintenance sheds. I just checked it out with Ross Wilson."

"Hell, Floyce, this is bound to affect the turnout!"

Mr. Floyce wasn't in the mood to argue. It was going to be a long day. "You have a tremendous grasp of the obvious, Eljay. Look, just you concentrate on gettin' yourself and KayDon to your pollin' place. That's two votes we can't afford to miss."

Every now and then in the midst of barking orders to his charges over the phone, Mr. Floyce had to keep a disturbing thought from rising to the surface of his brain—one that was triggered by Jo Nelle's comment that they might have overstayed their welcome.

"Damn Murphy's Law!" he exclaimed out loud at one point.

He had gotten elected that first time around on the heels of a devastating storm—not ice way back then, but driving winds and rain with a touch of hail for dramatic effect. What if he got turned out of office now by another unusual meteorological event—both of them functioning as the bookends of his political career?

"Damn it all!" he exclaimed again in spite of his best efforts to remain calm. Then he began another round of calls to Brother Thompson, Pastor Harris, and some of his good ole boy contacts down in Ward Six.

★

Mr. Choppy's polling place—the social hall of First Presbyterian Church—was just a short three blocks from his modest bungalow on Pond Street. He had no intention of dragging his little Dodge out into the weather and instead was setting out on foot in his hiking boots and pea jacket to cast his vote for himself. Who knew? A part of him played with the fanciful idea that it even might come down to that one vote with the weather being the obstacle it was and all.

Despite the fact that Second Creek had seen more than its share of unusual storms over the years, the town was not particularly adept at dealing with ice. It was still a relatively rare occurrence this far south, but that did not deter Mr. Choppy and scores of other Second Creekers from taking it on as if it were merely routine. For his part, he intended to put one foot gingerly in front of the other from the moment he walked out the door. But here and there along the route to his polling place, he found himself wincing at several fender benders out in the street. Or perhaps they were cars still frozen in place from the onslaught the night before. There didn't seem to be any injuries involved, but whatever the case, Second Creek was hardly about business as usual on such an important day. Instead, things were on the order of a logistical nightmare, and Mr. Choppy found that worrisome.

Once safely on terra firma inside the church social hall, he approached one of the poll workers and asked the inevitable question: "Has the voting picked up any? The last thing I heard over the radio was that the turnout was still light."

"A little bit," the middle-aged woman replied. "Just in the last hour or so, we've gotten more of a decent turnout. But you could've heard a pin drop in here most of the mornin'."

Mr. Choppy gave her a less-than-convincing smile and got in the short line marked A–H. It took less than five minutes for him to reach the poll workers' table, where he announced his name to Mavis Trenton, one of his former Piggly Wiggly regulars. An ample woman with an appetite and smile to match, she had often brought him new customers. It was contact with people like this that he missed the most following the closing of his store.

"Here you are, Mr. Choppy," she said, locating his name on the rolls and then watching him sign in with an admiring expression on her face.

"So good to see you again, Miz Trenton," he replied. "It's one crazy day for an election, huh?"

"Fit only for penguins, I'm afraid. In fact, I think I must have some penguin genes considerin' how easy I got here compared to most." Then she gave him a quick wink. "The best of luck to you today."

He returned her wink and walked over to one of the voting booths, pulled the curtains, and at last confronted what he now viewed as the biggest decision of his life. It even eclipsed his proposal to Gaylie Girl in the sense that he had at least had some experience in dealing with her before. If he actually ended up winning this thing, he would have to deal with a whole new set of tasks quite unlike any he had ever encountered. He could talk the talk all he wanted, but he would have to walk the walk if he turned Mr. Floyce out of office. The old adage about being careful what you wished for suddenly hovered above him, but it felt more like a halo up there than a glib bit of conventional wisdom. Yes, *halo* was the right word and the right image. He was in the social hall of the church whose gold-plated hand pointing to heaven had once been swept away by straight-line winds. A hand that he alone had been led to last summer by some unknown force or indefinable spirit that told him he had a mission to accomplish. Perhaps—as Mr. Gary Greene had suggested—there really was a Spirit of Second Creek to invoke.

Refreshed and undaunted by his thoughtful review of where he had been and how far he had come, he finally pulled the lever marked Hale Dunbar Jr. and let out a little sigh. There. It was done. He had followed through to the very end. Now it was up to the rest of the voters of Second Creek.

★

It had taken the road crews the better part of the day to make many of the Second Creek streets drivable again, but treacherous patches of ice here and there refused to cooperate with the city's most diligent salting efforts. Traveling even short distances remained a dicey proposition, and the police and fire departments had more than they could handle with all the fender benders and home space-heater accidents that continued to crop up everywhere.

In spite of everything, voting began to pick up steadily throughout the afternoon at all the polling places, but Mr. Floyce remained holed up in his office, fretting over his churchgoing Ward Six supporters. Many of them lived in neighborhoods that had been hardest hit by the storm, and even though he had recently gotten word from Sister Lula Mayes that Lower Winchester Road was open again, some of the streets feeding into it were still glazed over and quite dangerous to travel.

"I'm doin' the best I can, pickin' up this one and that one, but I don't know if me and Pastor Harris can carry 'em all in," she had told him once she'd finally been able to get to a phone.

"People are slippin' and slidin' all over the place down here, and we have to go so slow."

Mr. Floyce received much the same report from Brother Thompson, who indicated that for about a quarter of his Hanging Grapes congregation there was no way in or out for the time being. It might boil down to road openings versus poll closings for some of them. By five o'clock—with the polls open for only one more hour—Mr. Floyce began to get a sinking feeling that maybe the whole thing was slippin' and slidin' away from him, as Sister Lula had so aptly put it.

Jo Nelle appeared in the doorway just past five, looking pale and drained. "That taxi driver must run one of those wild kiddie rides at the state fair in Jackson during his spare time. Thank God I'm still in one piece. What a wife won't go through to vote for her dear husband!"

Manifestly exhausted by then, he wasn't in the mood to keep things from her and brought her up to date on the Ward Six transportation snafu.

"Well, I think that tale of woe calls for a drink," she replied, shedding her coat and collapsing into one of his great leather armchairs. "Pour me one from that stash I know you keep in your drawer. That is, unless you and Eljay have emptied it during all your meetings these past few months."

He gave her a scornful look but opened up the drawer and poured a shot of bourbon into two of his mother-of-pearl jiggers, handing hers over and downing his immediately. "You haven't by any chance heard anything from Minnie today, have you? She didn't leave word for me at home after I left, maybe?" he said while pouring himself a second shot. "Although she's got my cell number—I don't understand."

"Not a peep from her. I would have called you if she had. She didn't show up at all today? That's a first. I've always thought neither hell nor high water could keep her from her appointed rounds. I guess New Vista Acres must be pretty frozen over. Did you try callin' out there?"

He looked exasperated and said: "Of course. No answer. It's not like her not to even call. She's never even taken a sick day in the all the years she's worked for me." He mumbled something under his breath and shook his head.

"What's the matter?"

"I was just thinkin' about all those promises I made to give Minnie a raise. I just let it slip away from me somehow. Kinda the way I'm feelin' about this election right about now. Before last night, I thought it was safely in the bag."

The phone rang, and Mr. Floyce took his time answering it. "Prob'ly somethin' else I don't wanna hear about."

Jo Nelle watched the expression on his face change from annoyance to something resembling shock. She saw his eyes widening, brow furrowing, and jaw dropping, but still he did nothing more than wince and utter a pained grunt every now and then throughout what was obviously a long and involved monologue at the other end.

Eventually he said, "Thanks for tellin' me, Don." Then, after a pause, "No, I'm not all right." And finally, he hung up without so much as a good-bye.

Jo Nelle drained the last of her bourbon and sat up in her chair. "What was that all about? You look terrible."

He continued staring out into space, and when he began talking to her, it was as if she weren't even in the room with him. He was addressing some focal point in midair. "Minnie," he began.

"That was Don Hassett down at the morgue. He said Minnie and her husband, Charley, were drowned this mornin' on their way in."

The shot glass fell from Jo Nelle's hand as she jumped to her feet. "What? . . . Drowned? . . . How is that possible?"

His tone was nearly robotic, allowing for no hint of emotion. "As near as anyone can figure out from the tire tracks, their car lost traction and slipped off the road. Then it went slidin' down an embankment into a deep drainage canal full of ice. The car apparently overturned and broke through the ice, where they were trapped upside down and . . . drowned. No one even spotted the wheels stickin' up outta the water until late this afternoon. They were . . . under there all this time." He paused to shudder and quickly downed his liquor.

Jo Nelle moved to him quickly and put her arms around him as he sank back in his chair, staring silently up at the ceiling. "Oh, I just can't believe it, Floyce. It's just too awful. Those poor people."

"She was on her way to help me out as usual, I'm quite sure. I should have known somethin' terrible had happened. She would never have let me down. Never. Her and those little notepads of hers. I always had the sneakin' suspicion she'd recorded the creation of the universe on one of 'em."

"Poor little Minnie," Jo Nelle replied, her voice now trembling.

Mr. Floyce looked up at his wife like some sort of lost child, and the sadness in his eyes was apparently more than she could bear. She started tearing up and began to massage his shoulders.

"This doesn't look like it's gonna be my day, does it? We were just sittin' here talkin' about her a few minutes ago, talkin' about that raise I never gave her. And now . . . this."

"I know, honey, I know."

He mumbled something else under his breath and managed an ironic little chuckle. "I'm beginnin' to think you may have had it right, after all, this mornin'."

She stopped massaging long enough to frown. "What are you talkin' about?"

"That comment you made about a sign that maybe we'd overstayed our welcome. We got the ice storm. The uncertainty of the election. And now this. Minnie's gone. There's no doubt in my mind that I took her for granted, and now she's gone."

Jo Nelle resumed her massaging. "You can't blame yourself for this. It was a horrible accident on a day just tailor-made for accidents."

"That doesn't make me feel any better about the way I took her for granted. It only makes me feel worse now that I know I can't make it up to her."

"Does her family know yet?"

"Don said he had reached their son and daughter just before he called me. That dreaded phone call at some odd hour from a stranger. Prestridge's Funeral Home is handlin' the arrangements, and visitation will be day after tomorrow."

Jo Nelle sighed and glanced over at the clock on the wall. "Aren't you glad you called off that big to-do tonight at the Second Creek Hotel? Not many people would've showed up anyway in this weather. The polls close in about half an hour. I think it's time we went on home. There's not much more you can do. I think you've been here long enough."

He gave her a rueful smile, arched his brows, and said, "Exactly what I've been thinkin'."

★

All those who had been heavily involved in the Hale Dunbar Jr. campaign no longer had the luxury of monitoring the returns together, given the cancellation of the party at Evening Shadows. Instead, they were scattered throughout Second Creek listening to their radios separately and calling one another up as soon as new numbers were released. The Nitwitts, particularly, couldn't keep off the phones, irritating one another no end with the endless stream of busy signals they were bound to get under such circumstances.

"Who have you been talking to all this time?" Renza said, finally getting through to Myrtis after enduring redial for a couple of minutes.

"I've been talking to Laurie," came the reply. "Aren't you excited? There are only three precincts out, and Mr. Choppy is ahead by twenty-five votes. It's been nip and tuck all evening."

Renza maintained her huffy mood. "I was just calling to discuss it with you, that's all. Apparently, you'd rather talk to Laurie."

"Do you suggest I stay off the phone?" Myrtis replied. "I have just as much right to spread the good news as you do. Besides, I did try to call you, but your line was busy when I did. Just who were you talking to, may I ask?"

"To Wittsie, if you must know. Actually, I was checking up on her, but I didn't let her know that. She sounded fine."

And at half past six the totals stood at Mr. Choppy—378 votes, Mr. Floyce—353 votes.

At quarter to seven, it was Myrtis who was unable to reach either Renza or Laurie, settling instead to run things by Denver Lee. "Oh, dear," she began. "Another precinct has just come in, and Mr. Floyce has gone back on top. This seesaw thing is driving me crazy."

"Me, too," Denver Lee replied. "I hate things that go down to the wire. Oh, by the way, has anyone checked up on Wittsie?"

"Renza did and says she's just fine."

"Good. Well, I'm on my second Bloody Mary to steady my nerves. Has anyone heard from Mr. Choppy this evening?"

Myrtis said she hadn't. "I thought maybe it would be best to wait until it's over," she continued. "That way, I can either congratulate or console him, instead of just pestering him with partial scores. He's bound to be a bundle of nerves."

At that point, the totals stood at Mr. Floyce—428 votes, Mr. Choppy—404 votes.

At seven o'clock, Laurie and Novie made connections to discuss the neck-and-neck race. "I don't know how much longer I can take this," Laurie was saying. "Only twenty-four votes separating them with two precincts out. I just couldn't stand it if it ended up being one of those coming-so-close-and-yet-so-far things for Mr. Choppy."

"Have faith," Novie replied. "The radio said there was a minor glitch reporting the results in those last precincts, but we'd have the final result by quarter past seven. I hope this isn't so close it ends up like that god-awful Florida recount."

"God forbid. Powell and I haven't been able to eat a thing, though. I have this wonderful dinner prepared, but we're just picking at it listening to the returns."

"It could still go either way," Novie added. "The radio said those last precincts were either in Ward Six or Ward Four. There was some confusion. They also said the turnout was lower than expected because of the weather, which comes as no surprise. Do you think that favors us or Mr. Floyce?"

"Hard to say. But Powell keeps reminding me that we're stronger in Ward Four, and they're stronger in Ward Six. Keep your fingers crossed."

★

Mr. Choppy was pacing around his kitchen, staring at the clock as it moved to 7:13. Two more minutes until the quarter past results. Where were those missing precincts? In Ward Four or Ward Six? Never mind what the weather had wrought. The odds still favored Mr. Floyce. He had been four percentage points ahead going in, and the likelihood was that such an advantage would hold up no matter what. In other words, Mr. Choppy was preparing himself psychologically and emotionally for defeat. He knew what it was to lose a dream and somehow survive. He'd dealt with that for the better part of fifty years.

Then he sat down at his kitchen table and reflected a bit further. He'd also recently recovered that long-lost dream of his. Gaylie Girl had said yes to his proposal of marriage. So miraculous turnarounds in life were indeed possible. He mustn't concede this thing yet.

His heart pounding and his breathing shallow, Mr. Choppy turned up the volume on WSCM radio as the public service announcement on preventing forest fires ran out and the announcer said: "This is Rick Wentworth here at your Wonderful Second Creek Mississippi Radio Election Central, reporting your seven fifteen returns. We've been informed there's still a delay in getting the totals in from those final precincts. But the current results we have here show a razor-thin margin for the incumbent. At this point, we've got two different reports on where those precincts are, but we're working on that right now. However, we have been told that we should have the votes in any minute now. Meanwhile, we'll emphasize again, as we have over the last hour or so, that the turnout today was somewhat lower than expected, due obviously to the weather. Poll workers have indicated that there were some precincts where up to a third of the registered voters failed to show up . . ."

Mr. Choppy turned the radio down a bit and tried to steady his nerves. He took a few deep breaths, but that really didn't seem to help all that much. His blood was full of adrenaline, his brain full of random images.

Icy streets. Crews shoveling salt all over the city. A finger pointing to heaven. Gaylie Girl looking down upon him from Lake Forest like some sort of long-distance angel. He wanted so badly to be able to call her in just a few minutes and tell her he'd won. That, he thought he could handle. But he wasn't so sure about calling her up and having to tell her he'd lost. By a few votes, no less.

Rick Wentworth continued to babble over the radio. ". . . and as we said, ladies and gentlemen, we are expecting the vote from those precincts any minute now . . ."

Mr. Choppy began an involuntarily mantra in his head. Five words. Over and over again. Let it be Ward Four . . . let it be Ward Four . . . let it be Ward Four . . .

For if those precincts happened to be in Ward Four, rather than Ward Six, with the tally already as close as it was, he knew that he at least stood a chance of overtaking Mr. Floyce in the proverbial photo finish and moving into the winner's circle.

". . . and now we have the votes in from those final precincts, ladies and gentlemen . . ." Rick Wentworth said.

Mr. Choppy quickly turned up the volume.

"... and the final tally for the Second Creek mayoral election is as follows: the incumbent, Floyce Hammontree—633 votes; and the challenger, Hale Dunbar Junior—651 votes. Hale Dunbar, Junior is your new Second Creek mayor by the razor-thin margin of eighteen votes. I'm sure many will be stunned by this outcome. Perhaps the weather played a significant role in the turnout. The last poll by *The Citizen* showed Mayor Hammontree ahead by four percentage points with only two percent of the voters undecided. Doing the math, you can easily see that even if all of that remaining two percent went to Mr. Dunbar, it still wouldn't have been enough to overcome Mayor Hammontree's lead. Nonetheless, the voters of Second Creek have spoken their independent minds, and it appears that Hale Dunbar Junior will be your new mayor. To some, perhaps a surprising result at the end of a very unusual and interesting campaign ..."

Mr. Choppy turned the radio off and let his emotions whirl around him. They were all in there begging for attention. Relief. Joy. Surprise. Humility. Anticipation. Even a sense of awe that he had actually pulled it off. Two dreams had now come true within a very short space of time. He decided to go for a touch of the trite and pinched his arm. Ouch. It hurt. He was awake.

Before all of it could truly sink in, the phone rang. Predictably, it was Powell, with Laurie on their extension.

"We did it, my friend, we did it!" Powell shouted. "We pulled if off just like we said we would five months ago!"

Laurie chimed in nearly simultaneously. "Congratulations, Mr. Choppy! We squeaked by, but we did it, didn't we?"

"I can't believe it. Those last precincts musta been in Ward Four—I kept chantin' it over and over. You shoulda heard me— let it be Ward Four, let it be Ward Four. And it was so close—

I mean, I was just wonderin' if Mr. Floyce might contest it, you know. I'm wonderin' if it's really over and done with. Can I really breathe a sigh of relief?"

"Don't cheat yourself out of the joy of the moment," Powell replied. "You've earned it. We all have."

It was then that Mr. Choppy truly felt the victory; and while keeping the phone to his ear with his right hand, he pointed to the ceiling with the index finger of his left. The Spirit of Second Creek had come full circle.

★

Mr. Floyce sat propped up in bed with his clothes on, listening to Eljay rant and rave on the other end of the phone. He'd been tempted to let the damned thing ring and ring and was now sorry he hadn't.

"Well, why the hell don't you want to ask for a recount, Floyce? I can't believe what I'm hearin'. When an election ends up this close, a recount's practically par for the course. A few mistakes here and there, along with a little greasin' of palms, and you could be back in bid'ness. I still think you shoulda at least gone to Judge Moreton and asked him to consider an injunction to postpone the election first thing this mornin'."

"I told ya, he wouldn've gone for it, Eljay. I know him like the back of my hand. We gotta accept the verdict."

There was a long silence at the other end. Finally, Eljay said, "I've never known you to give up like this, Floyce. You told me months ago that you'd be the one to decide when you stepped down. Is this gonna be it for you? Where's that feisty spirit? What the hell's the matter?"

Then Mr. Floyce told him about Minnie and her husband.

He'd wanted to lead with the news right after picking up the phone, but Eljay simply hadn't let him get a word in edgewise.

"That's terrible. I had no idea," Eljay replied, moderating his combative tone somewhat. There was another awkward pause. "I can see why you'd be down about that. Anybody would be. But you're not gonna contest this and at least ask for a recount? Don'tcha think Minnie would've wanted you to do that? No one supported you more than she did."

Mr. Floyce hesitated slightly. "I know . . . maybe I do owe her that. Maybe I'll think it over and sleep on it. I was gonna make an announcement tomorrow at my office, regardless."

Eljay continued to press. "Don't concede yet, Floyce. At least ask for the recount. Anything could happen." He cleared his throat pointedly. "And if by some chance you require my particular services, you know where to reach me."

"Yeah, I do."

The conversation essentially came to an end. Mr. Floyce folded his cell and tossed it aside just as Jo Nelle came into the room, smelling of cold cream and ready for bed.

"Who was that?" she said, climbing in beside him and putting his phone on the nightstand.

"Eljay." He thought it over briefly, wondering if he should tell her he was having second thoughts about everything. "He thinks I should ask for a recount."

Jo Nelle gave him a scowl while fluffing up her pillows. "You're not gonna listen to him, are you? Didn't you tell him what we've decided to do?"

"No, I—I didn't tell him. He said he thinks I owe it to Minnie."

"I thought we'd resolved this, Floyce," she replied, the anger clearly rising in her voice. "I leave you alone for five minutes, and you and Eljay have cooked up another one of your schemes. I know what he's up to. Who does he want you to pay off this time?"

Mr. Floyce wasn't in the mood to argue with her now any more than he had been earlier in the evening when they'd hashed everything out. "All I told him was I'd make an announcement at the office tomorrow. I didn't actually agree to anything he suggested."

"But you did agree to somethin' that I just suggested, and you should've told him so. You should've told him that we agreed to let go of all this, to let go of Second Creek once and for all. Nobody runs this town, Floyce. You only thought you had it under your thumb. But it makes its own rules. Just when you think you've got the place under control, it throws you a curve. We need to take our money and move on. Maybe even out to Vegas, where you can try your luck at that stand-up career you said you always wanted. You can't let Eljay talk you into hangin' on and tryin' to manipulate things one more time. What you really owe Minnie is to just let it go. Aren't you sick and tired of it all?"

Mr. Floyce knew it was useless. She had him by the balls again. He was never any good at contradicting her when she came at him with the unadulterated truth. Somehow, he managed a tentative smile. "Yes. I am sick and tired of it all."

She leaned over and gave him a peck on the cheek. "Then get undressed and come to bed. Let's try to get some sleep. Tomorrow, we begin the first day of our brand-new life."

Far too weary to muster any sort of protest and still essentially in shock from the news about Minnie, the emperor finally shed his clothes—the first step toward ending his long and eventful reign as mayor of Second Creek, Mississippi.

17.

THE DAY AFTER

Rick Wentworth of WSCM and Rankin Lynch of *The Citizen* stood in the hallway outside Mr. Floyce's office the next day, speculating on the announcement that His Honor would be making in less than five minutes.

"Betcha a meal at the Victorian Tea Room that he's gonna call for a recount," Rick said to his cohort. "With only eighteen votes separating them, it's practically a done deal."

The lean and hungry Rankin perked up, feeling that the somewhat overfed Rick was an easy mark. He'd won this type of drinks-and-dinner bet with his colleague before. "And I say he concedes sure as the sun came up this morning to melt the rest of the ice out there."

When they shook on it, Rick said, "Get ready to pay up. This man'll do anything to stay in office, or so I hear."

Just then, Mr. Choppy approached with Powell and Laurie behind him, offering a handshake to both men. "You fellas did a great job coverin' the election from start to finish—I just wanted to say that to both of you here and now, no matter what happens in a few minutes."

"You got any inside info on what Mr. Floyce is gonna be announcing to us?" Rankin said.

"Fellas, I'd rather leave that up to him, if you don't mind," Mr. Choppy replied. "He and I spoke over the phone earlier this mornin,' and I'd prefer not to steal his thunder."

Rick quickly switched his focus to Powell. "Aren't you Mr. Hampton, the campaign manager? I've been meaning to let you know how much I enjoyed all those press releases you sent me at the station. That was some good writing. You have no idea what sort of sloppy, run-on copy crosses my news desk all the time. I could swear some of these things are written by chimps— with their toes, no less."

But Mr. Choppy intervened before Powell could answer. "I'd like to say somethin' about that 'cause I think Mr. Hampton here would be too modest. But he not only wrote all my speeches and press releases, he gave me a whole new outlook on the English language, as well as some great tips on things you just don't think too much about. Things like posture and diction and even when and how often to kiss babies out on the campaign trail."

"As a former dance instructor, I do feel body language is extremely important to those in the public eye," Powell said.

"Can I quote you on that?" Rick said, just as a television crew from one of the Delta stations joined the gathering crowd.

"If you like."

"And I'll be makin' my own statement after Mr. Floyce finishes, so you'll be gettin' more quotable material today," Mr. Choppy said.

Rankin stepped up with a somber expression on his face. "Did you hear the news about Mr. Floyce's secretary and her husband? That Miz Minnie was always such a sweetheart to me whenever I came around. She sorta took me under her wing when I first joined the staff of the paper last year."

"Yeah, I know," Mr. Choppy began. "Mr. Floyce gave me all the details over the phone this mornin'. I was in shock. I guess I still am. I didn't know her personally, but she was more or less a fixture around Second Creek, and I owe a debt of gratitude to her husband for a few personal favors."

"It's unbelievable that they're both gone," Laurie added. "What a horrible tragedy!"

The door to Mr. Floyce's office opened, and a flushed Eljay Jeffers waddled out to address the group. "Ladies and gentlemen, if you'll come on in, Mayor Hammontree has an announcement to make. We'll wait a few minutes for all you media people to get settled and set up, and then we'll get started."

Inside the mayoral chambers, a couple of the city councilmen, all the municipal-department heads, and Jo Nelle flanked Mr. Floyce, who stood in front of his desk with a deadpan expression on his face. Only the distracting manner in which he kept stroking his mustache with his thumb and forefinger hinted at his nervousness.

"Ladies and gentlemen, I'll be brief this morning," he began, finally bringing his hands down to his side. "I'm sure you all know the results of the election yesterday. Perhaps it was a surprise to some of you, particularly the way it went down to the wire. But although the results were very close and perhaps subject to further scrutiny, I am standing here before all of you today to announce that I am conceding this election to Mr. Dunbar with my very best wishes. The results of this election will stand as is."

There was an audible buzz throughout the room, and Mr. Floyce waited for it to abate before resuming. "This was a hard-fought contest, and it's very clear to me that enough Second Creekers were ready for a change to put Mr. Dunbar over the top, bad weather or not. And who's to say whether a larger turnout would have produced a different result? What's not open to debate is the fact that someone else will now be in charge of presiding over our very special little town—guiding it into the twenty-first century. That person will be Hale Dunbar Junior, and this administration will do everything possible to make the transition as easy as possible for him. I now turn the floor over to Mr. Dunbar to say a few words to you as your new mayor."

A round of applause followed as Mr. Choppy stepped forward to address the crowd. "I want to thank Mayor Hammontree for his gracious words, and I willingly accept his offer to assist me in the transition in the coming days and weeks," he began. "He will bring a wealth of experience to the table, and I trust I will be an apt pupil in learning the nuts and bolts of municipal government. Above all, I pledge to those who voted for me and also to those who didn't that I will enter into this with my eyes wide open and my ear to the ground, listening for the Spirit of Second Creek to guide me, as I believe it has so far during this campaign. Together, we will do what is right for our town, moving it forward as well as preserving the best of the past. And now, if you'll hold any questions you may have for the time being, I believe Mayor Hammontree has something else he wants to say to you."

Mr. Floyce took the spotlight once again, but this time there were no carefully enunciated, well-rehearsed words delivered without a hiccup. Instead, the stress in Mr. Floyce's face was clearly evident, and the fact that he was struggling with something was lost on no one.

"I'd like to ask all of you here today . . . this is very difficult for me . . . I would ask you to join me, my wife, Jo Nelle, Mr. Dunbar, and the many municipal officials present in a moment of silence for Minnie and Charley Forbes. As you all probably know by now, they tragically lost their lives yesterday in a car accident . . . and Minnie was much more than a secretary to me all these years—" He broke off, unable to continue.

Jo Nelle grasped his hand and finished. "Ladies and gentlemen, shall we observe that moment of silence together now for Minnie and Charley? May they rest in peace."

The gathering immediately complied, paying their respects for perhaps a full minute or so. The tribute cast such a pall on the proceedings that at first it appeared none of the media would pursue the mayor or mayor-elect further, but Mr. Floyce soon gathered himself enough to thank everyone for their participation and then invite their questions.

Rankin Lynch was the first to rise to the occasion. "Mayor Hammontree, have you decided what you'll be doing next?"

"Getting my act together somewhere, I suppose," Mr. Floyce replied. "My wife and I have been discussin' it recently, and perhaps we'll head out West to see what opportunities might await us there. Second Creekers might like to think so at times, but contrary to popular opinion here, this is not the center of the known universe—though I suppose you couldn't tell it by the weather. Everything seems to happen here sooner or later."

Rankin looked and sounded puzzled. "How far out West? Are we talking California or points in between?"

"We haven't decided yet, but thanks for askin'."

Then Rick Wentworth stepped up and added a much needed note of levity to the mix. "Mr. Dunbar, do you think you're up to the task of emceeing the annual Miss Delta Floozie Contest as Mayor Hammontree has done all these years?"

Mr. Choppy allowed himself a polite smile before responding. "I look forward to it, although I have to tell you all here and now—I can't carry a tune. Perhaps Mayor Hammontree won't mind if we play one of his 'She's a Doozie, She's a Floozie' CDs in his place? I think that's the sort of continuity we'd all welcome."

"I'd be honored to leave such a legacy," Mr. Floyce replied as the two men shook hands, thereby dissolving any lingering traces of their recent rivalry. The Second Creek reign of Floyce Yerby Hammontree had officially ended, and the Hale Dunbar Jr. regime had officially begun.

★

It was Mr. Choppy's first time to visit Evening Shadows, and it was a little overwhelming to him, all things considered. Myrtis Troy had done a make-good on that Election Night celebration they'd had to postpone because of the weather, inviting everyone remotely connected with the campaign to partake of food, drink, and good company in Mr. Choppy's honor. The Nitwitts and Powell were present and in fine form, of course, as were the Book Sheriff and some of her staff members, Lady Roth minus the Susan B. Anthony garb, the Hunter Goodletts, Vester Morrow, Mal Davis, and several other headquarters volunteers who'd done the nitty-gritty work of the campaign from start to finish.

Myrtis had set two festive buffet tables on her back porch—
the first groaning with hot and cold hors d'oeuvres, three-bean
and garden salads, crudités and dip, shrimp and wild rice casserole, smoked oysters, a variety of cheeses, and petits fours. The
second table featured two gleaming silver punch bowls—one for
teetotalers and the other for those who liked things spiked a bit;
between them glistened an elaborate ice carving of a hand with
an index finger pointing to heaven.

"I can't believe you thought of that!" Mr. Choppy exclaimed
to Myrtis as she temporarily spelled her Sarah to ladle the spiked
variety of punch into his cup. "Who did it for you?"

"Guilty," Vester Morrow said, stepping up at just that moment.

Mr. Choppy sampled his punch and beamed. "I might have
known. It definitely has that Victorian Tea Room elegance, but
I had no idea you did ice sculpture. My poor brain is tryin' its
best to take it all in. I traveled that mysterious road to the gold-
plated hand, and it eventually led to this." He paused briefly. "It
gives me chills up and down my spine."

"Chills, thrills, spills," Vester replied. "That's what we're all
about here in Second Creek. A magic trick a minute. And now
you'll take your turn as the master magician."

Myrtis relinquished her punch bowl duties once again to
Sarah and took Mr. Choppy by the hand. "Now, Vester, don't
you dare monopolize our hero. I have big plans for him tonight.
But first, come this way and let me fix you up a little plate of
goodies, Mr. Choppy. You just have to sample my delicious
shrimp and wild rice casserole—it was Raymond's favorite, and
I'm sure you'll like it, too."

Over at the buffet table, Myrtis caught Laurie's eye. "Well, here
he is, Laurie. While I'm helping him with his plate, why don't you

go get that little present we have for him back in the guest room?" Myrtis quickly surveyed the porch and gestured to the crowd. "Girls, Powell, Vester, Mal, everyone. Please gather 'round. It's time."

"Now, you didn't have to go gettin' me a gift, Miz Myrtis," Mr. Choppy replied.

Myrtis began puttering around the food while Laurie made a quick exit. "Oh, but we did, Mr. Choppy. We Nitwitts did a little research and discovered there was that one special thing you'd been yearning for. Now, don't deny us the pleasure of giving it to you tonight. It'll put an exclamation point on your wonderful victory."

A minute or so later, Laurie appeared in the doorway, but there was no present in her hands. Mr. Choppy frowned and cocked his head. "Ladies and gentlemen, may I present . . ." Then Laurie stepped aside, gesturing in the manner of a television spokesmodel. " . . . Mrs. Gayle Lyons, known affectionately to our Mr. Choppy as Gaylie Girl, and soon to be known as the next First Lady of Second Creek, Mrs. Hale Dunbar Junior."

Gaylie Girl immediately sashayed in dressed for the Hollywood Red Carpet and struck a dramatic pose, while the crowd applauded enthusiastically. "Hello there, Second Creek. Hello there, Hale, darling. Great to be here at last—and I absolutely insist that you all call me Gaylie Girl!"

Mr. Choppy put down the plate that Myrtis had just handed him and moved quickly to her side, saying nothing at first but giving her a passionate hug and kiss. Finally, he gathered his wits about him enough to say: "I can't believe you're here. You said you didn't know how soon you'd be able to get down when we talked last night right after the election."

She pulled back momentarily and gave him an affectionate wink. "I really didn't know myself until your marvelous Nitwitt friends here called me up and hatched a plot. Let me just say that it's no wonder you won the election with these devious and efficient ladies behind you."

"Myrtis and I drove up this afternoon to pick her up at the Memphis airport," Laurie added. "We've all been just about to bust, waiting for this moment to arrive."

Mr. Choppy almost seemed to be blushing. "I won't even ask how you ladies engineered all this. But I should know by now that nothin' can stop the Nitwitts when they put their minds to something."

"We do have our ways," Myrtis replied, looking quite pleased with herself.

"Thank you all so much. This is a wonderful surprise." Then Mr. Choppy focused on his Gaylie Girl once again. "Well, how do you like hangin' with these Nitwitts?"

"Oh, I love it. I've even been elected an official member, Myrtis tells me. We've all been getting acquainted and gabbing like old friends from the moment I got here this afternoon. I feel right at home already."

"And we're going to do everything in our power to keep you feeling that way," Myrtis added. "You're going to be a very important part of Second Creek from here on out."

Lady Roth stepped up and gave Gaylie Girl's outfit the once-over. "I just adore your ensemble. The way it flows, the way you wear it. That aquamarine color is positively dreamy, but I have to ask you, dear, have you had theatrical training? The way you posed just now put me in mind of a flawless stage performance."

Gaylie Girl laughed. "I'm afraid the closest I came was accompanying my singing cousins on a tour way back in the forties.

That's how I met Hale, as a matter of fact. But I appreciate your compliments."

Then it was Powell's turn to put in his two cents. "If you don't know already, Gaylie Girl, it was Lady Roth's portrayal of Susan B. Anthony out on the campaign trail that likely cemented our support from many of the women voters."

"Oh, I'd like to think I made a difference," Lady Roth replied, clearly pleased with the attention. "But I have to admit I'm relieved to be out of those dowdy black clothes. Susan B. Anthony may have been a pioneer in many respects, but when it came to fashion, she was strictly in the closet with the mothballs. You and I simply must go shopping together up in Memphis sometime, Gaylie Girl. I believe we both have an eye for the smart and stylish."

"I'd be delighted, of course."

Eventually the excitement over Gaylie Girl's dramatic entrance died down, and everyone began mixing and mingling as they had before. It was Lovita Grubbs whom Mr. Choppy and his future wife encountered next.

"I've heard through the grapevine that you've been involved with your local library board up there in Lake Forest," the Book Sheriff began in between bites of her casserole.

Gaylie Girl smiled graciously. "Yes, I have been—off and on over the years. I've found that it's not unlike being in politics. We were always on the lookout for special projects to fund. A public library can never have too much money."

"Ah!" Lovita proclaimed, her eyes lighting up. "You've obviously been fighting the good fight. I hope you'll consider helping out down here as well, although I'm delighted to say that with our Mr. Choppy here in office, I'm quite sure the library will no longer have an enemy in the mayor's office."

"I can assure you I will listen to your budgetary concerns, Miz Lovita," Mr. Choppy replied. "The days of your havin' to fight tooth and nail for every penny are over."

"And I'll be more than happy to do what I can to help," Gaylie Girl added. "I enjoy philanthropic causes, and that would seem to fit right into my new role as a Nitwitt. Oh, I absolutely love that name. It's so unpretentious — so unlike Lake Forest!"

Lovita leaned in and lowered her voice. "Of course, we'll have to wait for a fire-breathing dragon or two to die off before I can get you on the board officially, Gaylie Girl. There are a couple I'd like to sic a few water moccasins on in the meantime."

A few minutes later, Mr. Choppy and Gaylie Girl found themselves surrounded by Renza, Denver Lee, and Novie, all of whom were lobbying for an expedition to rediscover the whereabouts of the gold-plated hand.

"You're bound to have some inkling of how to get there," Renza was saying while working on her third cup of spiked punch. "How many pecan orchards can there be out in the county?"

"Oh, lots and lots, I'm afraid," Mr. Choppy answered. "Next to soybeans, it's our biggest crop around here."

"Don't forget catfish," Novie protested.

Renza bristled. "That's not a crop, Novie. You don't grow catfish like you raise soybeans and pecans."

"You most certainly do," Novie replied. "Our Pond-Raised Catfish plant that we've had for eons does just that. Like the name says, they raise them in ponds."

"Did I mention I can have catfish on my diet, girls?" Denver Lee interjected.

"You have, and we already know," Renza said. "Catfish doesn't turn to sugar."

Denver Lee caught Gaylie Girl's eye and leaned in confidentially. "I'm prediabetic and trying desperately to avoid the real thing, you know."

"Well, when you get to be our age, you realize you can't just eat anything you want without paying the consequences."

"A moment on the lips, a lifetime on the hips, as they say," Denver Lee replied.

Mr. Choppy and Gaylie Girl exchanged amused glances, and he said: "If we wander in search of the gold-plated hand the way this conversation just did, I don't think we'll ever find it. At any rate, I feel very strongly that it will always be here with me in spirit no matter where it actually landed so many decades ago."

Wittsie approached the group, and an air of solicitousness erupted amongst the other Nitwitts.

"How are you doing, Wittsie, dear?" Renza said. "Can I get you anything?"

"Yes, we lost track of you," Denver Lee added.

"Oh, please . . . I had to go to the little girls' room. . . . I'm not helpless. . . . I mean, I'm doing just fine, really. . . ." Wittsie turned to Gaylie Girl and drew herself up. "In case they didn't tell you, I've recently been diagnosed with Alzheimer's . . . but I'm receiving treatment. . . . All of a sudden I feel surrounded by mother hens . . . not that I'm complaining, you understand. . . . I founded the Nitwitts, you know. . . . Probably the best thing I ever did in my entire life . . . Look at all we've accomplished . . . and having such good friends to look after you is a blessing. . . . "

"And now you have me to add to your list," Gaylie Girl replied with a cheerful smile. "I can't wait to attend the next meeting after I move down for good."

"And when will that be?" Wittsie said. "I forget . . . did you say . . . ?"

"Probably not for another month," Gaylie Girl said. "I have so many things to attend to and put in order in Lake Forest, including dealing with my impossible family. But I'll be down soon enough, and then Hale and I plan to get married in a simple civil ceremony."

Renza eyed her skeptically. "You are planning on inviting us, though?"

"Why, of course."

"And letting us throw a blockbuster of a party for you afterward?" Denver Lee added.

"Absolutely. I want to take full advantage of that legendary Southern hospitality I've always heard so much about. I'm going to plunge right into Second Creek once I get down here and never look back."

A few minutes later at the buffet table, Mr. Choppy took Powell aside. "Well, I think my Gaylie Girl passed her first Nitwitt test with flying colors. Miz Hampton tells me the ladies have been puttin' her through her paces all afternoon and on into the evening here, and she hasn't batted an eyelash."

Powell chuckled generously. "So I gather you think she's a keeper?"

"You better believe it."

"Good. I'll notify the press."

Mr. Choppy returned the laughter. "They'll find out soon enough for themselves. Me and Gaylie Girl, we're gonna make a helluva Second Creek First Couple."

★

A couple of hours later, the party had dwindled down to Myrtis, Mr. Choppy and Gaylie Girl, and Laurie and Powell. Full of good food, drink, and humor, the five of them were seated around the living room discussing the future of Second Creek.

"I was thinkin' that I oughta consider lettin' some of Mr. Floyce's department heads stay on," Mr. Choppy was saying. "I don't necessarily have to end up doin' things their way, but I can at least let them help me learn the ropes, and then I can take it from there."

Powell nodded thoughtfully. "Good idea. You'll be able to tell during the transition period who you can work with and who you can't."

"And if either you or Miz Hampton wants a position in my administration—"

But Powell cut him off quickly. "No, as I told you, that's not for us. We were just happy to help you pull this off. It was a labor of love. I really don't think either of us would be much good at actually having to run this town."

"But I could bounce things off both of you, I assume. You both gave me such great advice throughout the campaign."

"We'll always be ready to help out," Powell replied. "I'm sure you and the other Nitwitts will, too, won't you, Myrtis?"

Myrtis came to after an awkward silence. "Oh, excuse me. I guess my mind drifted off a bit. I was thinking about Raymond and his record shop for some reason. Of course—the Nitwitts will continue to support you in any way we can, Mr. Choppy."

"Ray's Rock and Roll and More," Mr. Choppy stated evenly. "It was all the rage at one time. I remember it so well."

Myrtis sighed plaintively. "Yes, that shop just took off out of nowhere, and I think Raymond got a bigger kick out of it than the kids who came in to buy records. Which reminds me—I have Raymond's prehistoric turntable set up out on the back porch. Would you all like to hear one of his favorite songs for old times' sake? It just seems like the sort of night for letting go and having a little fun."

"Why not?" Mr. Choppy said. "I think we've about talked Second Creek politics to death."

Myrtis rose from her chair and led the way, and soon they were all assembled out on the back porch, standing around the turntable. "This was one of the songs that started it all," Myrtis explained, picking up the needle and placing it carefully on the forty-five of "Sherry" that she'd just started spinning. "I was listening to it just this morning while Sarah was cleaning up for the party. I think she thought I'd lost my mind when I started singing along in falsetto."

"Frankie Valli? The Four Seasons?" Powell said. "I remember you told Laurie and me about that when we were scrounging around for interesting material to use on your radio spot."

Myrtis nodded enthusiastically as the song began, startling everyone with a repeat performance of her morning falsetto act.

"Oh, I haven't heard that record in ages," Gaylie Girl said to Mr. Choppy as Myrtis continued her solo sing-along. "My children were crazy about it, though. They wouldn't rest until I'd bought them the LP. At the time, I thought it would rot their brains, but I gave in. Compared to all that heavy metal noise these days, it seems rather innocuous now, doesn't it?"

Laurie giggled and gave Powell her dreamiest look. "And I was the proverbial bubbleheaded teenager right here at Second Creek High when that first came out in the early sixties. Call me Sadie Hawkins, but would you care to attempt some sort of dance, sir?"

"Delighted, of course," he replied, immediately taking her in his arms and improvising some steps. "We never danced to that sort of music up at Studio Hampton, but here goes."

"Good idea, Laurie," Gaylie Girl said. "Come on, Hale, let's show 'em how it's done."

And with that the two couples put on an exhibition worthy of *American Bandstand* minus Dick Clark and the television cameras.

When the record was over, Myrtis collapsed in a chair, laughing. "Imagine people our age acting like this. I don't think I've had this much fun in years, not even at any of our most rambunctious Nitwitt meetings. How about you, Laurie?"

"Well, I'm positive the six of us never spun Four Seasons records and carried on like a bunch of over-the-hill bobbysoxers, if that's what you're getting at," Laurie replied, catching her breath. "I guess I should be happy no one was around to snap our picture for posterity."

"I almost wish there had been," Mr. Choppy declared. "The Spirit of Second Creek would say to hell with doin' what people expect you to do, and I just spent a good deal of time, energy, and money provin' just that."

"So you did, Mr. Choppy," Laurie added. "So you did."

Myrtis rose from her chair and pointed to the clock across the room. "Well, kiddies, the midnight hour approaches, and I absolutely insist that you all stay the night with me. No use taking any chances on those roads, even if most of the ice is gone by now. I imagine there are still a few patches here and there. Anyway, I've got two beautiful guest rooms just waiting for you. Now, Gaylie Girl, since you've already got your things in one of them, why don't you show Mr. Choppy the way and mosey on up? Laurie, you and Powell will take the downstairs guest room on the other side of the house. I won't take no for an answer."

"But I didn't bring along any nightclothes," Laurie pointed out.

"Now, you know better than that," Myrtis said. "You and I are the same size, and I still have some of Raymond's pajamas lying around somewhere that Powell and Mr. Choppy can use. Don't try to wiggle out of this, any of you. This is not the time and place to stand on convention. We didn't win this election by playing it safe and paying homage to the status quo. We were rebels, so let's act like it."

Laurie eyed Powell shrewdly. "She's right, you know. And I'm pretty tired. Let's do it. Let's stay."

"No argument from me," Powell said. "It's been a long couple of days at the end of a long five months."

"Oh, and I've got toothbrushes and toothpaste galore from my 'buying things in bulk and telling everyone how much I paid' phase," Myrtis continued. "Breakfast tomorrow's on me here at the Hotel Evening Shadows, of course. After all these years of trying, I think this monstrosity that Raymond and I built has finally come into its own."

Mr. Choppy gave Gaylie Girl a little nudge. "Then show me to our room, Mrs. Hale Dunbar Junior-to-be. We've got fifty years of sweet dreams to catch up on."

A half hour or so later, the last light in the house was turned off and everyone was settled in warmly for the night, anticipating the dawn of a bright new chapter in the ever-surprising, ever-unfolding history of Second Creek.

ACKNOWLEDGMENTS

This second novel in the Piggly Wiggly series owes so much to the incisive input of my wonderful Putnam editor, Rachel Beard Kahan, who knows precisely when to be hands-on and when to be laissez-faire. I deeply appreciate the confidence she displays in trusting me to become the best writer I can be; kudos also to Eve Adler, editorial assistant. I never tire of thanking my hard-working agents at Jane Rotrosen—Meg Ruley and her assistant, Christina Hogrebe. To say that these women have my best interests at heart is a vast understatement. I also must mention the crucial role my research assistant and friend Will Black played in compiling the facts I needed to inspire and complete certain passages. I cite the cooperation of the public relations department of the Peabody Hotel of Memphis, Tennessee—particularly Kelly Earnest, the director. Last, but not least, I thank all the public librarians who continue to support me with library book talks, brunches, luncheons, and dinners, and I offer my Book Sheriff as a shining example of the good fight librarians fight every day.